This book was produced by Melcher Media, Inc.
170 Fifth Avenue, New York, NY 10010
Under the editorial direction of **CHARLES MELCHER**

Editors: **GILLIAN SOWELL** and **GENEVIEVE FIELD**
Researcher: **TERA KUNTZ**
Assistant Editor: **EMILY DONALDSON**
Video Editors: **MEGAN WORMAN** and **EMILY DONALDSON**
Editorial Assistant: **ELAINE CHANG**
Translator: **LORI THOMSON**
Manager of Development, Bunim/Murray Productions: **SCOTT FREEMAN**

Cover and Europe Season designed by
ALEXANDER KNOWLTON and **ANTON GINZBURG** @ BEST Design Incorporated

Islands Season designed by
TIKA BUCHANAN and **DAVID BLANKENSHIP**, Eric Baker Design Associates, Inc.

SPECIAL THANKS TO:
Cris Abrego, Aaron Ackermann, Amy Backes, Alicia Bean, Jeff Berg, Lisa Berger,
Duncan Bock, Jennifer Bohbot, Erin Bohensky, David Boyer, Cindy Bradeen, Eduardo A. Braniff,
Karin Louise Buckley, Mary-Ellis Bunim, Robert Caplain, Brian Carbin, Jason Carbone,
Lynda Castillo, Gina Centrello, Lona Chiang, Carmen Cuba, Michael Cundari, Tod Dahlke, Lamar Damon,
Dustin Ellis, Lisa Feuer, Toni Gallagher, Janine Gallant, Kate Giel, Richard Glatzer, Lisa Haskins,
Brian Hueben, J. Scott Jackson, Jeffrey C. Jenkins, Greer Kessel, Mark Kirschner, Andrea LaBate,
Maria Massey, Claire McCabe, Rebo McFadden, Michelle Millard, John Miller, Jonathan Murray,
Ethan Myatt, Clay Newbill, Donna O'Neill, Kim Noone, Ed Paparo, Renee Presser, Tom Ronca,
Donna Ruvituso, Laura Scheck, Paul Schneider, Robin Silverman, Donald Silvey, Danny Spino,
Liate Stehlik, Jennifer Stipcich, Jonathan Taylor, Rick Telles, Chris Thomas, Kevin Thomas,
Van Toffler, Stacey "Loopey" Toyoaki, Matt Van Wagenen, and Kara Welsh.

An *Original* Publication of MTV Books / Pocket Books / Melcher Media

POCKET BOOKS, a division of Simon & Schuster Inc.
1230 Avenue of the Americas, New York, NY 10020

ISBN 0-671-01536-2

First MTV Books / Pocket Books / Melcher Media trade paperback printing November 1997

10 9 8 7 6 5 4 3 2 1

Printed in the U.S.A.

ROAD RULES

PASSPORT ABROAD

ALISON POLLET AND LEIF UELAND

Produced by MELCHER MEDIA INC.

Designed by BEST DESIGN INC. and
ERIC BAKER DESIGN ASSOCIATES INC.

Based on MTV'S ROAD RULES,
created by Mary-Ellis Bunim and Jonathan Murray
in association with MTV

MTV BOOKS / POCKET BOOKS / MELCHER MEDIA

DEAR ROAD RULER:

On behalf of the entire staff and crew of MTV's Road Rules, we would like to welcome you to the cast! We are excited that you will be a part of our new season, and hope that the following guidelines will help you as you prepare for your adventure.

THE CONCEPT

The concept is simple: Five young strangers travel around the world completing specific missions, and we tape the events of their travels. You've been chosen because those who have met you feel you have something interesting to share and that you will be a compelling addition to the group's dynamic.

THE PROGRAM AND PEOPLE BEHIND-THE-SCENES

We have a large staff of dedicated professionals working on this project who have been strictly instructed not to socialize with the cast members. Our focus is your relationship with the other cast members, not your relationship with us. This will be difficult, so please respect their position until the end of the project. Anything more than "Hello" and "Good-bye" can easily develop into more involved conversation, which changes the reality of the experience.

You will each be given a pager to keep with you and turned on at all times. Feel free to give the number out to friends, but remember the main purpose is for us to keep in contact with you. You will be responsible for these pagers, and they must be returned when the project is over.

ROUTINE STUFF

1. VIDEOTAPING: Please don't look into the video cameras unless specifically directed to, and don't mention MTV when referring to this experience. You can call it "the project," a documentary, or come up with another expression. The less attention we draw to ourselves, the easier all of our lives will be. Please refrain from telling people about MTV or ROAD RULES while shooting. For your privacy, we caution you to use first names only while on camera.

2. PROVISIONS: As you know, we will be collecting your money and credit cards at the start of the trip. (They will be returned to you when you complete all the missions.) At the start, we will provide you with a stocked fridge and a set amount of money as a group. During various parts of the trip you will have the opportunity to replenish your money supply by working at different jobs that we have planned for you. This money can be used for whatever the group wishes (i.e., food, lodging, etc.).

3. TELEPHONE: You will be provided with a calling card that will allow you to make $50 worth of phone calls per week. Anything over this amount you will be required to pay for yourself (from the group fund).

4. RESPONSIBILITIES: You are responsible for the motor home and its contents (i.e., carpeting, light fixtures, appliances, etc.). Should anything be unreasonably damaged, the replacement cost will be deducted from your final payment. In addition, you will be responsible for all your moving and parking violations. Please drive carefully; the motor home is probably a larger vehicle than you are used to driving. Safety should always be a concern.

5. ALCOHOL & DRUGS: No illegal drugs. No drinking and driving. Basically, you must obey all local, state and federal laws. Do not break these rules. You have agreed to this in your contract.

6. VEHICLE: The vehicle is quite roomy. How the space is shared is up to the group. For lighting and camera reasons, the furnishings should not be re-arranged, but feel free to decorate with your own personal touch.

7. CREW AREA: We have a caravan of crew vehicles that will follow you. These areas are strictly off limits to all cast members.

Attached please find a list that should aid you in your packing.

Congratulations, again! We look forward to working with you.

Sincerely,

Mary-Ellis Bunim
Executive Producer

Jonathan Murray
Executive Producer

Clay Newbill
Supervising Producer

Rick de Oliveira
Producer

THINGS TO PACK FOR YOUR
ROAD RULES **ADVENTURE:**

Athletic shoes
(cross trainers)

Sweats

Good socks

Swimsuit

Jeans

Lip protection

Sunscreen

Toothbrush

Hair/skin products

Dental floss

Shaving razor

Hat/cap

Underwear

Athletic bra for women

NO WHITE T-SHIRTS
(They affect camera exposure!)

THREE

You've been picked for the road
trip you'll never forget. Survive the
adventures planned for you, and you
will be rewarded handsomely.
So empty your pockets, and we'll take
care of the rest. Throw out your
rules, **these are Road Rules.**

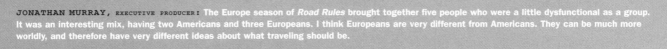

JONATHAN MURRAY, EXECUTIVE PRODUCER: The Europe season of *Road Rules* brought together five people who were a little dysfunctional as a group. It was an interesting mix, having two Americans and three Europeans. I think Europeans are very different from Americans. They can be much more worldly, and therefore have very different ideas about what traveling should be.

ANTOINE: Our group was subject to eternal conflict, yes, but it was also very balanced, very safe.

BELOU: I loved the group. We had a good time together—a lot of drinking, a lot of talking, a lot of hanging out.

ROAD

SEASON 3:

TRAVEL ✉ LOG

Meet Antoine, Belou, Chris, Michelle and Patrice as they embark on the voyage of their lives! It's love and adventure Euro-style as *Road Rules* crosses the continent!

CLAY NEWBILL, PRODUCER/ DIRECTOR: On the whole, this was the most attractive cast we ever had. They were all beautiful.

MARY-ELLIS BUNIM, EXECUTIVE PRODUCER: Having the production in Europe made it so that we had to preplan a lot more than we would were the cast traveling around the States. We had to have hotel reservations; we had to prepare their modes of transportation; and most importantly, we had to make sure they didn't run out of money. So more than any other *Road Rules* cast, this group was spoiled. It's the ultimate fantasy to be able to go across Europe and have adventures planned for you. Every day, you're pointed in the direction of something more fantastic that can happen.

MICHELLE: Our group was very chilled and laid back, but overall it was a total soap opera!

PATRICE: It was a really crazy bunch, and I'm really happy to have had the chance to meet them, because they helped me to think a lot about myself.

CHRIS: Our group was very touchy feely. A lot of hugging, kissing, holding. That was cool. I liked that a lot.

RULES

EUROPE

SYNOPSIS

EPISODE ONE

At the National Palace of Spain, two Americans, Michelle, 21, a former Dallas Cowboys cheerleader, and Chris, 19, an Ivy League fraternity boy, meet their European counterparts: Antoine, 22, a finance major from Brussels; Belou, 18, a Dutch hip-hop freak from Amsterdam; and Patrice, 21, a black model from Berlin. Season Two's very

EPISODE TWO

The cast travels to Carcassonne, in Southern France, via San Sebastián, where they stop for a couple of days. Antoine shocks one and all by shaving his head. There appears to be tension between him and Belou, especially when he shows up at her hotel door with a pile of clothes, including a bra. On the way to Carcassonne, Chris and

them to Roc et Canyon in Millau.

EPISODE THREE

The cast members reach Millau and settle into their temporary abode, a beautiful gite, where they drink and dine with the Roc et Canyon crew, with whom they feel an immediate bond. Chris and Michelle are affectionate, but rela- tions between Belou and

own Christian makes an unexpected appearance on a scooter, confiscates their money and credit cards and leads them to their new home-away-from-home—the Winnebago (inexplicably nicknamed, and henceforth referred to as, Pepe). The cast members receive their first clue and are off to Pamplona, where they embark on Mission Numero Uno— running with the bulls! The cast successfully completes their first mission and, over a celebratory dinner, are presented by a flamenco dancer with their next clue: to get on the road to Carcassonne, where they'll assist in Bastille Day fireworks preparations. But first, Belou, Antoine, Michelle and Chris ignite some sparks of their own!

Michelle take turns driving Pepe—and getting disastrous- ly lost. Their ineptitude sends Antoine on an angry and offensive (especially toward Patrice) tirade, and he insists on taking the wheel. Once in the medieval town of Carcassonne, they take on their task, helping wire the fireworks display around the fortress. The group takes pride in their work as they watch the amazing display, then they descend on the night, walking and talking. Belou and Patrice bond over the brewing antagonism they feel toward Antoine, and when Antoine interrupts their chat, Belou exclaims, "I hate you, but I love you!" The cast receives their next clue, a chain of carabineers directing

Antoine seem strained. After a turbulent phone conversation with her boyfriend at home, Steve, Belou seeks solace on a swingset outside the gite. There she cries, and calls for Michelle to comfort her. She makes cryptic vows to stay true to Steve and to begin the trip anew. Meanwhile, Antoine sits alone writing in his journal, seemingly unperturbed. The next day, the cast goes rappelling, and Patrice conquers his fear of heights. Then, in wet suits and helmets, they hike down a river, through waterfalls and rocks. During a quiet moment, Chris and Belou talk about the difference between love and fascination. Michelle does a loving etching of Chris. The cast is sad about their imminent departure from Millau, but their next clue—a broom and cleaning supplies—has them speculating as they head off to the Riviera!

EPISODE FOUR

After a teary au revoir to the Roc et Canyoners, the cast sets off for Cannes. Not only does Pepe stink but Michelle's haphazard driving has put a lovely dent in its side. Locating the yacht *Happy Fox* is a bit of a challenge, but the cast succeeds in finding their contact and setting about the first half of their job—scrubbing and scouring the boat for a private party. While on a speedboat ride with the yacht's owner, the cast discovers that the party is

toward a hotel; meanwhile, Antoine escorts Allyson home, where he gives her a courteous kiss on the cheek and leaves.

EPISODE FIVE

The cast bemoans their pitiful finances and sets off toward Lake Como. They arrive at their destination to discover that it's a water-skiing club, and that their next mission is to compete with the local team in a water relay race. During a training session the next morning the cast realizes that they're up against rather formidable competition. They try to maintain their confidence, and Antoine takes the lead, assigning positions: he and Belou will water-ski, Michelle will kayak and

find a clue telling them to compliment a stranger on the Ponte Rialto. They take a water taxi to the bridge, oohing and aahing at the sights. They find the right stranger and retrieve their clue: they'll be cooking! At their hotel, Belou has a screaming fit when she realizes she has lost her backpack. The others are not amused. At breakfast the next morning, Belou attacks Antoine, reaching for a knife on the table. The two take it outside, and threats of violence ensue. Thankfully, the fight dissolves—mainly because the cast has a mission to attend to: under the tutelage of world-class chef Fulvia, they are to prepare and serve a gourmet

actually for them, and that part two of their job is to comb the streets of Cannes for two dates apiece. (It's also then that they receive their next clue—to head to Italy's Lake Como, where they'll "race for a million!") There's competition in the air as the girls and guys go ogling. After a few near misses, and more than a couple of rejections, the gang finds their guests, who converge upon the yacht that evening for champagne and hors d'oeuvres. The party goes after-hours and moves to the beach, where Chris and Antoine go skinny-dipping with two of their invitees, Allyson and Melissa. After his dip, Chris snuggles with Melissa on the beach, and eventually they stagger into the night

Patrice and Chris will row. Antoine's leadership throws Belou for a loop, and over lunch she stages a massive tantrum. Patrice counsels her in a private tête-à-tête by the lake. Belou returns to the table and complains that there's no real team, and that she's not going to race. Yet after a bit of prodding, she decides not to abandon the others. Unfortunately, the cast races poorly against the expert Italians. They're defeated and broke, but they get their next clue— a toy gondola! They're Venice bound!

EPISODE SIX

The cast leaves Pepe to take a train to Venice. In their compartment, they

meal. Belou and Patrice remain with Fulvia while the others go shopping for ingredients. After successfully completing the mission, the cast members take a gondola ride through Venice and learn they will take a train to Milan. On the train, Belou receives wooden tulips: the cast is off to the airport and on the way to Amsterdam.

EPISODE SEVEN

The cast arrives in Amsterdam, where they're to stay at the house Belou shares with her boyfriend Steve. Unfortunately, Steve isn't eager to have house-guests, and while Steve and Belou argue, Antoine makes arrangements for the cast to stay at a hostel. Things are amiss between Belou and

Steve, but the gang does their best to have fun walking around the city. One night, while Steve's away, Belou cooks the cast dinner. A messenger arrives at the house and delivers the next clue—a pair of satin shorts, affixed with the address of a local gym. The next day, the cast arrives at the gym to discover they're boxing—each other. Chris beats a weary Patrice; Michelle and Belou tie; and Antoine, who in Belou's words "fights like a kangaroo," beats Chris. The cast receives the next clue—a stuffed seal—from a park juggler. They discover they will be going to Pieterburen, Holland, on a seal rescue. Belou and Steve continue to fight, and Michelle predicts the relationship won't last much longer.

be leaving Amsterdam for Paris, where everything will be new.

EPISODE NINE
The cast arrives in Paris and goes straight to legendary department store Printemps. Their contact informs them that their next job is to partake in a fashion show—as models! After fittings and runway lessons galore, the cast leaves the store and heads for the youth hostel, where Belou styles Chris's hair in dreadlocks. The next morning, the rest of the cast have their makeup and hair done at Printemps: Belou's is a work of art, Antoine's is orange! After hamming it up on the runway, the cast members are thrilled to discover that

The next morning, the cast embarks on a trip to a grand old château, where they meet two princes, one of whom hits on the girls. It's mysterious regional dining that evening, and the cast is horrified to discover—after the fact—that they've consumed the innards of a pig. As night falls, the cast convenes in one bedroom, where Belou gets uppity once again. "No one understands me," she cries. Her state of mind seems to infect Chris, who has an uncharacteristic breakdown regarding his inability to love. Belou concludes the emotional evening with an impassioned breakup call to Steve. Prince Phillip cannot understand the cast's emotional antics and scolds them for making noise. The

EPISODE EIGHT
The cast takes a train to Pieterburen. There they meet the heads of a seal rehabilitation center. They learn about the perils the animals face and help in the care of sick ones. Early the next morning, they help release two of the newly rehabilitated seals. They receive certificates and return to Amsterdam. On the train, they find Barbie dolls and learn they will soon be on a runway in Paris. They are psyched! Back in Amsterdam, Belou rejoins Steve. And Michelle, Chris and Patrice—desperately in need of dinner money—take to the streets, where they wash windshields and panhandle for cash. Belou and Steve exchange a tense farewell, and she expresses relief to

they're finally getting paid. Their next clue directs them to take a boat tour of the Seine, where they receive yet another clue, a miniature Winnebago. The cast then uses the GPS to try to locate Pepe. It takes much searching and a trip up the Eiffel Tower, but they finally find Pepe and their next clue—a reproduction of Mona Lisa, with a message on it: to go to the Loire Valley. The cast spends the night carousing in Paris, and Belou accuses Michelle of moving in on a man she's met, a gorgeous South American named Pablo.

EPISODE TEN
Belou decides she's falling in love with Pablo and spends the night with him.

next day, they search the château grounds for a series of clues, all of which direct them to the seaside town of Lacanau.

EPISODE ELEVEN
It's a terse good-bye to the princes as the cast heads off to Lacanau. They're elated to reach the beach paradise, where they're greeted by expert surfers Schmoo and O'Connell. The cast takes lessons and attends a night party on the beach. Patrice, Antoine and Chris adopt new looks for the fete, but only Patrice's bleached-blond do goes over well. Feeling out of sorts, the guys leave the party early. The next day is a surfing bonanza, and although Belou gives him a run for his money,

Antoine wins the surf competition (and his very own *Road Rules* surfboard!). The cast receives their next clue—they'll be jumping. They travel to the French town of Lourdes, where they're shocked to discover that their contacts are the Roc et Canyon crew. They're ecstatic! The cast goes bungee jumping off the Pont du Napoleon. Patrice has conquered his fear of heights and jumps without a moment's hesitation. Over dinner, the cast receives their next clue—to head back to Spain, to the party town of Ibiza!

EPISODE TWELVE

It would seem that Michelle and Chris's relationship is getting steamier when— en route to Ibiza—the two

a car. Chris plays nurse. After all, Michelle is "his sweetheart." The cast loves paragliding, and when they complete their mission, they receive their next clue. It's a rather confusing one: a bottle of mustard, goggles and camouflage clothing.

EPISODE THIRTEEN

The cast predicts that paintball will be their next mission. Yet, when they arrive in the small town of Buñol, they find that the whole town is raging. The streets are teeming with people, the store-owners are covering their windows and doors with large plastic sheeting. Their local contact sets the cast straight: they'll be participating in the Tomatina

when their rewards surpass their expectations: high-tech entertainment centers and envelopes full of cash for all! They celebrate with a final feast in the glamorous suite of a hotel, where they engage in perhaps their most difficult mission yet: saying good-bye. The next day, Michelle is the first to leave on a morning flight to Dallas. She presents the team with a farewell letter, which they read over breakfast. Patrice is next. The cast deposits him at the train station, then proceeds to the airport. Antoine and Belou board flights to Brussels and Amsterdam, respectively, and Chris picks up a rental car: he's off for a semester in Rome.

have a tender moment. Is it more than a friendship? Beautiful Ibiza offers a sensory explosion for our Road Rulers, as they embark upon their next mission: to promote the town's hippest party places. They flyer the streets, hit the nude beaches and talk up the hot spots to local revelers. That night, they use the cash they made to soak up the island's wild nightlife. Chris hooks up with an English girl, and admits to being jealous when Michelle makes out with a random guy at the bar. In the club, Patrice hears the DJ make a special announcement: it's their next clue, and they're going paragliding! The next day, they ride scooters to the paragliding site, and Michelle crashes hers into

festival, an annual tomato-throwing fest. After a commencement ceremony involving a greasy pole and a ham, the rowdy crowd engages in a bloody tomato battle, and the Road Rulers scramble to defend themselves. Michelle and Belou, immediately stripped of their layered T-shirts, are uncomfortable and miserable, while Antoine and Chris are in tomato-hurling ecstasy. Patrice tires of the whole experience rather quickly and leaves. After the festival, the cast receives their next—and final—clue. It's back to the bullring in Barcelona where they'll collect their handsome reward. The cast members are wild with anticipation as they enter the bullring, and thrilled

CASTING

Antoine

NICKNAME: Twanner

HOMETOWN: Brussels, Belgium

BIRTHDAY: May 1, 1974

SIGN: Taurus

CURRENTLY LISTENING TO: Trip-hop

FLUENT IN: French, English, Italian and Dutch

PET PEEVE: When people neglect the environment.

ODD JOBS HE'S HAD: Car salesman, home renovator, bartender, waiter, horseback riding teacher at a girl scout camp

CARMEN CUBA, CASTING DIRECTOR: Antoine was difficult to interview. He was really evasive. I would ask him questions and he would answer me with a question that he wanted me to answer. We were doing the casting interviews in a hotel room, and in order to have enough space for the cameras, we'd had to push the bed up against the wall. When I finished interviewing him, I asked if I could leave him alone so he could do a confessional, which is step two of the interview process. He was alone in the room for five minutes, and then he called, "I'm done!" We walked in the room, and he'd put the bed down, undone all the sheets, slid under the covers and pointed the camera toward himself. He was like, "Why don't you guys come and join me?" We thought it was genius, really funny, but again, he'd avoided talking about himself by creating a situation that was entertaining.

ANTOINE: **My family is incredibly fractured. I have four brothers and sisters, but none of them are from the same father or same mother or anything.** I've never known my parents as a couple, and I've always had to find my way on my own. Maybe that's why I love traveling so much. My feeling is that the more you travel, the more you're able to travel. The more you travel, the less you take in your backpack.

Moving around doesn't allow for the longest relationships. I spent a year at college in Manchester, and that's where I had an absolutely wonderful relationship with a girl. It lasted a year, and it completely turned my personality around. She's someone who's very important to me.

There's also a girl in Brussels who I really love. Every time I go there, we have long conversations and it's very deep. We don't even kiss. I love her and I think she loves me, and that's the way it is. If one day we settle down in the same city then we'll think about it, but for now, it's good.

Casting Scoop

Antoine showed up at an open call in Rome and was initially rejected, because the casting people were looking for an Italian!

[CASTING APPLICATION]

Where do you see yourself in five years? What is your career goal? In Vietnam or China or Bali. Most important to me is to stay on the move, see the world, do business and have fun.

What are your worst and best characteristics? Best: Very energetic, up, and great at making first contact with people, very international personality. Worst: I cannot settle down or commit myself to just one country or one person. But as long as I've got variety, I'm okay.

If you could only pack one backpack for a trip, what would be in it? I always travel with just one carry-on in which I take: My roller-skates, one book, a journal, letter paper and my fountain pen. One shirt, one tie (you never know), one pair of orange PVC pants. The rest I'll find on my way.

Do you work out? No work out! Sport to me is cycle in the woods, snowboard down mountains, swim in the ocean or dance your soul away in nightclubs. Your heart's gotta be with it!

What habits do you have that we should know about?
I have a smile on 80% of the time I am awake.
No habits other than that.

Have you traveled around Europe? Where? Describe some experiences you've enjoyed and some you didn't.
Loved Ireland, England, Holland (such a greatly open-minded and relaxed country— especially Amsterdam), France, Spain, Portugal, Italy, Greece. I did not enjoy southern Germany where I did not hook up with people too well.

CASTING
ANTOINE

What is the most interesting place you've ever visited? What makes it the most interesting? Manhattan is the most incredible place on earth. Everything that the world is made of, you can find a sample of it on this twenty-mile-long strip.

What is the most important issue or problem facing you today? Do I go on to become an actor, a barman, a new-age traveler or a businessman?

Describe how conflicts were handled at home as you were growing up (Who won? Who lost? Was yelling and/or hitting involved?). My parents divorced when I was two years old. Almost all my family is like that, but never any fighting. You go your way, I go mine, in dignity. We all speak to each other without resentment or anything of the sort.

What are your thoughts on political extremism?
You think whatever you want about whatever you choose to make your cause.

Name two living people who you would like to meet, and tell us why. Neil Armstrong. Wouldn't you love to fly 3,000,000 km away from the earth? Fidel Castro. Maybe he'd tell me about some adventures he went through and give me good ideas.

What do you do for fun? I live and breathe for fun.

If you had three wishes, what would they be? 1. Keep the faith for all my life. 2. Keep my drive on until I die. 3. Get on *Road Rules*.

Belou

NICK NAME: Bubba

HOMETOWN: Amsterdam, Holland

BIRTHDAY: October 26, 1977

SIGN: Scorpio

REAL NAME: ElisaBEth LOUise

FAVORITE GROUPS: A Tribe Called Quest and KRS One

PERSONAL HEROES: Gandhi and Bob Marley

I played by myself a lot.

CASTING VIDEO

My second casting call, in London.

BELOU: My mom ignored me when I was a child, so in a way, I guess you could say I had a bad youth. Then again, when you look at people like Steve, my old boyfriend who was homeless throughout his childhood, I had a good youth. As a child, I was very difficult to handle. I could just scream for hours. Say we were in the supermarket, and my mom said I couldn't have something—well, I would roll around in the aisles just screaming and screaming until I got it. **My mom worked in a café, and I would see her for three hours a day.** She sent me to this after-school program, which I went to until I was nine. I blamed her for leaving me alone so much, and I really hated her. By the time I was seventeen, I knew I needed to move out of my mother's house. It was just too much pressure living with her, screaming all the time. I moved in with Steve. And then I went on *Road Rules*....

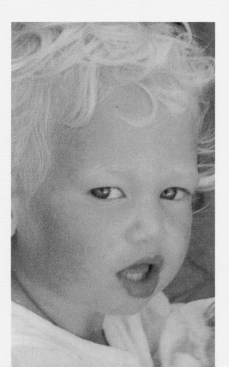

CARMEN CUBA, CASTING DIRECTOR: When Belou arrived at the second casting session, in London, she was totally freaked out, because she'd had a really crazy morning. She'd lost her passport the morning that she was supposed to get on the plane, and her mom had to go through this whole process within an hour of getting this whole replacement thing, and she'd thought she was going to miss her plane. She wore a jacket during the first half of her interview, but halfway through, she took it off to reveal that she was wearing a T-shirt that said Goddess. **Everyone looked around the room at each other. It was like we were all thinking the same thing: "Oh, my God, she is a goddess."** Not only because of how beautiful she was but because of how much she'd been through and how much she'd persevered. At one point, Mary-Ellis Bunim, the executive producer, said, "I can't believe you're only eighteen, with everything you've been through." And she said, "You can't? Well, why not?" She wasn't afraid to throw it back to people. She was just awesome.

[CASTING APPLICATION]

What are your worst and best traits?
Best one: I try to get the positive out of everything. Worst one: When I'm mad, I'm really mad, and I always want to be right! I can scream a lot!!!

If you could pack one suitcase for a trip, what would be in it? My music, a pen and paper for my lyrics and my video camera (and some clean underwear!!).

How would your boyfriend/girlfriend feel about your leaving for eight weeks? Would you be faithful? Yes, I will be faithful!!!

How important is sex to you? Do you have it only when you're in a relationship, or do you seek it out at other times? What's the most exciting/interesting place you've ever had sex? Sex for me is experiencing a natural thing. If I'm attracted to someone, that's the first thing I'm thinking of, but that doesn't mean I will do it. I'm a dreamer! My most exciting experience was in the woods!

What is the most important issue or problem facing you today? The devil is money! There are people dying because of money. You've got to find the future in yourself.

Me imitating Madonna at age 15.

What are your thoughts on abortion?
Right now I would have an abortion. You can't raise a child if you're not ready.

What are your thoughts on other sexual orientations?
Always use a condom. What else is there to say?

Where do you see yourself in five years?
Still being busy bringing my message out to the world.

I've really grown up a lot.

AMSTERDAM,
Holland

CASTING
BELOU

Where do you see yourself in ten years?
Being a film director and people are getting my message.

What are some ways you have treated someone who has been important to you that you are embarrassed by or you wish you hadn't done? Dissing someone I loved for someone else. Still thinking about that a lot.

Do you work out? If so, how often and what types of activities do you like to do? If not, how do you stay in shape? I meditate and weight lift at home. I use my bicycle a lot to go places. And I dance, of course.

Describe a major event or an issue that has affected your life.
Hip-hop!!! That's my state of mind.

What's the best thing about being out on your own? No parents!

Have you traveled around Europe? Describe some experiences you enjoyed and some you didn't. I've been to Greece, France (Paris), Spain, Belgium, Portugal, and Turkey. It's all about tourism. I'm always searching for the real thing.

Describe a recent major argument you had with someone. Did you win? Do you usually win? An argument for me is not about winning. I had an argument with my mom. She thinks I'm a loser. I want to make her see I'm not.

If you could change one thing about the way you act, what would it be? That I could stay cool in a hectic situation.

NICKNAME: Big Bro

HOMETOWN: Swampscott, MA

BIRTHDAY: June 14, 1976

SIGN: Gemini

FAVORITE TV SHOW:
The Simpsons

**PREFERRED FASHION
STYLE:** Retro

DRINK OF CHOICE:
Good beer

**FAVORITE ROAD RULER FROM
THE PAST:** Kit

CHRIS: At age three, my family moved to Germany, because my father was serving as a naval orthodontist. At age six, when my mom, my sister and I took a trip back to the States, my father called and told my mother not to come back, because he was in love with another woman. At the time, I didn't realize what a big deal the whole thing was. I just would see my mother crying a lot. She got remarried to my step-father ten years later. They're divorced now.

All of this has made me very scared to fall in love. I never have fallen in love, and maybe that's because I haven't met the right girl. Maybe it's because I don't let myself fall in love, or I'm too afraid to. I don't know. I know that I'm going to have to let myself go at one point. I know now that I'm more attuned to falling in love than I used to be. I used to go and get with girls that I knew wouldn't call me the next day and who I wouldn't have to call, low maintenance hook-ups. My freshman year in college was ridiculous. We would go to frat parties, and it was always the same thing. I got sick of it. Sick of the macking. It lost its flavor. I think I'm getting more mature about the relationship thing.

JILL HIGGINS, CASTING COORDINATOR: Chris walked up to my station at the open call, and he was the only one of four hundred people who looked me straight in the eye, shook my hand and said "Hi, my name's Chris." Hardly anybody at these open calls does that. I immediately put a circle on the number on his application. Then, when I was interviewing him, he grabbed my wrist so he could look at my watch to see what time it was. He seemed very at ease with himself and the whole situation.

Casting Scoop

Chris found a flyer for the Philadelphia open call in the men's room of a dorm. He went on a lark with two friends— neither of whom made the finals!

JONATHAN MURRAY, EXECUTIVE PRODUCER: We were all really impressed with Chris after the first casting tape. When the camera went in really close, his eyes seemed to tell a lot about him. He has a really wonderful way of speaking, a great sensual voice. There's a sexiness about him, a real magnetism, and it really came across in the interview process. He's very articulate, pretty deep and has some really interesting thoughts about the world and his own situation, regarding his willingness to commit and get involved in relationships.

Chris

This picture is about strength. It helps me through the hard times.

[CASTING APPLICATION]

Describe your most embarrassing moment. This was when I was taken advantage of by a girl at Penn who was someone I would (in a mildly coherent state) never fool around with. I remember some of it, but was told the whole story by my friend, who witnessed it (most of it, that is).

What are some ways you have treated someone who has been important to you that you are embarrassed by or wish you hadn't done? I have never told my father that I love him. We have a problem communicating our feelings—not to other people, but to each other. The history of the relationship is complex, and is evolving and evolving more and more each day. He knows I love him. I'm just embarrassed 'cause I haven't told him.

Describe how conflicts were handled at home as you were growing up (Who won? Who lost? Was yelling and/or hitting involved?) I grew up with my mom and sister. Saw my father about four hours a week. My mother is very trustworthy and liberal, so she never hit us, but would punish us by conventional methods (send to room). She always made it clear to us exactly why we were being punished. She was an incredible single mother. My sister won all the fights up until about the time I reached thirteen.

Describe a major event or issue that has affected your life. The divorce of my mother and father has greatly affected my thoughts on love, marriage and the notion of love being for "life and longer." It has made me very cautious about love and the mutual dependence associated with it.

Do you work out? If so, how often and what types of activities do you like to do? If not how do you stay in shape? I work out about five times a week. Basketball, swim, lift weights, play tennis. I love to be in shape, makes me feel energetic and healthy. Also love sports.

How would you describe your best traits? Enthusiasm: I have a lot of energy and I love to laugh. Passion: I'm searching for passionate moments and new adventures. Honesty: Sometimes brutally so. I'll always say what I feel. Risk-taking: This is why I'm filling out this application. I'm looking for adventure and am willing to throw myself head-first into the search for it. Altruistic: Love to make other people happy.

What habits do you have that we should know about? I bite my nails. I'm messy. I think I'm addicted to cotton swabs.

What habits do other people have that you simply cannot tolerate? I have a hard time with people who snore. Other than that I'm a pretty tolerant guy.

How important is sex to you? Do you have it only when you're in a relationship or do you seek it out at other times? What's the most exciting/interesting place you've ever had sex? Sex is important to me, but sensuality is more important. I don't think that sex has to include penetration. The best part of being with someone is kissing them. I've only slept with two women in my life. Release of sexual tension/energy is very healthy and important to me. Tried to in a moving car—did not work.

What are your thoughts on other sexual orientations? I know that I felt uncomfortable once when a homosexual man started hitting on me, but I have no problem at all. I would very much like to have a long talk with someone who is gay to find out how it is, and how hard it must be.

Where do you see yourself in ten years? I would love to be married to a working woman and have three children, hold a fun, exciting job and be happy (most important!!!).

CASTING

The Many Faces of Michelle

CASTING VIDEO

CASTING VIDEO

CASTING VIDEO

CASTING VIDEO

NICKNAME: Mich Mich
(or Texas)

HOMETOWN: Dallas, TX

BIRTHDAY: January 14, 1975

SIGN: Capricorn

FAVORITE DRIVING CD:
The *Rent* soundtrack

DRINK OF CHOICE:
White Zinfandel

Michelle

Michelle

Casting Scoop

Michelle had been considered for Road Rules season two, but with her southern accent and wacky wit, there was a concern that she was too much like Kit, from season one!

CLAY NEWBILL, PRODUCER/DIRECTOR: When I met Michelle, I was surprised that she was ever a Dallas Cowboys cheerleader. When you think of a Dallas Cowboys cheerleader, you think of the big hair, the big chest, the legs, and she doesn't have any of that. She's a very attractive girl, but she's not what you think of as your typical Dallas Cowboys cheerleader. And that's why we were interested in her.

MICHELLE: I had a pretty angry relationship with my mom when I was in high school, and I used to write about it. Every day in ninth grade, I'd go to study hall and I'd never study. Instead I wrote poetry. Just getting it all out. There was some pretty freaky stuff. A lot of it was about death and bleeding and sorrow, and I guess it was just my way of dealing with it. My mom was oil and I was water. We just did not mix. She was trying to hold on too tight, and I was kind of wild. At that point I was really feeling fire. She would say, "Don't stay out past ten," and I would come home at eleven thirty. I'd be smoking cigarettes and drinking beer. That was the big thing in ninth grade.

Things got pretty bad. We pulled hair, we bloodied lips; although that didn't happen too often. Usually it was just screaming and yelling.

I wanted to take off when I was sixteen, but I thank the Lord that I didn't, because I wouldn't have what I have with my parents now. My mom is one of my best friends. I love my mom.

I was raised Catholic, but I don't claim it. I definitely believe in something up there, but to me, whether you're Jewish, Christian or whatever, it's all the same. **It's all about love and goodness and believing that something else is out there.**

[CASTING APPLICATION]

What is the most challenging thing you have ever accomplished? How did it make you feel? What would you do differently today? Trying out for the Dallas Cowboys cheerleaders and making the squad. It's a long, complicated process. It was one of the best experiences of my life. I would change my opinion of myself when I was cheering if I could go back. Suddenly I felt fat, not pretty or funny enough. It took a lot for me to accept myself and love myself for me.

If you could only pack one suitcase for a trip, what would be in it? The normal stuff. Clothes, makeup, my dancing shoes and some good tunes, like "Flashdance." And if my girlfriend Julie would fit, I'd stuff her in, too, because I'm always laughing when she's around.

Describe your most embarrassing moment. I have this retainer with two false teeth on it. It can be removed to be cleaned and stuff, so as you can see, it's not hinged to the roof of my mouth. I was at a gathering at a friend's house, and my friend Becca accidentally knocked me in the mouth while we were boogying down. My teeth flew out and down to the floor. It was bad. I recovered my teeth and laughed about it ... but only much later.

How important is sex to you? Do you have it only when you're in a relationship? Do you seek it out at other times? What's the most exciting/interesting place you've ever had sex? Sex is definitely not that important to me. Don't get me wrong— I enjoy it, but I almost like closeness and cuddling more. I've had sex outside of a relationship once only. It's just not on my mind that much. The craziest place was on the hood of my car, parked on a street, with cars driving by. What can I say?

Name two people you would like to meet and tell us why. 1. MADONNA. She was a dancer, she's brave, she's smart. **2.** My mother's real dad who died when she was thirteen. She loved him. I'd like to meet him and love him too.

What's the best thing about being out on your own? Finding your independence and accomplishing things on your own.

What's the worst thing about being out on your own? Not having someone there to save your ass when you've done something wrong.

What's your greatest fear? Why? My greatest fear is the fear of losing touch with what's really important in life. I never want to sacrifice my happiness for material or career aspirations. I never want to forget to smell the flowers of life along the way. That would suck.

If you could change one thing about the way you look, what would it be? I would change the way I look at myself. Then I wouldn't care if I have a dimple on my cheek in the wrong spot or that I have a bump on my nose.

If you could change one thing about the way you act, what would it be? I would never take what I have for granted. Why does it always take something to happen to make me remember? For instance, I didn't appreciate my false teeth until I flushed them down the toilet by mistake.

CASTING
Michelle

CASTING

Patrice

Patrice wanted to be on Road Rules so badly that he showed up at the hotel the casting people were staying at "just to say good-bye." He was pummeling them with questions as they were walking out the door!

NICKNAME: **Superburschi**

HOMETOWN: **Berlin, Germany**

BIRTHDAY: **November 1, 1974**

SIGN: **Scorpio**

PREFERRED FASHION STYLE: **Avant-garde, classic and casual mix**

FAVORITE *SINGLED OUT* HOST: **Carmen Electra**

FAVORITE GROUP: **New Edition**

FAVORITE CAR: **Porsche**

To: Mary-Ellis, Jonathan, Clay, Rick
From: Carmen
Subject: Hello from Italy!

The finalists turned out to be really great as well. None of them seem to fit the "typical" German image, but apparently there just does not exist such a thing. From what we've heard, this generation is doing its best to be as far from typical as possible. We have a black German who has not traveled anywhere except to Amsterdam and Paris, which is highly unusual for this age group (it seems). He's another one we found in a club—he's got a wonderful look, and his personality is warm and friendly.

CASTING VIDEO

CLAY NEWBILL, PRODUCER/DIRECTOR: I met Patrice at the second round of casting, in London. I had seen a lot of videotape on him and couldn't believe the way he looked. He looks like a statue. I mean, the guy just has a fabulous body and chiseled features. He looks like a model. My first thought was: "This guy is going to be tough and probably unlikable because of the fact that he is so attractive." What I found when I first met Patrice face-to-face was that he was actually very warm and very, very likable. He had this great innocence. He was kind of wide-eyed in how he looked at things—sort of like someone who'd been deprived of experience. When I called to tell him that he'd been selected, he was so excited. He told me that he was running back in forth in his apartment. But he was also concerned. He thought that all of the people were going to be so cool and calm except him. I told him, "We want you to be yourself. If you want to react, react. Have confidence in yourself!"

PATRICE: My father is from Congo, a French colony in Central Africa, and my mother is a white German. It is very difficult to be someone with such skin who is living in Germany. If you ask most people what it means to be German, most likely they will say you have to be blond with blue eyes. So it's quite a strange thing for me to say I'm German. My parents got divorced when I was thirteen. I never really had a stable family. Living through a divorce gives you a unique perspective. Suddenly this harmony is destroyed. You're so hurt. All you want to do is avoid getting hurt again. I guess you could say that that's why I appreciate solitude so much—the moments when I can really savor myself and really be by myself. When I don't feel comfortable around people, I tend to hide a lot of things about myself. I do this in two ways: Either I talk a lot, or I stay in the background and say nothing.

[CASTING APPLICATION]

What do you think are your best characteristics? Please describe them. I'm one of the nicest assh**es; it takes a moment to recognize that I'm nice. I'm confident (I know who I am). I'm romantic in love and life. I'm curious—I have to know everything.

What do you think are your worst characteristics? Please describe them. Laziness. Being funny (I overdo it sometimes). Being direct. I talk a lot.

What are some ways that you've treated someone who has been important to you that you have been proud of? When they need me I'm there and do as much as I can. That's what friends are for.

What habits do other people have that you simply cannot tolerate? Hysteric people is what I hate. Also selfishness.

Name three living people who you would like to meet, and tell us why. Michael Jackson—I still want to know how he really is. Luc Besson—I want to have a part in one of his films. New Edition—party! party! party!

If you could only pack one backpack for a trip, what would be in it? Portable CD player, condoms, chocolate bars, a couple pairs of trousers, T-shirts, socks, and fresh underwear.

PATRICE

How would your boyfriend/girlfriend feel about your leaving for eight to ten weeks? Would you be faithful? Nobody is faithful one hundred percent.

Describe how conflicts were handled at home as you were growing up (Who won? Who lost? Was yelling and/or hitting involved?). Shouting at each other was normal, but a solution was found that way.

Tell us about some places in Europe that you have always wished you could visit. London, Milan, Rome, Venice, Turkey.

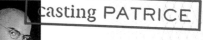
casting PATRICE

Patrice

What do you do for fun? Watching movies, playing videogames, eating, nonsense (tricks and jokes), sex.

If you had three wishes, what would they be? Health, peace in the world, love.

What is your greatest fear? Racism, because it's everywhere.

Have you ever hit anyone in anger or self-defense? If so, tell us about it. I was nine when I hit my best friend. I was so angry that I made him bleed out of his nose. It took one hit. Since then I've been afraid of hurting people.

If you could change one thing about the way you look, what would it be? I would like to have smooth clear brown skin.

What are the most important issues facing you today? Unemployment, racism, pollution, the Taiwan and China conflict.

How do you feel about abortion? It's a she thing. As a man, I have no right to dictate to a woman what she should do with her body.

CLUE *Go to the National Palace of Spain to meet your travel mates.*

Go to the National Palace of Spain to meet your travel mates

First Impressions

CHRIS: In terms of my travel mates, the first impressions are only good. I'm starting to see how we five wound up in this camper. There seems to be all the elements necessary to a unique, exciting group dynamic.

BELOU: Antoine gave me a kiss on the cheek, and I thought, "Oh, a kiss." When I met Antoine for the first time, I felt nothing. I thought, "Hey, nice guy, very spontaneous." On our first day, Patrice opened his toiletry bag, and I had to laugh. There was a little bit of makeup to cover up pimples, and everything was so neat and organized. He had five deodorants and four toothbrushes. Everything was practically in alphabetical order.

MICHELLE: When Chris saw Belou for the first time, he said, "What a bunny."

bunny \bun′nē\ n., pl. -nies. a babe, a cutie, usually used **Definition** by guys in reference to girls.

ANTOINE: Before I met everyone, I thought I was going to be the weaky, the quiet one. I thought the guys would be a bunch of Rambos.

PATRICE: On the first *Road Rules*, there were three girls and only two guys. And then on the second season, there were three guys and two girls. I was expecting it to be three girls and two guys again. Antoine and I were standing there, waiting to see who would show up. When I saw another guy approaching with Michelle, I was so disappointed.

MICHELLE: Chris wasn't what I expected him to be. I expected him to have this Boston accent and to be or look more New Yorkish. He was definitely too cute to be from Boston or New York, I thought.

Christening Pepe!

WHAT WAS WAITING INSIDE PEPE:

POLAROID CAMERA
FILM
A GPS (A COMPUTERIZED
   MAPPING SYSTEM)
TRUNK WITH MISCELLANEOUS
   BOOKS (INCLUDING A COLORING
   BOOK WITH CRAYONS)
DIARIES
SUNGLASSES
ROAD RULES MANUAL
LAPTOP COMPUTER
PHONE CARDS
HIKING BOOTS
SPORTSWEAR
CASSETTE (WITH FIRST CLUE)

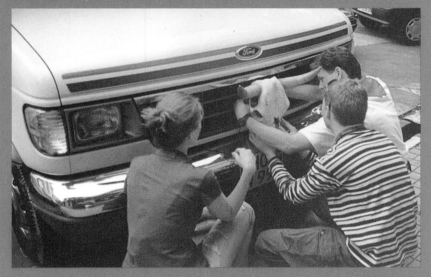

Barcelona is full of the inspirational designs of architect Antonio Gaudi y Cornet. Check out the Cathedral of the Holy Family and Guell Park. Modern artists Pablo Picasso and Joan Miró also worked in Barcelona for a while.

PAGE

25.

**BARCELONA
–PAMPLONA
312 miles**

Catch their work—as well as Renaissance and Baroque paintings— at the giant Art Museum of Catalonia. For late- night walks, snacking and bar-hopping, walk Barcelona's Las Ramblas.

BELOU: *The bulls—they're, like, five meters from me! I don't have the guts to look!*

ANTOINE: *You feel like you're being pushed and squashed! It's the biggest rush of adrenaline ever!*

CHRIS: *I just jumped over a few people who were getting knocked on their heads! That was really cool!*

mission 1

Run for your life as you run with the bulls!

CLUE

Welcome to Road Rules 3, The European Adventure! All right guys, let's get down to business. Just follow the clues you receive, and when you complete the missions, you can expect that handsome reward. Best of luck. Okay, let's get rolling! There's a place in Spain in the dry summer heat where running from creatures will be your first feat:
Festival de San Fermín
7 a.m.
Plaza de Santiago

ANTOINE: Running with the bulls was a truly great mission. Truly a challenge! A great way to start our trip!

MICHELLE: Belou and I were, like, two of the only women. There were almost no women running, and that was really freaky. We were so afraid we'd get knocked down. The crowd doesn't give a f**k if you're a woman or not. When there's a bull coming toward your rear end, you're just running!

CLAY NEWBILL, PRODUCER/DIRECTOR: Our first mission was a challenge to film. There's this long passageway called the Corridor of Death, and it was too narrow for us to have cameras set up there. We had set ups before the corridor and after it, but none in the alley itself. So when the cast started going down it, we took two cameras and followed them. I was really frightened. I was thinking, What if one of the cast gets knocked down by somebody else and gored? That didn't happen. What did happen is the cast walked too late, and the bulls had already passed. We ended up getting some great shots of other people getting gored by the bulls, and other people running with the bulls, but we barely got any footage of the cast. **What we got on camera was more like strolling with the bulls.** Belou and Michelle were basically window-shopping. Luckily, the bull-running takes place over eight days, so I had the opportunity to talk the cast into doing it a second time. "You guys were great," I said, "but would you mind running again?"

PATRICE: The only reason that I did it again was that I didn't want to be a chicken, and that's the truth. I was scared the first time we ran—even though nothing happened. I mean, that's something the cameras didn't get—my fear when I was about to go down the Corridor of Death. When they told us later that they had nothing on tape and asked us to do it again, I was like, "What?!?" But Chris said, "Yeah, no problem." And Antoine said, "Yeah, let's go and do it." So I was like, "Okay, yeah, I'm going to do it, too."

MARY-ELLIS BUNIM, EXECUTIVE PRODUCER: The footage from Pamplona was both exciting and horrifying. I couldn't believe how close the camera guys got to those bulls in the arena. The final irony was that we were asked to edit out any moments of contact between the bulls and people for the MTV Europe version of the episode. Europeans are even more sensitive to animal rights issues than Americans.

Fireworks!
BELOU'S BOY 1

BELOU: That night in Pamplona, Antoine started it. We were standing looking at the fireworks, and it was incredible. It was so beautiful. And I don't know, there was something there. Antoine grabbed me and just started to kiss me on the shoulder. He started it, he really started it. I remember Chris and Antoine coming in our room with roses that night. We spent the night together in one bed with Chris and Michelle, the four of us. We laughed and we talked, but we didn't really do anything. I mean, we didn't have sex. The next morning, we stood up, and I told Antoine, "I am sorry. I have a boyfriend. I don't want anybody to know about this." I think that he had something like a crush, you know. He said, "Yeah, no problem." The cameras were there the whole next day, and I put my sunglasses on, and I acted like nothing was going on. I think it made Antoine mad. It made him feel like a joke.

Antoine and Belou, sitting in a tree, K-I-S-S-I-N-G.

ANTOINE: Belou's a very sensual person, and I can be very sensual when I want to, and we just happened to be sensual at the same time. It was just a splendid moment, a very sweet one, but that's as far as it goes.

CHRIS AND MICHELLE GET TOGETHER: 1

CHRIS: Michelle and I made out. I don't know what Antoine and Belou were doing. I didn't listen or pay attention. That just seemed normal to me. When you live the college life ... I've hooked up with a zillion people. Once I was on a cruise ship, and there were four girls in the room, and I was with one girl. The room was, like, tiny, and my head was hitting the top of someone's bed who was sleeping above. So that stuff doesn't bother me. That first night, I was, like, **This trip is going to be mad!**

PATRICE: I didn't feel lonely when Michelle and Chris and Antoine and Belou got together. I thought Michelle and Belou were really cute, but they weren't my type. Also, I wanted to concentrate on the trip. Dating a girl is something you can do any day of the week. I knew the trip was going to be a unique experience. I didn't want to miss a minute of it.

TRAVEL ✉ LOG

Our Road Rulers avoid the bulls' horns, but they run straight into Cupid's arrow. Will Chris and Michelle mug their way through Europe? Will Patrice stay solo? Will love cast its spell on Antoine and Belou? Or will cuddling on camera lose its charm?

The processions, parades and nonstop partying of the San Fermín festival happen between the sixth and fourteenth of July every year, and the biggest attraction is the encierro or running of the bulls. The average bull weighs half a ton and can run the 848-meter course in about two minutes—about twice as fast as the average human!

PAMPLONA–
SAN SEBASTIÁN
73 Miles

SPAIN
PAMPLONA

☆ The Road Rulers had a full night out on the town which began with dinner and flamenco dancers at Don Pablo (Navas de Colosa, 19-B) and ended with drinking and dancing at Bar Utopia (Calle Nueva, 117).

MICHELLE: Right after Belou and Antoine mugged in Pamplona, Belou was convinced she didn't like him. But that didn't last very long. A day later, she was like, "Michelle, I think I'm falling for him." Bam, bam, bam. For the next few days, they hung out with each other nonstop. Unlike me and Chris, who just went on being friends, and didn't really go for the fooling around thing, they were together all the time. Coupley, kind of.

mug \mug\ v. **mugged; mugging.** 1: to fool around. **Definition** 2: to get together, hook up. 3: to make out (and perhaps a little bit more)!

BRUCE TOMS, DIRECTOR: Something happened in San Sebastián that was very dramatic for everyone involved. We got little bits and pieces of it—Antoine shaved his head, and there was something about a lost charm and a note, but it all happened on days off, and the cast was pretty cagey about telling us about any of it. The cast has made a promise to let us into their lives. In San Sebastián, they kept us out. After San Sebastián, the group was never the same.

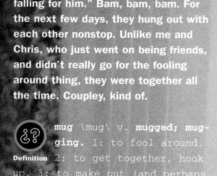

Shaved!

CHRIS: We didn't tell the cameras we were shaving Antoine's head, because we thought it would be funny. It was a mistake, I guess, because I think they were upset. You can get a shot of Antoine saying, "All of a sudden, I shaved my head last night," but you don't have the actual footage.

BELOU: I know why Antoine shaved his head. In San Sebastián, we were staying in this really expensive hotel. That was nice and all, but we were really bored. We were ready for our second mission. We were ready for action. Antoine was very bored, and he said that he wanted to do something bold. And so Chris and I started shaving. What a mistake, because **after he shaved his head, Antoine changed into this maniac, into this aggressive person.** It had to do with the crummy attitude Antoine had toward the crew. I mean, at first, in Pamplona and San Sebastián, I shared it with him. The cameras really bothered me, and so Antoine and I would interfere with the crew, scream at them and stuff, because we wanted things our way. I realized pretty quickly that I had to play by the rules. But Antoine, he never stopped blowing things up ...

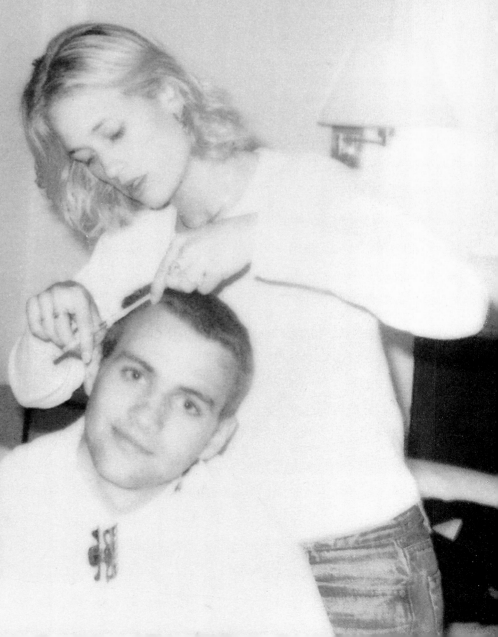

Emergency Meeting

CLAY NEWBILL, PRODUCER/DIRECTOR: It was in the first few days of the trip that Antoine realized that he didn't like having the cameras on him. Belou was wigging out, too. She did not understand why the camerapeople and the crew wouldn't chat with her. After Antoine shaved his head, and the tension level was pretty high, Bruce and I sat down with the entire cast to work things out. **Belou voiced her antagonism. She said, "The crew, they work like dogs, and it's like they're stupid robots."** It really upset me, and I tried to re-educate her on the point of the show. "Listen," I said, "they're not stupid, and the only reason they're doing what they're doing is because they have been trusted not to interact, and they're professionals."

JONATHAN MURRAY, EXECUTIVE PRODUCER: We've never had a cast try to live two lives—one in front and one behind the camera—as much as the Europe cast. It was very, very frustrating. We've taken steps in both casting and how we shoot to make sure it doesn't happen again.

Lost Charm

ANTOINE: I'm fine with the fact that people and things appear into your life, and then they disappear. That's why I don't get very attached. To anything. To anyone.

MICHELLE: Okay, here's the real reason Antoine and Belou went bust. We were all down on the beach, drinking and hanging out and talking in a circle. Chris, Belou and I decided we were going to go skinny-dipping in the ocean. Belou was wearing this necklace with a cross on it that Antoine had lent her. It meant a lot to him, I don't exactly know why—some girl gave it to him or something. I don't know if he asked Belou if she wanted to wear it or if she asked if she could. All I know is that he gave it to her and said, "Whatever you do, just don't lose it." Well, when we went skinny-dipping, she didn't take the necklace off. She came out of the water and the necklace was gone. She started freaking out. She ran up to the room completely hysterical. I went after her and found her in the shower crying, "He's going to kill me, and I care about him so much!" She was like, "I can't tell him, Michelle. Will you tell him for me?"

I went down to the beach and just spilled it. "Antoine," I said, "I really don't know how to tell you this, but Belou lost your cross. She's absolutely hysterical that you're going to hate her." He was strangely calm. He said, "That's fine, I'm not going to hate her." He stayed down there on the beach and kept partying. I told Belou about his reaction, and she was really relieved. "Really?" she said. "He's okay with it?" And I was like, "Yeah."

I guess Antoine really wasn't okay with it, because when Belou went back down to the beach, he was really cold to her, and then she went to hang out in his room with Chris and Patrice, and he asked her to leave. So it all kind of happened from there; it all kind of spiraled downward. **The lost cross, that's where it just started to blow up.** And then, of course, there was the letter.

WHAT BELOU WOULD LOSE DURING THE NEXT TEN WEEKS

- Her passport (three times—not counting the time in casting!)
- An earring
- Her Pharcyde tape
- Her black towel
- Her cigarettes
- One shoe
- Her backpack—containing passport and airline tickets home
- Her ID (twice)
- Her slippers
- Her sneakers
- Her headphones
- Her grip, and her composure, but not her soul!

THE LETTER

Belou,

Short & simple:
If you need to put your feelings in someone's hands, don't put them in mine. If you need someone to take care of you, don't rely on me. There are things I can't do with anyone. People I have long and sturdy relationships with are people who rely on themselves and go their own way, without getting involved with me too deeply. I can't get involved with anything right now. I don't want to; there's no point. In September, I'm hoping to move to Vietnam. Keep your life and your feelings to yourself and we can do great things together. Indeed, I think you are a lot more than just a cute little girl, but I am not trying to get into you or to let you get into me. Let's not be foolish, but make the two next months as pleasant as possible.

Antoine

CHRIS: I guess the letter was the beginning of the end. If the letter's what it sounds like, I would be pissed if I were Belou.

PATRICE: She seemed to be really upset about everything, not only the lost charm but also all the feelings she and Antoine shared. He just replied that she should know that, to him, it's not huge, nothing at all. That's what boys always say: "It's not really that important to me."

MARY-ELLIS BUNIM, EXECUTIVE PRODUCER: My take on Belou and Antoine's relationship is that they got together, but she pulled back because she got nervous about betraying Steve on camera. Then Antoine got defensive and attacked. I think that if they each had reacted differently that next day, there might have been a relationship that could have gone somewhere. They had a lot to share with each other. I would have loved to see them fall in love. That would have been a fascinating story to witness.

BELOU: I think that in a way Antoine was in love with me. He just denied it. Maybe Antoine was really shocked by how upset I was about the locket and how that meant I cared about him, and that's why he wrote the letter, I don't know. After I got the letter, I knocked on his door. It was late, and we were whispering. I said, "What the f**k are you telling me? You have such a wall around you! You won't let anybody come to you! You won't let anybody love you ever!" And he agreed. He said, "No, I won't. No, I won't." And I said, "Let me come to you. Please, take my hand. Come on, let's be friends. Let somebody love you. Let somebody into you." He said, "I can't, I can't!" And we just started to get so crazy, standing there in front of each other. **He said, "You're like an angel who has come to me, but I can't let you in."** And I said, "What if I am an angel and I want to help you? Why won't you let me?" And he said, "It's not the right time. You're not the right girl." And I said, "Why not? Why is it not the right time? Why am I not the right girl?" He said, "Because you are too young, and you are too naive, and you have Steve." After a while we just said goodnight. It was a big drama—whispering, and crying, and yelling. I was crying and he was yelling. **No cameras. Big drama, only between us.**

MICHELLE: Belou was crushed by the letter. I couldn't believe it, either. He'd seemed so into her. The next day, in the Winnebago, on the way to Carcassonne, there was this huge tension. It was like we were with a whole new Antoine person we didn't know. Belou was trying to feel him out, and he wasn't gonna pay attention to her. He wouldn't have any of it.

BRUCE TOMS, DIRECTOR: The day we drove from San Sebastián to Carcassonne, I was filming in the cast Winnebago, and because of the tension, it was one of the worst days of my life. They got lost, and Antoine screamed at everyone. Not to mention that we were on the road for twelve hours and that because of the fridge and the bathroom—despite the no-dump rule—the Winnebago stunk.

ANTOINE: I bitterly regret that I got so mad at everyone because we could not find the way. And I hate watching this episode of me getting angry and telling people off. The fact is, I think I'd slept three hours all night because I'd spoken with Belou so much.

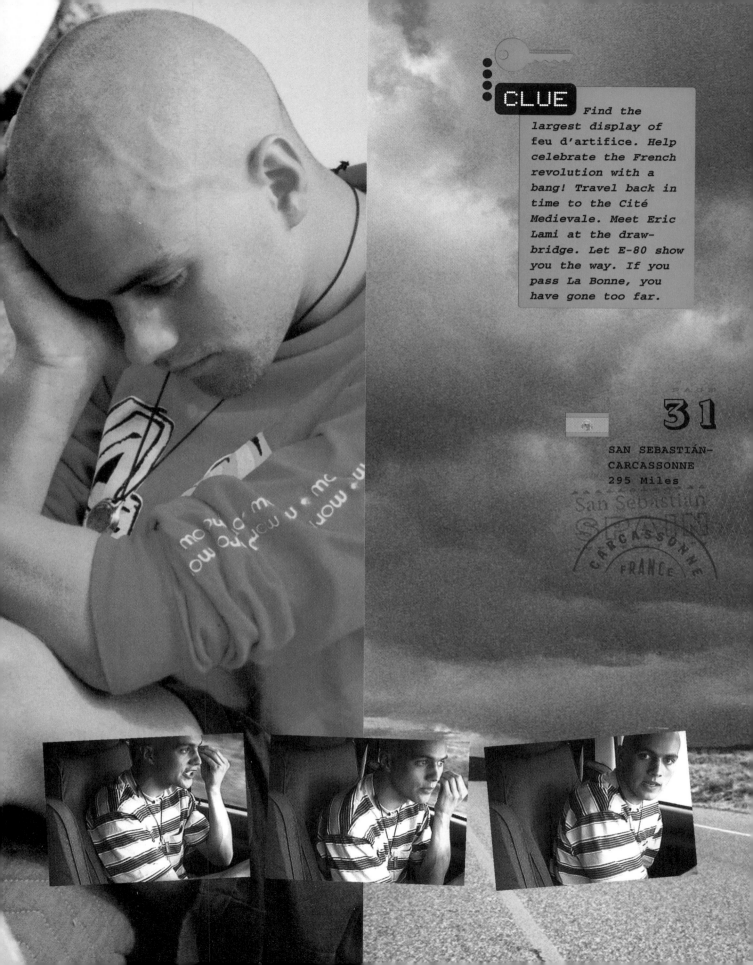

CLUE

Find the largest display of feu d'artifice. Help celebrate the French revolution with a bang! Travel back in time to the Cité Medievale. Meet Eric Lami at the drawbridge. Let E-80 show you the way. If you pass La Bonne, you have gone too far.

31

SAN SEBASTIÁN–
CARCASSONNE
295 Miles

San Sebastián
SPAIN
CARCASSONNE
FRANCE

ANTOINE

JONATHAN MURRAY, EXECUTIVE PRODUCER: I think the trip was difficult for Antoine because he was used to doing his own thing. I think he felt to some extent that the production was compromising his personal journey.

MICHELLE: Antoine was the father figure of the group. When he would spew out facts and point out things, that didn't bother me. I had never been to Europe, and I was pretty ignorant about things, and I wanted to hear, I wanted to learn, I wanted to know. Belou would say, "I want to do the trip, and I want to learn on my own, in my way." It got to her; it didn't get to me.

PATRICE: Antoine, well, he's a disturbed child, in my opinion. He always tried to be the center of attention, and that got on my nerves. Michelle was always saying that she saw him in a father-type role. That annoyed me so much.

CHRIS: I would say we became friends, Antoine and I. He had an adventurous spirit, and I liked that about him. We could have a lot of fun together. But if he were someone at my high school, I don't think I would have gotten to know him. We would have just said hi in the halls or something.

CLAY NEWBILL, PRODUCER/DIRECTOR: Antoine travels using a backpack, and I'm talking about something the size of your bookbag at school. He's that experienced a traveler. He likes to go someplace and absorb as much as he can there and be challenged intellectually. And once he feels he has learned as much as he can learn in a certain amount of time, he's ready to move on. Antoine never cared about "the handsome reward" we were offering. The reward for him was traveling to all these cool places and meeting these people and experiencing these things.

MARY-ELLIS BUNIM, EXECUTIVE PRODUCER: I think Antoine's whole philosophy on life is that the best defense is a great offense. He has a protective wall around him, and if anybody gets too close, he pushes back first. If he sees that people are getting to the real Antoine, he throws up a smoke screen.

BELOU: I think Antoine will make a great dad. I can just see him at the head of some big wooden table with good food and wine, taking visitors and talking all night. He'd have everybody listening to him and laughing about him and asking him questions. He would love to just talk about history and about the house that he bought, about whatever.

ANTOINE: I never was a group person. I've come to like it very much now. So I guess you could say that *Road Rules* did indeed change me. I'm rather a solitary person, and for the first time, I really had to be part of a group and take the group into account.

Still, I guess I spend too much time making sure I'm happy with everything that's going on instead of making sure everybody else is alright. But there you go.

Often I need to be alone with myself. I need to hide away from everything now and then, because that's when I recoup my drive. And my drive is something vital to me. Chris has commented that I have a hard time letting people get close to me, and it's true. It's less true now, thanks to this trip.

I miss the road. Like waking up in hotels and unpacking and packing. Like going to tiny restaurants and eating tapas for next to nothing. It's the little things I miss.

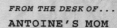

PAGE

33

THE CAST
AND CREW on

ANTOINE

CARCASSONNE,
FRANCE

mission 2

Feels like French
Fourth of July! The
fireworks show is in your
hands! Don't blow it!

MICHELLE: We didn't exactly have
the best seats. There was soot falling
in our faces the whole time.

PATRICE: Right now I'm like
a lone soldier, the outsider,
but that's okay, 'cause it's
the real me.

FROM PATRICE'S JOURNAL:

BRUCE TOMS, DIRECTOR: There
was a time when Patrice turned to me,
because things really sucked for him.
This was in Carcassonne, after the fireworks. And you don't really see this in
the show, but Patrice does not enjoy
the fireworks. I think he's almost crying in the background. It really upset
him when they were late for things.
They had to meet their contact for the
fireworks before the sun went down.
Patrice kept saying, "We gotta go, we
gotta go, we gotta go." And right when
they needed to go, Antoine stepped
into the shower and made them ten or
fifteen minutes late. The sun went
down, and they missed their contact
and got in trouble. Patrice spent the
rest of the evening brooding while
everyone was having a great time
watching the fireworks go off.

CHRIS: We took a break from driving to hang out in this amazing field.

CLUE *Reach new heights with these tools. Retain what you learn for future Road Rules. Roc et Canyon, Millau—on July 15th.*

MILLAU, FRANCE

BELOU: During the trip, Patrice would often bump into people's personalities. He'd isolate himself. He always had to have everything in control, and sometimes it set him apart from everybody. Like if we had to be out by 6:00 a.m., we'd wake up at 5:30 a.m. Patrice would wake up at 5:00 a.m. Or sometimes he'd just be very particular. Like once, in Millau, we wanted to go shopping. I was going to cook that night. We all went into the car. Patrice was talking to this girl that worked at Roc et Canyon. And we said, "Are you coming with us shopping?" And he said, "No, I'm not coming, because you're always doing cheap shopping." So we were like, "Okay, Patrice." So we went shopping, and we just bought our things. And I said in the supermarket, "If Patrice is going to say one word about the food—whether it's wrong or right or whatever—I'm going to totally freak."

And everybody was making jokes: "He's going to do it! He's going to do it!"

So we came back, and the first thing Patrice does is step into the car, go into the bag and search for what we bought. He took the bread out and went, "Ooh, you bought old bread!" in this very annoying way, like a little child. And I just collapsed. We were both in the backseat of the car, and I just pushed him. "Shut up!" I said. "You have no right to talk about the bread. We bought bread. You didn't want to come. You just eat what we bought, whether you're happy with it or not!" And we had a whole fight. He said, "You don't have the right to push me." And he started pushing me, and we had a big fight in the car. Everyone loved the food that night. Everyone except Patrice.

CHRIS: That was the point where everyone was sort of annoyed with Patrice. Wherever we were, he got overexcited, like a little kid in a candy store. He wasn't letting people get their words in, and he was spouting off about America. We were not happy with him, and he sort of got the vibe. I remember once he went out walking with his headphones and didn't come back for a while. Belou, Michelle and I finally caught up with him. We had this huge talk. Belou was like, "You don't listen to people, you have to try to listen better." That seemed pretty ironic—Belou telling someone to listen better; but still, it was a good conversation.

LAMAR DAMON, STORY EDITOR: I think that Patrice was often misunderstood. I think his language skills were lacking, and that put up barriers for him. When I watched footage of him, I could see that he was desperately trying to get his point across, but he couldn't. Occasionally, he would talk too much, or too fast. Effie from Season Two had similar problems: she wanted to communicate, but she just couldn't do it with ease.

Journal Entry

MICHELLE: I am already starting to mix days together. Patrice is going to drive me crazy. I can already feel myself getting testy with him. This could be a long trip for me with him. He is very hyper and just talks, talks, talks!!!

Bastille Day is July 14. Carcassonne, known as the Cité Medieval, was featured in 1991's Robin Hood, Prince of Thieves.

PAGE **35**

CARCASSONNE–MILLAU
149 Miles

CARCASSONNE FRANCE *Millau*

FRANCE

The cast stayed at a youth hostel: Auberge de Jeunesse (Rue Vicomte Trencavel—just off Rue Cros Mayrevielle.)

CHRIS: Patrice had some insane eating habits. When he had to eat, he had to eat!

mission 3

Get extreme as you rappel down some serious cliffs, dive into moving water and swim to safety!

CHRIS: The big thing about rappeling and canyoning was Patrice getting over his fear of heights. And he did it. It was really amazing. When we were standing there, he was trying to do anything to allay his fears. I even heard him singing a Take That song, which was pretty funny. I mean, you can't get much worse than cheesy British pop.

PATRICE: It's something you should really not do—sing a Take That song in public. Especially at this moment of truth.

MICHELLE: Rappeling and canyoning was great, except for the fly factor. I was pulling a Belou on the flies. They were all over you. We were climbing up this hill with all our equipment, and I was just cursing. I had had it with that whole thing. And while we were canyoning, the tour guys were definitely being sexist. To Belou and me, they were like, "Why don't y'all rappel down, and the men can jump." Typical.

pulling a Belou \pul-ing a be-loo '\ n. 1: freaking out.
Definition 2: having an unexpectedly huge outburst, the magnitude of which is disproportionate to the cause. 3: losing it.

ROAD RULES CASE #0000001

RICK DE OLIVEIRA, COORDINATING PRODUCER: The Road Rulers, they're having a great time, and Patrice got over his fear of heights, which was great, but all said, the filming of Roc et Canyon was brutal. We were having to scale mountains to get certain shots. It was intense, and the crew was exhausted and beat. And then the cast, after they've had this amazing adventure—I caught them sneaking around and trying to snag food from our crafts service table. Unbelievable.

MICHELLE: *I should have worn hiking shoes.*

PATRICE: *I just checked the view and saw nothing. Just some trees. If something's going to go wrong, it's over. Game over. Hasta la vista!* ▼

BELOU: *I lost my grip at one point, and I was hanging there, holding my brakes and struggling to get my grip back again. I'm a little bit shaky right now. I gotta admit it. But I loved it.* ▼

MICHELLE: *This is good stuff! The water! The rocks! We're scaling walls! We practically bodysurfed down rocks and waterfalls! I mean, you feel like freakin' Spiderman!* ▼

ANTOINE: *I just did twelve meters down, and I went pretty fast. I'm quite happy! The others said that I look like a frog going down the mountain. That must be in my roots somewhere.* ▼

CLUE Have we got a job for you. A Cannes job. Locate the yacht, the Happy Fox.

RICK DE OLIVEIRA, COORDINATING PRODUCER: This is something very typical that Antoine would do: the cast had to get to Cannes by a certain time, and on the way, he started telling them that St. Tropez was so much nicer and that's really where they should be going. He almost had them all convinced that they should be going there instead. Of course we'd put a lot of work into setting everything up in Cannes.

PAGE

37

MILLAU–CANNES
289 Miles

Millau
FRANCE

Cannes
France

TRAVEL ✉ LOG

Could it be that a rocky mission has actually put our cast at ease? Think again! It's all about drama as the cast heads to the beach for some clean-livin' fun and a few close encounters of the Canuck kind!

Job #1

SWAB THE DECKS!
SCRAPE THE BARNACLES!
WASH THE LATRINE! PUMP THE
BILGE! THEN TROLL THE TOWN
FOR TWO DATES APIECE.

Allyson and Melissa

BELOU: Allyson and Melissa, I loved them, but I mean, they were like maniacs!

MICHELLE: I liked Melissa and Allyson, but they were not the kind of girls I could hang around all the time. They were too much talkers. Always having a story. And Allyson would finish her stories, pause and then go: "No, I'm lying." And she would have been lying the whole time.

MELISSA: Then there was Texas—Michelle. She was a huge cheese, but you couldn't help but love her.

Journal Entry

Come to Our MTV Yacht Party!

MELISSA: I'd actually been set up with Chris before. He had been visiting a friend of mine in Montreal who thought we'd be good together, and we ended up spending, like, forty-five minutes talking at a bar. I knew he was going to be on *Road Rules* in Europe, but I didn't expect to run into him. When they called us at 8:15 p.m., Allyson and I freaked out. We weren't even showered, we had to be ready for MTV and we thought the boat was leaving at nine. **Two girls with forty-five minutes to get dressed and showered. It was like Mission: Impossible.** I liked the group. Michelle was the peacemaker, the neutral one. She's everybody's friend. I had some amazing, amazing conversations with Patrice. There might have been something there, but nothing really came out of it. I thought he was a bit strange in the way that he was very to himself. And I don't think he would have done anything about it if there was anything between us.

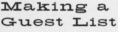

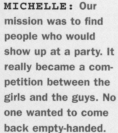

Making a Guest List

MICHELLE: Our mission was to find people who would show up at a party. It really became a competition between the girls and the guys. No one wanted to come back empty-handed.

ALLYSON: So we got on the boat and met everyone. It was cool; it was chill. It was a little uncomfortable having the camera right in your face at first. I made myself busy, though. I was being sleazy. **I had a crush on Antoine the minute I saw him. I wanted him right away, to be blunt.** He's a very good-looking boy. A little crazy, mind you. But let's face it, he's stunning. I loved Belou. She's a crazy, crazy girl. There was some kind of connection between Melissa and me and Belou.

BELOU: We tried to find dates in a gay bar. Oops!

ALLYSON: I had one conversation with Patrice. It was about the rest of the group, but he didn't have the nicest things to say about anyone.

Chris and Melissa

CHRIS: When I was with Melissa, now that was a time I didn't want a camera on me. I didn't want a microphone on me. I didn't want what I was saying recorded. So I did censor myself a little. I wanted to be alone with her. Not necessarily to have sex with her, but just to talk with her without that knowledge that's always there, whether it's conscious or subconscious, that there is someone there recording your actions and your words.

We had fun. The thing is, I think she's spoken to many people about her experience since. Apparently she's really proud of her story, or she had no shame in telling anyone. It's all over.

MELISSA: I just know that the night that I was with Chris I felt that when the camera was on he was kind of preplanning the conversation by asking me certain questions. I felt like I was being interviewed. I think we were both sketched out. It was really annoying—the cameras were in our face, and we just wanted to be alone. So the cameras finally left, and he just came back with me to my hotel room. Nothing really happened. We just hung out. Instead of Pepe, we gave him a nice bed to sleep in, and then nothing really evolved after that.

Antoine and Allyson

ALLYSON: Antoine and I wanted to get away from the cameras and everything. So he yells out, "Anyone want to go swimming?" Chris, Antoine and myself went in the water. They went skinny-dipping. I didn't. I was wearing Antoine's shirt. He and I swam out to this rock island. He just started kissing me or whatever, and it was very nice. He's a good kisser. He's a very good kisser. Good with the hands, too. And then I said, "I'm going back to my hotel. I'm freezing, I'm wet, mascara's dripping down my face." We left discreetly—or so I thought. We were walking back to my hotel room. Everything was cool; I was having the best time with him, talking, and all of a sudden, boom, camera's in my face. For a second I thought Antoine just wanted to get me back to the room so he could look cool on camera and have a girl. We were talking without moving our mouths, very low, so the cameras couldn't understand us. And I was like, "What is going on?" And he was like, "I didn't plan this." I was so nervous, I was a little impaired, I didn't know exactly what to do. So he whispered to me, "When we get to your hotel room, just say goodnight to me. I'm gonna hide, and then I'll come back." We get to my hotel. He says, "Thank you for a very nice night," gives me a kiss good-bye and leaves. The camera is still there. I'm like, "Good-bye, it's over." The cameras still didn't leave. They just kept taping me. I was like, "I'm going to my room." They tried to go in with me. I was like, "No, good-bye." I got upstairs and immediately called one of my friends from Montreal, because I was freaking out, like, "He's not coming back, I don't know what the hell just happened." About fifteen minutes later, there's a knock on my door. Antoine comes in my room, and he goes, "You don't know what I just did. I had to run and hide in this alley so the cameras wouldn't find me!"

ANTOINE: I was hiding in bushes, running down the street and trying to stay away from the cameras. I kept asking people on the street, "Have you seen a camera crew?" People thought I was crazy. "We're right in the middle of Cannes. It's three in the morning, and you're asking us if we've seen any camera crews?"

RICK DE OLIVEIRA, COORDINATING PRODUCER: We knew Antoine was hiding from us, but we decided to let him have his fun. It was late. We'd gotten enough coverage.

CLUE *Race for a Million in Cash. Go north to Lake Como. See Vittorio at Club Morgan, Franzione Crotto #10 2250 Lezzeno, Italy.*

PAGE

39

CANNES–COMO
284 Miles

The cast hung at Cannes public beaches, Plage du Midi and Plage de la Bocca. The cast camped out at grounds right near Cannes: Caravaning St. Louis Campground in La Roquette/ St. Louis.

TRAVEL ✉ LOG

A high-stakes and high-stress mission finds the group in a state of total duress. Belou combusts. Patrice comforts. Antoine combats. And Chris and Michelle ... communicate (?!?!). It's drama Italiano as the cast competes for spending money and comes up lira-less.

LAKE COMO, ITALY

← mission 4

Row! Kayak! Ski! All in the name of competition, glory—and cold hard cash!

CHRIS AND MICHELLE GET TOGETHER: 2

MICHELLE: One night, everybody was off somewhere, and Chris and I were just hanging out talking, mainly because he felt this need to tell me about what had happened between him and Melissa in Cannes. We started listening to Enya, got in a really good conversation, then started mugging. It was no big deal. Sometime later on, Chris said that it was in Como that he thought our relationship might go somewhere, but that the next day I was very standoffish and cold to him and wouldn't even make very much eye contact with him. I felt terrible when he told me that. I'm always putting up walls.

 ## Road Rules Casualty

MARY-ELLIS BUNIM, EXECUTIVE PRODUCER: In Lake Como, we planned to do interviews in the backyard of a mansion that had a farm and a glorious view of the lake and the mountains. I arrived to find that filming had been delayed an hour and a half because there was a rooster on the grounds who was just carrying on to no end. Every time the crew would roll tape, the rooster would scream. Finally I said, "Take twenty bucks, buy the rooster, take him out to the country and board him for the day, then bring him back. Do whatever it takes, as long as the farmer feels that his rooster's going to be okay." Our associate producer went off, and suddenly we didn't hear the rooster anymore. I was thrilled, but it was a bit strange. **It was like he was just cut off in mid cock-a-doodle.** Our associate producer came back, and he had this horrible look on his face. Apparently he'd bought the rooster, but the farmer hadn't understood we still wanted him alive. He'd just killed him right then and there. I felt horrible. I don't know whether it was a language problem or why it happened, but it was not the way to solve a production problem. I was horrified. I think the cast was, too, because it got out.

Belou's Grandmother

BELOU: I found out in Cannes that my grandmother died. I was really in pieces when I heard it, although I knew she was very sick. Before I went on the trip, I'd said good-bye to her at the hospital. I had a really great relationship with my grandma, my dad's mom. I remember I was with Allyson and Melissa when my uncle called to tell me, and they were so sweet to me. They were like, "Oh, Belou!" And Michelle and Chris and Patrice, everybody was hugging me. And I remember that Antoine was sitting in the Winnebago, and he couldn't hug me. He couldn't say anything. He finally said, "I am sorry for you." That's it. He didn't know what to do. With that exception, everybody was really with me at that moment. We went out to eat, and I remember that after we had dinner I called my dad.

Right after the Lake Como mission, I went to Amsterdam. The funeral, it was very beautiful. I was with Steve, my friends, my dad, and my mom for two days. And then I flew back to meet everyone in Milan. I was a day late, because I missed my flight—I'd left my passport at home.

PATRICE: Lake Como, I think, was the place that we really all had a problem with each other. **Belou went nuts at lunch.** I was really mad about the group itself. Everyone was so selfish. I was disappointed by them. I was disappointed by Chris. He was getting mad at Belou, and he was just in this kind of groove. At that moment, I was really an outsider, and I just didn't know how to explain it myself. I just didn't belong to this whole party. There was Belou, who was repulsed. And there were these three guys who had just had enough of this problem. I was right in the middle.

CLUE *Take the train from Milan to Venice. P.S. Remember to bring the GPS. When you arrive in Venice, compliment a stranger on the Ponte di Rialto to receive your next clue.*

CLUE *Venezia will test your creativity. Cut loose your apron strings as you aim to please. Call Fulvia.*

PAGE

41

LAKE COMO-
MILAN-VENICE
42 miles by
Pepe and 187
miles by train

MARY-ELLIS BUNIM, EXECUTIVE PRODUCER: It was frightening to see the reactions of people in the restaurant around us who weren't with the group. We were functioning in a very low-key way. There was a director. There were even two cameras cross-shooting. But the *Road Rules* crew people, as usual, were careful not to draw attention to themselves, so it was very quiet. And then suddenly Belou leapt out of her chair screaming. She had the full attention of the restaurant.

BRUCE TOMS, DIRECTOR: I think Belou's big blowup in Lake Como was a result of built-up frustration. She hadn't really gotten over everything that had happened between her and Antoine, and she'd just found out her grandmother had died. She was a wreck.

ANTOINE: In France there is a theory that one should never write laws when one's blood is warm. That is my philosophy. And so when Belou would blow up, I—for the sake of harmony, for the sake of making the whole thing bearable for everyone—would just carry on and take the lead. That tended to make Belou crazy, because it showed that I did not want to pay attention to what was bothering her. After we lost the mission in Lake Como and Belou left for Amsterdam, we had a day off, which was actually really great and really relaxing. Chris and I swam the whole length of the lake, with Michelle and Patrice rowing in the boat next to us. I think altogether it was five miles or something. We ate on the other side, and we were so tired. It was so great! I think it was an hour and a half in the water. It was so cool. But it all went crazy again once we got to Venice.

Lake Como is at the foot of the Swiss Alps and is surrounded by small Italian villages. Check out Ostello La Primula, the youth hostel located in the neighboring village of Menaggio. Go to the gardens at Villa Carlotta. Or catch the view of the Alps and the lake towns from Punta Spartivento ("the point that divides the wind"), which is on the outskirts of Bellagio.

BELOU

JONATHAN MURRAY, EXECUTIVE PRODUCER: I don't think we realized Belou was going to feel as much as she felt. She's just this whirlwind of emotions. She can't help herself. I think she can be maddening to travel with, yet at the same time I think some of her travel mates were almost jealous that she felt things so strongly.

CHRIS: There's no real way to explain Belou. Flamboyant? A little. Psycho? Sometimes. Smart? Yes, in her way. Spiritual? More so than I would ever be.

PATRICE: I don't know how to explain it in English, but in German, we have this expression *Olde Weis*, which means "people who pretend to be older than they are." That's Belou to me. But I think she changed a lot over the trip, really grew.

MICHELLE: I love Belou. She was definitely my baby. She was always forgetting her cigarettes or forgetting something. Sometimes I'd wash her clothes out for her. Belou's tantrums and her spats were surreal. With the trip and an unhealthy relationship behind her, maybe she'll be better. I think it'd be really good for her to be alone, without a man in her life.

ANTOINE: Belou has this incredible sense of spirituality. It's a gift from God, and something worth cherishing. Sometimes she boasts about it too much. But I think she should follow her feelings, because they are good. I think they will lead her to happiness.

MARY-ELLIS BUNIM, EXECUTIVE PRODUCER: Belou is on the verge, I think, of great things. But first she has to realize that she doesn't have to define herself through the man she's with. She can be alone. She's a complex girl, and I think she's very bright. There's so much life experience that she needs, yet she thinks she's very sophisticated. I'd love to keep a window into her life over the next ten years. **That girl is going to just explode!**

BELOU: I learned so much from *Road Rules*. How to keep myself stable. How to take a step back and take a deep breath when you really just want to scream. I'm less of a fighter now than I used to be. Being on the road with the group, I really learned the value of silence. I just loved the traveling. All the people. All the learning, learning, learning.

It really feels like therapy being around four other people day and night. I've never had brothers and sisters. I've never had people around me all the time. Being with the group helped me to find peace in myself. **The whole time on the road, I felt like I had to yell for people to hear me, to see who I was. Now I don't feel the need to scream at people to show them who I am.** If people don't agree with me, if they don't see the real Belou, I smile and walk away.

BELOU'S POEM

A strong willed woman
So much, so little
A disrespected woman
with undivided attention
From the man

Giving all and standing naked
Seemingly trying to
  hinder something
A man blows his horn
And she comes running

She hurts when he
Gets into his routine
I am using my strength
In this dark space

My soul gets weaker
Under this influence
And the man has lost his soul
And doesn't have the energy
To see my strength

There are no lessons for him
He'll continue to blow his horn
He will no longer step
  over my line
I am the unknown.

FROM THE DESK OF...
BELOU'S MOM

I really didn't like the way that Belou seemed to get so emotional whenever she couldn't find what she was looking for fast enough or whenever things didn't go her way. I do, however, realize that this is who Belou is. I am so proud of Belou, and I am constantly encouraging everyone to look at Road Rules. I would like to thank the whole Road Rules crew; Belou has really had a wonderful time. She has become more relaxed, and she seems to be able to keep her emotions better under control. Basically speaking, she has become more independent. She has really grown up.

THE CAST
AND CREW on

Mission **5**

Cook a gourmet meal!
Serve it up with style!

That's Amore

 BELOU: Let me tell you about how crazy Antoine is making me. I attacked him during breakfast in the hotel, because **that loud Belgian just won't take me seriously!** I'd just woken up and walked to the breakfast room to eat breakfast (obviously). I said, "Good Morning," and what I got from him in return was an attitude. So I responded in an angry tone of voice by saying, "Good morning, Antoine!" Antoine (with his stupid attitude) then began to give me this little sarcastic laugh of his, and that was the straw that broke the camel's back. So I asked him in a nice way to please take me seriously, but he then began to laugh even harder.

So what did Belou do? I grabbed him by the collar, and the fight began. Boom! The cameras were in our faces. Chris was trying to tear us apart, and Michelle was screaming, "What the f**k is going on!?" So it was huge!

Everything has changed in the group. It's not going as smooth as it used to. The fight is between Antoine and me, but I sometimes feel that the others think that they have to take sides.

ANTOINE: I saw Belou, and she was right next to the canal. And the first thing that came to me was, "I'm just going to push her into the canal. And if I have to dive in with her, I will." The only reason I didn't do it was because we both had microphones on, and I didn't want to ruin them. I just held myself back. I really wish I had not. Because I would have found it great to be in the water, both of us being punished for being childish and being silly people who cannot get along with each other.

Here's the thing: I never had a crush on Belou. I very much liked Belou in a protective way. At one point on the road, I wanted to take her under my wing. But she wanted more and more and more, and she was pissed off. Sometimes I'd be so sweet to her. I'd take care of when she was late or losing her stuff. But other times, I didn't want to look at her, because I wanted to have myself to myself. And that she couldn't stand, and she couldn't understand. She thought I was hiding something, and the rest of the time, she thought I was faking it.

What Really Happened with the Knife

BELOU: After I grabbed Antoine in the restaurant, I grabbed for this knife on the table and held it up. I just want to state for the record that I was never going to use that knife on Antoine. I just picked it up because it was the only thing there.

FULVIA'S RECIPE FOR
RISI E BISI
(SOUP WITH PEAS AND RICE)

(SERVES FOUR)

3 tbs butter
1/2 cup processed pancetta
1/2 cup rice
1 small onion, finely chopped
4 cups boiling salted chicken broth
1 lb fresh peas or thawed frozen
  peas, cooked in 2 tbs butter
1 tsp ground fennel seeds
4 tbs Parmesan

In a large shallow pan, heat 1 tbs of butter and sweat the pancetta
for about 5 minutes. Add the rice, cook briefly while stirring and add
the onion. Cook gently, gradually adding the hot broth. About ten minutes into the stirring and pouring process, heat the peas and add to
the rice. Stir continuously.
  After about twenty minutes, remove the pot from the heat, add 2 tbs
of butter and the Parmesan cheese, and "shake"* the rice. Sprinkle with
the ground fennel seeds, stir and serve.
*Shaking means holding the pan by the handles and dragging it up and down on
  the table, so the rice starch comes out and makes the rise e bisi velvety.

FULVIA: It was a wonderful day, because I had the new experience to work with the five participants of the program *Road Rules*. I liked them very much. **I was touched by their enthusiasm and their seriousness!**

CLUE *You're going to Belou's! Linate Airport–Milan. Air Alitalia Flt. 116. LV Milan 5:35 p.m., ARR Amsterdam 7:20 p.m.*

VENICE–MILAN–AMSTERDAM
187 miles by train and 600 miles by plane

The open-air Rialto Market is located in the Rialto district at the end of Ponte Di Rialto. The market has been around for centuries, and it used to be the place to go for fabrics, gold and silver. Now, it's the place to go for daily needs. The best time to go is on a weekday in the early morning. It's closed on Sunday and quiet on Monday.

ROAD RULES CASE #0000002

MICHELLE: Things were really tense when Chris, Antoine and I went to the Rialto market. We couldn't find some of the ingredients we needed, and it put Antoine in a foul mood. Then, when we went to the regular supermarket to buy some frozen peas, the lines were

so long that Chris and Antoine got frustrated, and stole a bag of frozen peas. I had to leave the store, because I was too squeamish.

MARY-ELLIS BUNIM, EXECUTIVE PRODUCER: I don't know anything about the peas, but I warn the casts that if anyone gets caught committing a crime, they are on their own—we won't cover for them.

J'accuse!

CHRIS: Apparently I served one of Fulvia's guests a glass of water with a dead spider in it. Obviously the crew had planted it there. I mean, I highly doubt that in a house that nice and meticulous there'd be dead bugs in the cupboards. In my interview, I accused the crew, and they laughed, but I swear to God they did it. It was a conspiracy. They drew their plans against me.

CLAY NEWBILL, PRODUCER/DIRECTOR: Not true. I swear to God. Believe me, if I had planted it there, I would have gotten a story out of it. The woman would have noticed and made a big scene about it and humiliated Chris. Now that would have been good!

BELOU'S
BOY 2

BELOU: In Venice, the cameras missed something. One night I met Ben, and he was a really special guy, a friend of Chris's from school. We had a philosophical conversation about things. We talked deep. And I don't know, in the end he asked me, "Can I kiss you?" And I said to myself, "Belou, should I?" He said: "All night, I'm yearning to kiss you." So we went outside and he kissed me, and then he ran away. I screamed, "Will you write me?" And he answered, "I shall!" We never wrote. It's a good thing nothing really happened, because—even though I didn't know it at the moment—I was going to see Steve soon.

Staying with Steve

PATRICE: I was very nervous to meet Belou's boyfriend, Steve, and when I did I was really surprised. He acted so weird. I couldn't understand why he wasn't happier to see Belou and why he was so unhappy to see the cameras.

CHRIS: Steve didn't want us or the cameras in his home. I find that a little strange. He's a struggling artist. In my opinion, what could be better than international exposure? A chance to talk about your music on television? I would have thought it was a dream come true for someone trying to make it in the business, but I guess I see the world a little differently from Steve-O.

ANTOINE: **When I walked into Steve's house, I said, "Hello, I'm Antoine." And he looked at me knowingly, like, "Oh, so it's you."** He needed to run an errand, and I said, "I'll come with you." So we went out alone. To talk. He asked me why there was so much tension between me and Belou. I said, "You know Belou, right? She's uncontrollable, and the less you react to the way she is and the colder you behave, the more crazy it makes her." And he completely agreed with me. We spoke in faith and showed each other respect.

I was happy to not trouble him by staying in his house. He wanted to see Belou alone. When he's with Belou, he wants to be the boss and tell her what to do and everything, and he doesn't want to see other people interfere between him and her.

Hip-hop!

BELOU: I was in middle school when these boys in my class put a rap together and performed it. I was like, "Whoa, what are these kids doing? I want to do that, too!" I started to go out when I was thirteen. I had a lot of older friends, and we started going to this hip-hop café, the Devil. My best friend Shorty and I hung out there every weekend and sometimes during the week. That's where Carmen from *Road Rules* found me. It's the closest thing I have to a permanent home in Amsterdam.

MICHELLE: I thought Steve was too protective of Belou. I could already tell he was going to go crazy when *Road Rules* aired. It was almost like a father-daughter relationship. It was almost like he was her daddy in a way. She needed his approval and his protection, and she was very dependent on him.

BELOU: It was a very difficult time for me when we were in Amsterdam. Things were not as I would have wished for them to be with Steve. It was really really hard, and I did really want them to work out.

CLAY NEWBILL, PRODUCER/DIRECTOR: **The first time I saw Steve, I didn't like him. It was obvious to me from the way he was acting that he didn't care about Belou. He was standoffish; he didn't touch her; it appeared to me that he was not in the least bit happy to see her. He blamed his odd behavior on the cameras, but it was clear to me that there were other issues there. He never listened to Belou, and he didn't appreciate her.**

Belou's Hip-hop Phrases

 Definition blastin' \bläst'in\ adj. 1: relaxing. 2: kicking it.
dusted \dus'ted\ adj. messed-up.
skins \skinz\ n., pl. derogatory word for girls.

Belou's Hip-hop Look

BELOU: I remember when Antoine figured out that I was into hip-hop. It was early on in the trip, and I needed to go change my clothes. He came with me. He was like, "Whoa!" because I changed into my hip-hop clothes, and he had never seen them before. He was like, "Great, great!" I remember he gave me a compliment. He said, "Oh, excellent! And here I thought you were, like, haute couture."

 Journal Entry

MICHELLE: I'm kind of depressed right now. I'm trying to chalk it up to PMS because I know I'm supposed to start soon, but I don't know. I miss home. I miss having an adult conversation with someone. The boys all seem so young. All they really talk about is girls and getting laid. I find myself wanting to hang out with people on the crew for some real conversation, but I can't. Things are more relaxed now, but there's still that invisible line we're not allowed to cross. I feel very lonely at this point in time. I don't feel I have anyone to really share all these magical experiences with.

AMSTERDAM
HOLLAND

The Road Rulers stayed at the youth hostel Vondelpark (Zanpad 5 1054 GA, Amsterdam)

 **CLUE** Meet Ruud Van Der Linden Friday at 11:00 a.m. at Albert Cuypstraat 241, Amsterdam.

PATRICE'S HOOKUP

PATRICE: I didn't spend the first night in Amsterdam in the youth hostel. Instead I spent it with this girl who Chris and I met in a fast-food place. Her name was Mareyjke, and she was really nice. I don't like blondes that much, but I think Amsterdam is the place with the most beautiful blonde women. Definitely. I would describe Mareyjke as a nice person. I should say she is a boy's dream. She is well built, blonde and a stewardess. She was really not a bimbo. She was really confident and smart. I'm really sad about the fact that I don't have her address or number, because I know I will not be able to find her place again.

Chris was really great that night. Mareyjke had a friend, Truca, who Chris did not like, but he hung out with her and paid attention to her, so that I could be alone with Mareyjke. He called it "taking the grenade."

 Definition take the grenade \tāk the gri-nād'\ v. 1: to cover the blast for your friend. 2: to sacrifice your real desire in the name of friendship: Truca was the grenade, therefore I jumped on her so that Patrice could make away with her friend.

AMSTERDAM,
HOLLAND

mission 6 ←

Slip in a mouth guard, suit up in satin and bob and weave your way to boxing glory!

Be a contender!

Boys Will Be Boys!?!

Chris: **Antoine's competitiveness with me— that bugged me. If I had wanted to floor him, I could have.** I was thinking, "If you just stuck to the rules, you know you would lose." He had to find some way around the rules in order to win, and he tagged me a few times, and it pissed me off.

ANTOINE: **Who cares about who wins and who loses?** I mean, I had a blast. I think I won fairly against Chris. If he thinks he could have clubbed me but didn't, well, I'm sorry for him. If that's the kind of consideration he carries when he's in a fight, he's not up for many wins.

Patrice: I think everyone thought I was a wimp. It really got on my nerves that I lost. I guess that's really my male ego. But Antoine won, so you cannot take it that seriously.

Girls Will Be Girls!?!

ANTOINE: *I think I'd put my money on Michelle.*

PATRICE: *But you know Belou can kick ass!*

ANTOINE: *Michelle's more reserved, and she pays more attention, and she's less crazy, you know?*

CHRIS: *I'm gonna put my money on Michelle, on the calmness factor and the quickness factor.*

ANTOINE: *The communist factor?*   **CHRIS:** *Calmness, the calmness factor.*

PATRICE: *No, Belou's an animal. Belou's gonna kick her ass, that's for sure. I saw her really exploding. I know how it is.*

CHRIS: *But I think Belou will explode and get out of control, and I think Michelle will use the intelligence and the quickness to counter.*

ANTOINE: *That's right. I put my money on Michelle.*   **PATRICE:** *We will see.*

FELIX VAN DER LINDEN, head of boxing school:
Women are more often afraid to hit. They are less powerful than men.

ANTOINE
AKA TWANNER
Height: 5'9"
Weight: 130 lbs
Advantage:
Well, David beat Goliath
Handicap:
Lacking in poundage

BELOU
AKA BUBBA
Height: 5'5"
Weight: 119 lbs
Advantage:
Can kick ass! (see Venice)
Handicap:
"I can't hit one of my best friends!"

CHRIS
AKA BIG BRO
Height: 6'2"
Weight: 190 lbs
Advantage:
Full-on bulk
Handicap:
A lot of beer and cigarettes the night before!

MICHELLE
AKA TEXAS
Height: 5'9"
Weight: 116 lbs
Advantage:
Calm, cool, collected
Handicap:
"I can't punch her cute little face!"

PATRICE
AKA SUPERBURSCHI
Height: 6'1"
Weight: 179 lbs
Advantage:
Long reach!
Handicap:
Partied hard with Mareyjke the night before.

BELOU: The guys were saying that it was not really a tie between me and Michelle, and that Michelle won. I don't know. They called it a draw, and I still ask myself, "Is it because we were girls?" I gave Michelle a couple of hits, and she gave me a couple of hits. What I didn't like was that the guys were really siding with Michelle.

MICHELLE: Boxing was weird, because during the match, the trainer told me I was really good-looking and told Belou she had great legs and stuff. He asked me out and gave me his number, but I never did anything about it.

PATRICE: I met this girl named Edith at the boxing mission. She was a friend of one of the trainers. I don't know what happened to me. It was something I never would have done before, but I just went up to her and said, "Hey, what about your number? Why don't we meet?" I was really mad, because at one point Antoine started to flirt with her. I was like, "Hey, hey, hey, there's a limit." Some rules are international rules. Never mess around with the girl of somebody else. That was his competitive side.

Anyway, I ended up hanging out with her. We spent the night together at her place. It was a really beautiful place. We hung out on the roof, which had this beautiful view of Amsterdam.

CHRIS: The girl from the boxing thing, she seemed to really like Patrice. We met her, and Michelle was like, "I think she really likes Patrice." And Antoine was like, "Oh, she really likes everyone she meets, you know? Couldn't you tell?" He couldn't stand not having the spotlight.

ANTOINE: I love competition! I love competition! But only if it's true competition—like boxing or swimming! I find it so degrading to compete over a girl. I hate that. I don't like being fake and underhanded. I like competition only if it's in the open.

 CLUE *Ride bikes to Vondel Park. Find Bert the Juggler near the statue of Jus Vanden Vondel. Take this gift with you. Be there by 6:00 p.m. tonight.*

 CLUE *Lend a helping hand and receive a seal of approval. See Lenie Van Het Hart, Hoofdstraat 94A, Pieterburen.*

PAGE
49

AMSTERDAM-
PIETERBUREN
129 miles by
train and 22
miles by car

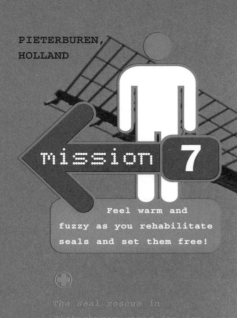

mission 7

Feel warm and
fuzzy as you rehabilitate
seals and set them free!

*The seal rescue in
Pieterburen cares for common seals and grey seals
harmed by the extreme
pollution of the Waddensea,
a unique wetland ecosystem.
The center is busiest
during "pupping season,"
which is June and July.
It takes about 2.3 hours
to get to Pieterburen
from Amsterdam.*

*To whom it may concern,

Pieterburen, 4th August 1996

Patrice,

has been working in the Seal Rehabilitation and Research Centre Pieterburen
for the period:
3 and 4 August 1996

During his practical training at the SRRC, he has been involved in the following
activities:

-participating in the daily work of seal husbandry:
cleaning, preparation of food, assisting with feeding and hygienic procedures
-assistance in releasing two rehabilitated seals

Patrice has been a pleasant person to work with, always helpful and available
whenever necessary.

On behalf of the SRRC staff.

Lohe
(Director SRRC)*

*The Road Rulers almost
did another mission when
in Pieterburen, and that's
mud-walking, which is a
popular sport in the
Netherlands. The place to
go for it is Wadlopen
(Stichting-Wadloopcentrum-
Postbus 1, 9968ZG
Pieterburen.)*

THE EVOLUTION OF PATRICE

MICHELLE: When we were on our way to Amsterdam, Patrice was going to play a joke, and he jumped off the train. He came back, knocked on the outside window and started running back and forth in front of the window. Oh, my God, it was so funny, because the train actually started moving! We were going nuts, and if the conductor wasn't going to stop, we were going to pull him through the skinny little window. It was hysterical, it was classic, because he was joking like it was going to happen, and then it started happening. He had suddenly become the jokester, and that was hysterical.

PATRICE'S
HOOKUP **3**

PATRICE: *I'm going to Paris and all I've got to wear is this seal tee shirt!*

PATRICE: On a day off in Paris, I met a Swedish girl named Jenny, and I asked her if she wanted to hang out in a café with me. Of course, I had to explain that I wouldn't be alone, and that there'd be cameras. Unless, of course, I could dodge the crew, which was my plan. The next day, I tried to pick the right moment to leave the group and go by myself and pick her up. But then Rick asked me where I was going, and I had to tell him. He called a camera team, and they followed me to Planet Hollywood, where I picked her up. It was the most embarrassing moment. At Planet Hollywood, the people were just desperate to see celebrities, so when people saw me, they were like: "Who's this? Who's this?" I think Jenny had a problem with the camera, because she left pretty quickly. She gave me her number, but I didn't think

PATRICE'S
HOOKUP **4**

she had that much interest in me. Well, that night, we went back to the youth hostel, and Chris and I met these Italian girls. It was a beautiful night, and we were all hanging out, and we just had a really romantic night. The next day, Jenny and I actually ended up meeting again. We spent the whole day together without the cameras there. I ended up having a really good time, and suddenly got a really bad conscience. I was thinking, My God, what if she sees the show and sees that I kissed her and the Italian girl one after another? I had to tell her. She wasn't really happy about it. The truth is that the Italian girl didn't mean anything to me.

MICHELLE: Whenever random people we met asked me why cameras were following us around, I said we were doing a travel documentary. I think the guys would say they were with MTV. That always helped them pick up girls. I think Patrice got caught by the crew doing that a couple of times.

CLAY NEWBILL, PRODUCER/DIRECTOR: Of anybody, Patrice changed the most over the course of the trip. He gained a lot of self-confidence; he saw more and experienced more. What he had perceived as weakness in himself was, perhaps, just inexperience. He became very outgoing—especially when approaching women on the trip.

TRAVEL LOG

A heartwarming mission gets our cast's seal of approval and sets their hearts a-pumpin' as they head Franceward in search of love, Parisian style (or in Belou's case … South American!) Love abounds and francs await as our cast goes cosmopolitan! Get ready to work the runway, sweeties!

AMSTERDAM–PARIS
327 miles
Pieterburen
HOLLAND
PARIS

CLUE

Down to your final guilder? Time to work on a runway. Return to Amsterdam and take a ride on the TGV to Paris. See Malilee Elis at Printemps, 64 Bd. Haussman, 4:30 p.m.

BELOUS BOY 4

Journal Entry

BELOU: I met three really cool and tough South American guys, with whom I went drinking on a bridge in Paris. We talked about life in South America and about religion. I must say that I really like one of them. His name is Pablo, and I think he feels the same way about me. I realize that I'm going to have to keep my distance.

Antoine Has a Moment

MICHELLE: I remember one night we were in Paris, and I wasn't feeling well. Antoine's family was in town. He said to me: "Please come to dinner with my family, I would love you to." It was so sweet for him to invite me to go out to dinner with his family, but I really felt terrible. Well, before he left, he was like, "Here's some money if you want to go and get a soda." He was making sure I was all set. And then, just as he was about to walk out the door, he turned around, came back and kissed me on the cheek. It was the sweetest thing. It completely touched me.

JONATHAN MURRAY, EXECUTIVE PRODUCER: Patrice has a lot of stereotypically German traits. I think he's very easy to travel with in that you know exactly what to expect from him. I think he's difficult to travel with because you can't stop and smell the roses—Patrice has to be on schedule.

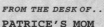

BELOU: I love Patrice. He was always there for me. Always available to talk. In many ways, Patrice is like a little child. Sometimes he can be so sweet, and sometimes he can be so annoying. **Sometimes you just want to grab him and say, "Oh, I love you Patrice! You're so sweet! But just be quiet!"**

CHRIS: I think Patrice has a really good heart. He means well, and he's someone I'd always want to have on my side. He's also a perfectionist, though. To a bad point. If there were fifty good things about somebody, and one bad thing, he'll notice the bad thing first. Once, this beautiful girl walked by us on the beach, and he was like, "She has too much hair on the back of her legs."

FROM THE DESK OF...
PATRICE'S MOM

I am proud of my son Patrice. It was difficult for me to comprehend why he would have wanted to do Road Rules. He probably did it to stand out and be recognized.

Patrice and I used to disagree about the way he always let things get to him. Since the show, I've found that he doesn't let things bother him as much.

I think that the cast has enormously helped Patrice with his outlook on life. He's really worked on his self-esteem and become a totally positive person.

MICHELLE: Patrice annoyed me at the beginning of the trip. I was like, "This guy is just talking to hear himself talk. He is going to drive me insane. He's anal!" I couldn't believe he was chosen to be on this trip, because he was really not a rough-it, tough-it kind of guy. At some point he started turning around. He became this whole new Patrice. I was proud of him. Not for being who I wanted him to be, but just because he was happier. He was trying new things. He was more open. He was laughing. I loved his laugh. His laugh was the best.

ANTOINE: Patrice is someone who craves happiness and harmony—a good aim in life, I would say. He also craves really nice cars and good clothes, but above all, he wants everyone around him to be happy.

THE CAST
AND CREW on

PATRICE: I changed a lot. I have become much more confident about myself. *Road Rules* was such a new experience. To me it wasn't really about being on MTV; it was about seeing so many things I hadn't seen before Maybe it's how I was raised or something, but during the entire trip— even until the end— I felt this pressure. **I felt it was my duty not to disappoint the people who'd given this great gift to me.** I always felt conflicted. During missions, I was often thinking I wasn't going to make it. Or I was feeling that people were going to hate me, that I was getting on everybody's nerves because I was asking so many questions.

Really, I just wanted to learn, I wanted to see a lot of things. I wanted to understand everybody and everything.

By the end of *Road Rules*, I realized that I didn't need to be so concerned with what everyone thought about me and that I didn't need to be so hypercritical.

You do your best, and that's all you can give.

PARIS, FRANCE

Job #2

SLAP ON SOME LIPSTICK, BAT YOUR EYELASHES AND WIGGLE YOUR HIPS! BE A MODEL! DON'T JUST LOOK LIKE ONE!

F—f—f—fashion!

PATRICE: I loved it on the catwalk. What I didn't like was all that nonsense, all those stupid people. This Frenchwoman kept telling me to relax, that I didn't have to be so excited all the time.

But then, when something didn't fit, she'd go crazy: "We cannot change, we cannot change!" While the show was going on, she was flipping out.

CHRIS: At the fashion show, this woman told me and Patrice that we should try modeling and that we should check out this agency in Paris. Well, we went the next day, and it was closed. A few weeks later, I called. She was like, "You want to be a model?" And I said, "Well, I'd like to try." And she was like, "That's great, but we only represent women." I still want to look into it.

MICHELLE: I think that Patrice and Chris got kind of an attitude after the fashion show. Kind of like this confidence that they didn't have before. I had a lot of champagne. I just needed to loosen up. But I had to pee so bad like 20 minutes before we were supposed to start the show, and the show coordinator wouldn't let me. My bladder is, like, the size of a pea, so I was about to pee in my pants! I probably was walking like a fool down the runway. After the show, we found out there was bathroom right there backstage. Ugh!! The story of my life. **I guess you don't see the fact that I'm buck naked.** You had to be, because you had to change so fast. You couldn't wear panties or a bra with those clothes. It didn't bother me, because I'm used to doing quick changes on the side from dancing and from shows. At one point, there was a woman pulling on my dress, and Antoine was buckling my shoe. But by that point it was no big deal, because we had all seen each other anyway.

CLAY NEWBILL, PRODUCER/DIRECTOR: **The Road Rulers dusted the Printemps models! Just blew them away!**

How to Get Chris's New Do

(THIS WORKS ONLY IF YOU HAVE SHORTISH HAIR!)

1. TAKE A BAR OF WHITE SOAP AND MOISTEN IT WITH YOUR HANDS

2. SCRUB HAIR WITH SOAP UNTIL IT IS COATED BUT DRY. BE CAREFUL NOT TO USE TOO MUCH SOAP (YOU SHOULDN'T BE ABLE TO SEE IT)

3. PUT A LITTLE BIT OF SOAP ON YOUR FINGERS EACH TIME YOU GRAB A PIECE OF HAIR

4. TWIST TWO PIECES OF HAIR TOGETHER BETWEEN SOAPY FINGERS, THEN PULL THE HAIR DOWN TOWARD THE SCALP. PULL HARD! (THIS SHOULD HURT A LITTLE BIT)

5. REPEAT STEP 4 UNTIL ALL HAIR IS DREADLOCKED. DREADS SHOULD LAST AS LONG AS YOU DON'T WASH YOUR HAIR.

CLUE *Catch the 4:30 p.m. ferry. Bateaux Parisiens will be your guide as you cruise the Seine. X marks the spot. P.S. Look for big clues in small packages.*

CLUE *Trouvez Pepe. North 48, 51, 563. East 217.427*

For cool boutique shopping in Paris go to Le MARAIS ("The Swamp") on the Left Bank. For couture culture, check out Boulevard St. Germaine. If vintage is your thing, check out Société OH LUMIÈRE, Friperie Second Hand Clothing (2 avenue de la Republique 75011 PARIS.) The gang scored a bunch of cool duds here, including Chris's brown suede jacket.

BELOU: *I invited Pablo to come see the fashion show, and he did a bunch of sketches of it.*

Another Letter

CHRIS: The biggest problem I had with Belou was that she didn't listen to me—to a point where it was absolutely ridiculous. She was always interrupting and interjecting. Of anybody on the trip, Belou taught me the most, but I still feel that she herself has a lot to learn. That's why I wrote her the letter. I felt like it was my turn.

BELOU: In Paris, Chris gave a letter to me, and it came out of nowhere. I still have a hard time understanding that letter. Sometimes he could keep such a distance from me that I didn't know what he wanted—if he wanted me to get close or if he wanted me to keep distance.

Au Revoir, Steve! Bonjour, Pablo!

BELOU: I really never fell in love with anyone before Pablo. We felt like we were twelve years old—butterflies in the stomach and pain and everything. It was so incredible. I don't know how to describe what I felt, but it was something special. It was terrible to say goodbye, but I had to move on. We rented a hotel room the last night in Paris. We had been in front of the cameras the whole time, and you know, he wanted to get me into bed. We spent the night at the hotel, and we agreed that we were not going to have a heavy goodbye. We were just going to say a very normal goodbye. I knew I would be with him again. And even though I didn't know it quite yet, it was over with Steve.

As for Antoine, well, his dad came to visit in Paris, and I met him. His dad said to me, "Hey, you're Belou! Antoine just loves you! He just loves to fight with you! He's fond of you! He can't stop talking about you!" I was like, "Whoa!" I remember Pablo saying to me, "Can't you see that Antoine has a crush on you?" I remember Antoine used to tease Pablo all the time. He'd go, "Hey, Macho! Hey, Macho!" Pablo didn't like it. He was like, "Come on, I'm not macho." Antoine just kept saying it... "Hey, Macho!"

TO BELOU,

Unbridled passion, mixed
With an intelligence beyond your years
A loud voice, with a soft heart
That I can see in all your tears
A kindred spirit
So different, with so much to teach
So similar, with so much to learn
A fight means nothing
Unless it's followed by a kiss
A hug means little
Unless it follows your tears
That smile, in which I can see
So much love, passion and emotion
Has become my teacher, my guide
The arguments, so fierce, so bitter
Have given me both hope and despair
My temper, so calm and concealing
Is intended to teach, to instruct
In the way that needs no words
In a manner which need not be said
For words mean little
Unless they are spoken from the heart
Words can lie, a gesture cannot
You are my teacher
As I am yours
Two paths crossed for a reason
Two lives with so much instruction
Could not cross for any other reason
You will learn, as will I
That there is wisdom in both our ways
We cannot ignore that which is opposite us
We may fight
But we cannot ignore
Your time into mine
Black time into white
Together we will stand
Divided we will fall
Learn from me, as I have from you
My sweet, my only Belou
Time will only tell us what we seek
People will tell us what we don't want to hear
Fakes will tell us what we want to hear
Only life, only life
Can tell us what we need to know
I will be there for you in the good and the bad
From the ecstasy to the depressingly sad
My heart cries more than my eyes
But let that not tell you how hard I try
I'll be there in good and in strife
To Belou, friends for life!

Sincerely,
CHRIS

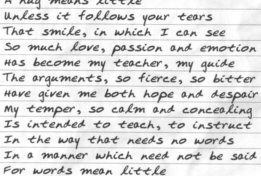

ATOP THE EIFFEL TOWER

Où est Pepe?!?
Avoid duress and use your
GPS to find the Winnebago
and your next clue!

59

PARIS-TOURS
167 miles

PARIS

CLUE Trouvez Pepe.
North 48, 51,
563. East 217.427

BRUCE TOMS, DIRECTOR: My impression of Chris is that he's still discovering his own power, his boundaries. I think he's a really kind person, and he's a whole lot of fun. He's definitely got the good old boy thing going on. I think

ANTOINE: Of all the people in the group, I feel the most for Chris. **He's extremely sane and extremely healthy, and someone who will always know right from wrong.**

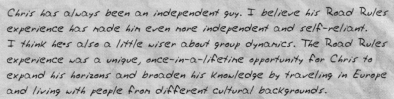

FROM THE DESK OF...
CHRIS'S MOM

Chris has always been an independent guy. I believe his Road Rules experience has made him even more independent and self-reliant. I think he's also a little wiser about group dynamics. The Road Rules experience was a unique, once-in-a-lifetime opportunity for Chris to expand his horizons and broaden his knowledge by traveling in Europe and living with people from different cultural backgrounds.

All that said, watching Chris on TV is somewhat surrealistic. On some level, I feel like a Peeping Tom. To be honest, it makes me a little uncomfortable. There are a few new things I've learned about Chris that have surprised me. He's a bit wilder and more of a ladies' man than I had realized, but for the most part, Chris handles himself just like the son I've known and loved for twenty years!

PATRICE: To me, the most surprising thing about Chris was that he'd lost his virginity at the age of nineteen, only one year before we met. I found that really strange, because he was really handsome and really knew how to impress girls.

MICHELLE: Chris is so intelligent and so knowledgeable and so giving. I find that all very attractive. But at the same time, he's so fratty. Who can drink the most beer?!? Party, party, party! I was attracted to Chris, and I am attracted to Chris. There was a chemistry, but I know—and I knew—that there would be no future thing.

BELOU: I had a hard time digging into Chris, getting to know him. I think he was a great actor. He always gave the impression of being happy and perfect, but I think something inside was killing him really badly.

CHRIS: **I'm an exhibitionist.** I like being in front of a crowd. I like having a camera on. My friend once bet me five bucks to get up in front of a packed audience in a movie theater and dance in front of the screen during the previews. I did it.

All the same, being on camera was a little overwhelming. You have to wear a mike all the time. You have to alter what you're wearing so it can't be seen. Sometimes, if you want to tuck your shirt in, you have to leave it out. These are little things, but they make a difference.

The first morning, when I woke up in Pamplona, there was a camera in my face. For all I know, I could have been drooling; I could have had snot coming out of my nose. This camera was, like, three feet away from my face. And I was like, "Oooh, this is gonna be a long eight weeks." But the truth is, you get used to it. You get desensitized.

It's impossible to go into an experience like *Road Rules* and come out and be exactly the same. I don't think I changed in any major way, though. I didn't become more nice. I didn't become more sympathetic. I didn't learn how to deal with people better. I was just practicing old skills.

mission 9

Be a royal glutton! Just don't puke on the princes!

CHRIS: I have a feeling that the two princes aren't going to miss us too much. Someone who makes me eat pig balls shall not be forgotten, or forgiven.

The Princes

PRINCE LOUIS: The cast seemed to forget that they were in a public place and that they had to be cautious about the noise. **They got a bit out of their minds.** The boys apologized. The girls did not. It seemed to me like quite a solid group, with the guys acting as leaders and the girls taking it more at ease.

ANTOINE: I wonder why the others think that the princes had no right to be angry. I really understand why they were angry. Our behavior surely did not fit the place. It's not like in America, you know? You don't bend over for customers just because they're customers and because they have money. In France, if you're at a bar, and you don't say, "May I please have a drink," you might find a waiter who will not serve you. Rightfully so, I believe.

PATRICE: At the beginning, he had a reason to be mad. But after every one of us apologized, I can't understand why he kept up his bad mood against us.

Château de la Bourdaisière
37270 Montlouis-sur-Loire
Indre-et-Loire
Tél: (16) 47 45 16 31
Fax: (16) 47 45 09 11

Dîner du 14 Août 1996

Salade Tourangelle
Escargots Farcis
Rognons de Veau Madère
Assortiment de Légumes
Salade
Fromages
Tarte Tatin
Vins Montlouis Sec
Chinon
Café

Michelle's Big Secret

MICHELLE: At the château, we had this massive conversation where a lot of stuff came out. It was very difficult to sit there and see Belou crying and Chris crying and for me not to. But I really don't like to cry in front of other people if I can avoid it.

Actually, I was really laughing at one point in time last night. I mean, just thinking about the fact that we pissed off a prince—two, at that—and disrupted a castle was a bit amusing to me.

I'm only growing fonder of the group as each day passes. Unfortunately, I'm growing fonder of one of the crew members as well. I'm growing soft on all of them actually, but one in particular I'm very drawn to. He intimidates me in a way, and I'm drawn to that. It's been a while since someone's made me nervous or jittery when I'm around them. I've realized I've forgotten how love feels—I can only remember lust.

TRAVEL LOG

Their runway days behind them, our cast members are model travelers no more! Having eaten a royal meal of pig guts, and perhaps a drop too much vino, they find themselves getting royally emotive! Belou may have found Prince Charming in Paris, but she still wants the group to understand her. Chris thinks he'll never find Princess Charming, and cries on Belou's shoulder. Patrice plays mediator; Michelle has a secret; and Antoine gets a kick out of it.

BELOU: They were not at all princes. One was very grumpy. When I got really upset that night, he accused us of making too much noise with our acting. And we said, "But we're not acting! It's real!" And he said, "Then why are the cameras on? Stop acting!" When Michelle said we were having a personal crisis, he didn't believe us. He kept saying that if the cameras were there, we had to be acting. We were like: "But the cameras are always there."

Royal Baths

MICHELLE: The baths at the château were amazing, and we all took advantage of them. One day I was soaking in this big huge tub. I had my headphones on, listening to Alanis Morissette, and I guess I had the windows open, and I didn't know the crew was down there filming. And I was just singing, "You Oughta Know." All of a sudden, I heard, "Quiet up there!" I was so embarrassed!

One day at the castle, I remember that I opened the door to the boys' room, and Patrice didn't have anything on. Oops. I was like, "I'm sorry," and he was like, "That's okay, I was just getting out of the bath." I had never seen Patrice before, and I was thinking, "God, he's really good-looking. He's got a really great body." Chris and Antoine, they would just walk out of the shower, just drying their things. No big deal to me. I mean, if you've seen one, you've seen them all.

CLAY NEWBILL, DIRECTOR/PRODUCER: At one particularly heated moment during a very intense conversation the cast was having while at the château, Antoine was trying to speak with Patrice. He was trying to make eye-contact with him, but there was a cameraman in his way. So what does he do? He slides down the bed real quick and kicks the cameraman. Like a dog. Like some sub-human. It took a lot for me to not just grab him at that moment and say, "What the hell do you think you're doing?" It really pissed me off. I pulled him aside, and I told him, "Antoine, if you ever touch anybody on the crew again, you're outta here!" I said, "This guy's out here working so hard, and you know all of his work is hopefully gonna make you look good, and you treat him like this!"

ANTOINE: We'd been speaking for something like two hours, and it had been the most intense conversation. At one point I was speaking with Patrice, and then the cameraman got right in front of me, so I couldn't see him anymore. And so I moved, but the cameraman moved as well. **Hell, no! I never kicked him. I just moved forward quickly and pushed him with my foot!** Of course it was very untactful and everything, but I spoke with him and apologized. Was it such a big deal?

MARK JUNGJOHANN, CAMERA OPERATOR: Antoine? Apologize? Antoine is Mr. I-Would-Never-Apologize.

BELOU: That's so Antoine. When he had a fight with me, he kicked the cameraman. Why? Why doesn't he kick me? That's what he really wanted to do. But he always blamed his anger on the cameras. There's some kind of grudge there, and it kept building up.

CLUE Pack up Pepe with the swiftest of speed. Tomorrow morning it's off to the beach, and your next mission you will reach. Lacanau.

PAGE
63

TOURS—LACANAU
167 miles

THE CHATEAU
FRANCE

The Loire Valley is famous for its wine. Sancerres and Pouilly Fumés are the most expensive. Cheaper wines are Touraine Sauvignons and Vouvrays!

The Microphone Incident

MARY-ELLIS BUNIM, EXECUTIVE PRODUCER: It's a very tough thing to live in the eye of a camera. There's no privacy whatsoever. They have to remember to turn their microphones off when they go to the bathroom. That's a tough way to live, and there's a level of paranoia that's a natural reaction to all of these people staring at you all day long. You wonder, "What are these people going to do with all this tape? How are they going to edit it? How am I going to end up looking?" The crew tries very hard to foster a relationship with the cast so they'll really trust them, but it's hard.

PATRICE: I still feel really bad. Actually, at the moment I did that, I didn't think it was such a bad thing. I did it because I wanted to be loyal to Chris. Because the two girls we were talking to were not absolutely my type. But I figured, "Hey, if Chris was going to talk to them, stay with them." I just want to check out the situation. When Rick came over, it was like, "Wow, we're caught!" There was just senseless fighting between Antoine and Rick. That was so stupid, but it was also so typical of Antoine. I had no problem saying sorry, but not Antoine. Afterwards, he was also mad at Chris and me. He said, "I did that for you." But really he did that for himself, just to be the person who was right.

CHRIS: In Lacanau, Patrice and I met two girls on the beach, and we were so sick of being followed by the cameras. **So we did the unthinkable: we turned off our mikes** and started talking and saying sly, flirtatious things. And then Antoine came over, and he had his mike on, and through him, the crew was able to locate us and pick up our conversation. Rick, the coordinating producer, showed up, grabbed our mikes, and duct-taped them so we couldn't switch the buttons. He was like, "We trust you guys, and you broke our trust." And we were like, "We're sorry. This is the first time, and it will be the last time. We made a mistake, and now we're apologizing for it." Antoine hadn't really done anything, but he was the one who ended up getting into the biggest fight with the crew about it. **Antoine actually left the show for a day.** He went and hung out with some friends who lived in the area, and then came back for the surfing mission.

MICHELLE: When the guys took their mikes off to hit on some girls, I was so pissed. They were like, "Hush, don't tell anyone." I felt like they were getting me in trouble. I was just like, "You f**kers knew what this trip was about." So I busted out, "Why don't y'all just quit thinking with your d**ks and start thinking with your heads!" And that started a spat, to say the least. I just thought, My God, have you not gotten enough nooky yet?

CHRIS AND MICHELLE GET TOGETHER:

CHRIS: After the mikes incident, Michelle was disgusted with Patrice and me, because all we would talk about was girls and about how we would get them. She told us both off. Belou told us off, too, but when Belou yelled at me, it never meant anything. It was like hearing a baby crying: after the first few times, you're desensitized. I didn't want Michelle to be upset at me, so I said, "Can I talk to you?" We went out to the beach with a sleeping bag, and we just had an incredible talk.

MICHELLE: Chris and I have never been as close as we were that night on the beach. I know that Chris is not any great love or soul mate or anything like that. He's more than a friend, but a friend first. Definitely a friend first. I desire no more than that. I don't want anything more than that.

There is one person I desire more and more everyday. The more I get to know him, the more I want to know.

Chris told me that if he won, he was going to give the surfboard to me. He said he had no use for it in Boston, and he knew I wanted one for California. I was really touched, and I know he was sincere.

MICHELLE: *I want that surfboard!*

Patrice's new coif!

MICHELLE: *I'm feeling the heat, and if you can't take the heat, you gotta get out of the kitchen! I've caught a few waves, I was doing the big kahuna, hanging ten, riding 'em!*

mission 10

← Go on a surfin' safari! Compete for a *Road Rules* surfboard, and don't wipe out!

CLUE *Jump with-out a net!*

PAGE

6 5

LACANAU–LOURDES
194 miles

LACANAU FRANCE
LOURDES
France

ROAD RULES

CHRIS: *I want revenge for the boxing trophy! I'm ready to show that the U.S.A. is truly dominant: the Belgians can no longer own what I should own, what is rightfully mine, and I will bring it back to my country. Thank you.*

The Road Rulers rented their surfboards at Lacanau Surf Club (Maison de la Glisse, Boulevard de la Plage — 33860 Lacanau Ocean.) The boys got their hair dyed at one of Lacanau's pre-miere salons, Salon du Daniel Darsonville.

SHAPED BY OG
ERIC BECKER

CHRIS: *Captain Competition pulled out another victory!*

BEACH PARTY

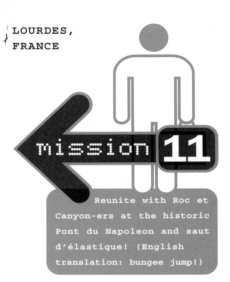

mission 11

Reunite with Roc et Canyon-ers at the historic Pont du Napoleon and saut d'élastique! (English translation: bungee jump!)

TRAVEL ✉ LOG

Could it be, with only a few more weeks to go, that our cast has gotten a wee bit jumpy?!? Patrice discovers that blondes do indeed have more fun, as the cast put one over on the crew! Big time!

ANTOINE: *Belou felt like a bird. Well, I felt like a missile. All my muscles were contracted and tense. I thought I was gonna go down straight, hit a rock and completely bust it!*

MICHELLE: I wore the headcam during one jump, and the body pack. It was so heavy, it was like Michelle and child. They had to duct-tape it around me. I rebounded so much higher when I was wearing it. I didn't have the strength to lift myself up. And I thought my head was going to explode. I'm not kidding. The blood, my eyes—there was all this pressure behind them. And for the next two days, I would bend down and the room would swirl.

ROAD RULES GETS BUZZ KILLED!

BRUCE TOMS: We were in some small village in France, and we'd been driving all morning, and we stopped for lunch. The crew Winnebago and the cast Winnebago need to travel simultaneously, so the cast stopped for lunch also. They were running out of money, so they had to go to a fast-food place instead of the place we went, which was moderately expensive. I gave one of them, I think Antoine, a walkie-talkie in case there was some kind of emergency. Well, while we were eating lunch, they devised this whole scheme. When we got to the place they went to eat, they weren't there. Instead, they had turned the tables on us and left us a clue. In order for us to locate them, we had to drive all through this area in rural France, picking up clues and figuring out routes. It ended up taking us a couple of hours, and it wasn't good, because we were late for our next mission. On the other hand, **a lot of the tension that was building up between the cast and crew burst.**

It was a really good laugh.

CLUE #1

Atac was just a crack. Get some gas, that's where I was. There shall be your next clue. It will tell you what to do.

A full tank here should be cheaper than a full stomach there.

Think where. Mikky D in the place to be.

CLUE #2

A full tank here should be cheaper than a full stomach there. Think where. Mikky D is the place to be.

BELOU: *You don't feel your feet. You're flying. It's like a bird. It's freedom. Man, it's unbelievable! I've no words. It's freedom.*

CHRIS: *You get a little blood in your brain when you're dangling around there, but man, it's so worth it! I would do it a hundred times over.*

PATRICE: *My eyes almost popped out! I was flying! Superburschi to the rescue!*

LOURDES-
BARCELONA-
IBIZA
338 miles by
Pepe and 197
miles by boat

LOURDES

France

IBIZA

SPAIN

In the nineteenth century Lourdes was home to Bernadette Soubirous, a religious woman who had visions of the Virgin Mary. Today there are three churches near the site of Bernadette's visions: Notre Dame de Lourdes, St. Pie X, and the Church of the Rosary.

CLUE #3
Sorry, we ate it all. Here is a condom, though. We may be at the tire warehouse across from Atac.

MAP OF
AREA

CLUE #4
Trouvez Pepe!
N. 46°33.267
E. 0°20.128

FINALLY
DISCOVERED
ATOP PEPE

Job #3

*RAVE ON, ROAD RULERS!
FLYER THE BEACH AND
CLUB YOUR WAY TO SOME
HARD-EARNED CASH.*

LAMAR DAMON, STORY EDITOR: The single most difficult episode to put together was the Ibiza show. We wanted to focus the show on Michelle and Chris's relationship, which seemed to be simmering. The two of them had been flirting for two months, and when we finally thought they were going to actually go for it, they went and fooled around with other people entirely. We had to wonder: was there a subtext there? Was Chris fooling around with that girl to get his mind off Michelle? Was Michelle fooling around with that guy in the bar to get back at Chris? Or was she trying to get her mind off something else?

Scamming!

BELOU'S BOY **5**

BELOU: **Ibiza was a very strange vibe—a lot of sex going on, a lot of loving girls and boys.** I started talking to a guy named Steve one night at the club. He had a very weird accent, and I couldn't understand a word he was saying. Well, that night in the bar, we started to kiss. I spent a lot of time with him. No sex—we kissed and we talked. It was a strange situation. I can't really say that it was love. Because I had really already decided Pablo was the only one.

MICHELLE: I got pretty sloshy, and I ended up mugging in the club with this guy Christian. We were kissing, and all of the sudden the camera was in our face, with lights and everything. We immediately split apart. Then the cameras would go away and we'd be back together, and we'd be kissing again. It was like a game; we were trying to totally avoid the cameras and still try to mug.

CHRIS: In Ibiza I met this English girl. She lived in a tent and had had this amazing life. She was really great. Of course, when Antoine saw me with her initially, he got competitive. He was like: "Yeah, she's really cool looking. Do you like her?" I said I did, and then he went and talked to her, but I don't think she was into him at all.

PATRICE'S HOOKUP 5

PATRICE: I met another girl in Ibiza, and we really got along. It didn't really get on camera, so I was pretty happy. I didn't want the girls I met to be on camera. I just wanted to keep them safe somehow.

Reunited!

ANTOINE: In Ibiza, Chris, Michelle, Belou and I had one really great night. We ended up in the gay part of Ibiza town, where the atmosphere was really sensual and natural; you just start talking about stuff in ways that you've never really done before. Chris was holding Michelle and walking next to Michelle, and I was walking next to Belou, and we went back to the room. I really don't think it was a big deal. We just fooled around when it fit us. I think it was the same for Chris and Michelle. Very often—when there was only the four of us—our discussions turned much more sensual, much more intimate. It was like we were two couples—although we weren't really couples at all!

MICHELLE: One night, Chris and I were out on the balcony hanging out, and we were kissing or something. I mean, it's not like Chris and I were constantly touching. Our relationship was more about friendship. We could lay in each other's arms and cuddle and never kiss. Anyway, that night, we were looking out into the streets, and Belou and Antoine were in the bedroom together. All of a sudden we noticed that they were being kind of kissy-huggy on each other. Chris and I were like, "Goodness gracious sakes alive!" It wasn't a big deal—whatever creams your Twinkie, as far as I'm concerned. But talk about coming full circle. This trip had come full circle, completely.

creams your Twinkie \krēmz yōr twing′kē\ v., pl. **-kies.**
Definition 1: makes you happy. 2: alt. dings your dong.

CHRIS: I think Michelle's and my relationship was based on mutual respect. There was no plasticness to her. She knew what she liked. She wasn't afraid to talk about anything. She was open and honest and fun. And it didn't hurt that I was attracted to her. I'm assuming she was attracted to me, too.

MARY-ELLIS BUNIM, EXECUTIVE PRODUCER: Michelle and Chris emerged from the trip with a close relationship, a lot of mutual attraction and respect. Everyone was kind of rooting for them to fall in love, but for whatever reason, it never happened.

mission 12

Fly like an eagle!

PAGE **69**

IBIZA-VALENCIA 137 miles by boat

IBIZA SPAIN

SPAIN VALENCIA

CLUE *Here is the mostaza. Now you make the ketchup. Take the ferry to Valencia and head for Buñol, Spain. Meet Michael at 9:00 a.m. sharp.*

Michelle Finally Breaks

MICHELLE: I guess one of the main reasons I didn't really pursue something with Chris was that I was interested in someone else.

Journal Entry

MICHELLE: It's the next-to-last day, and I am ready to be home. I'm starting to not be able to deal with things anymore. I'm becoming very cold, very bitter. I can't be strong anymore. I just can't do it. I don't know anything anymore. I feel like I'm losing my mind. I'm trapped, and there's no one for me to talk to, to cry to. I'm sitting on the stairwell of the eleventh floor—because the terrace wasn't open—sobbing. I've never felt so alone. The only one I have to hold me now is God. I feel so bad that I always turn to him in my times of trouble. I have everything, but nothing. I'm in total confusion. I'm falling for a man I hardly even know. At this moment, right now, sitting here, I feel so lost.

I can only be strong for so long, push it all down inside; then one day it's going to have to overflow, because there's no more space in that hole I've created inside. That's when the wall comes down. That's when I'm a child. There's this huge part of me I never let out. I'm scared, I'm lonely, I'm a trembling child that only wants to be held, to feel loved and secure, to collapse in someone's arms so I don't have to be independent and strong anymore.

MICHELLE: The truth is there was a certain person on the crew with whom I had a chemistry. It was just one of those things when you meet someone and you have an instant connection. I carried it with me during the whole trip, although it intensified during the second half. The only person who knew how I felt was Belou. Not Antoine and not even Chris. Maybe I told Patrice at the end of the trip, I'm not sure.

Nothing was ever talked about, and nothing ever happened. I knew that it would have interfered with the production of the show. I knew he would never have done anything about it. I never acted on it.

After the show was over, we made a lot of jokes about it. We acknowledged the tension, but we realized that the timing wasn't right. And by that point, I had a boyfriend who I really loved.

BELOU: It was the end of the trip, and we were in a hotel, and I was looking for Michelle, who wasn't in her room. I went up the stairs to the pool, and I saw Michelle sitting in the corner, writing, tears running out of her eyes, crying. I was like, "Michelle, what's going on? Come on, come here." I mean, I was really happy that I was there that moment, that time, because I had the chance to give back to her one time.

She just collapsed. Because she is always smiling. She's always up. I said, "Michelle, what's going on?" And she said, "I don't know, I just gotta cry, I just feel sad, and I ... I don't know what to do with the rest of my life." She just felt sick about everything. About the fights we'd had. And I was like, "Gee, Michelle, you need to sometimes just let go and just tell people what bothers you. You don't have to cry, but try to show a little emotion when something is bothering you."

JONATHAN MURRAY, EXECUTIVE PRODUCER: I think that between the cast and crew there's often a Romeo and Juliet thing going on. There's a wall in between them, and they can't cross it.

We are documentarians who are supposed to be as unbiased as possible. I think the crew understands that. If they want to act on feelings for cast members, they can't. It truly does impede production. So much so, that we've built into their contracts a clause stating that they cannot have relationships with cast members during the production or six months after it.

As far as I'm concerned, the cast can do no wrong. It's perfectly fair for a member of the cast to develop a crush on a member of the crew, and it's fine if he or she tries to go for it. On the other hand, it is not okay for the crew member to respond. It's difficult, though. When you're told, "Don't, don't, don't," you tend to wanna, wanna, wanna.

VALENCIA
–BUÑOL
27 miles
by Pepe

SPAIN
VALENCIA

BUÑOL
SPAIN

mission 13

Get saucy as
you attend the annual
tomato-throwing fest!

PATRICE: I had the feeling that I did something wrong, leaving Tomatina thirty minutes before it was over. It was too much. I didn't feel so well, because I couldn't see anything through those goggles, but I didn't dare to take them off. I was blind. **There was tomato on my clothes and in my eyes, and I just wanted to get out and breathe some air.** I had the feeling Clay was mad at me that I got out, that I didn't give him the pictures that he wanted. I didn't get in trouble, but I felt terrible. I didn't dare say anything to him.

TRAVEL ✉ LOG

It's the last mission, and things are getting a wee bit juicy! Chris and Antoine just wanna have fun, Patrice goes AWOL, and Belou goes PC. As for Michelle ... Could it be that she's too crushed out to have fun?

JONATHAN MURRAY, EXECUTIVE PRODUCER: I went to Tomatina. I got to run the Elmocam, which is this tiny camera that we placed on a big long pole. And I was on a balcony, sweeping this little camera over the crowd. What I didn't realize was that I would become a target. I was pelted with tomatoes!

BELOU: I'm at a tomato-throwing party, and it's s**t, man. It sucks. It sucks. There are so many f**king people who need this f**king food, and the whole street is filled with it! I'd say there are surely one million salads you could make from these tomatoes!

MICHELLE: I never thought that I could be tortured with food. Like, I saw 9½ Weeks, the movie. It's like eroticism with food—you know, food for fun. But this is torture with food!

ANTOINE: It's very scary. You can feel the tomatoes flying at you! You're ducking all the time!

MICHELLE: I was in my bra and shorts at one point in time. Belou was smart. She happened to wear one of my sports bras. Tomatina was fun for me for the first ten minutes.

CHRIS: Both studs in my ears were torn out, but I wasn't really aware of it when it happened.

CLAY NEWBILL, PRODUCER/DIRECTOR: I wasn't angry that he dropped out. I wish we had gotten a shot of him, though. With the exception of Patrice, Tomatina was a real bonding point for the cast and crew, our last mission and all. Early on in the fest, I bumped into Antoine. We were both staggering around, looking like, "Geez, is it over yet?" I looked at my watch, and I said, "Antoine, we've got forty more minutes of this. It's only been twenty minutes; there's forty minutes left." And he started screaming into the air, "Everyone stop this! This is silly! I'm a finance major! Order!" And I said, "Wait, let me try, I'm a director: Cut! That's enough! We've got enough! That's a wrap! Everybody go home!"

CLUE *You've earned these and much more. Head to the bull ring in Barcelona to retrieve your just reward.*

BUNOL-VALENCIA-
BARCELONA
258 Miles

The Tomatina Festival takes place every year on the last Wednesday in August. Tomatoes start flying at 11:00 a.m., and cleanup crews take on the soupy mess at 1:00 p.m. The festival takes place in the town square of Buñol, a small city (only one pension!) about three hours from Madrid and a half hour from Valencia. La Tomatina is but one of many events that take place during the course of the week. On the night before the tomato brawl, there's a giant paella (a rice and seafood medley) cooking contest!

MICHELLE

JONATHAN MURRAY, EXECUTIVE PRODUCER: Michelle was vibrant, fun and easygoing. I think she's probably one of the easiest people to travel with in the world. And it's a good thing she was, because she was traveling with Belou.

CHRIS: Michelle is an incredible person. She's so caring. She looks out for other people before she looks out for herself. We were sort of set apart from the rest of the group. **Whether we were supposed to be the next Kit and Mark, I don't know.** Whatever. We were both such altruists, and we were always trying to keep things peaceful. Maybe if we weren't always worrying about keeping everyone else happy we would have had time to go at it ourselves. Michelle deserves the best. She really does. She should get it. She will, I think.

BELOU: Michelle is a pretty smart girl. She was very sweet to me. She was the one that was always there for me. She always wanted to help everybody and wasn't really against anyone. Sometimes she was irritated. Michelle, when she is irritated, takes a step back. She locks herself up in a room, and that's where she tries to get rid of her irritations. And then she comes out of the room again with a big smile.

PATRICE: Michelle. She's the all-American girl. The way that she smiled, for example, when she didn't understand something. That's what you expect from TV.

MARY-ELLIS BUNIM, EXECUTIVE PRODUCER: Michelle has a perpetually sunny disposition. She's a lot of fun to be around. She's a born diplomat. It takes quite a lot to push her buttons, but she's not a doormat. She kept the group morale up a great deal, and she has wonderful energy that kept them going.

MICHELLE ROUGHING IT

ANTOINE: I thought Michelle was a bit of a buffer in the group. She understands people, and she tries to understand people before she reacts to anything anyone says.

FROM THE DESK OF...
MICHELLE'S PARENTS

We noticed an even greater maturity when Michelle came home. We recognize that her strong sense of self is reflected in her behavior on the program, and she has always been relatively secure in her values. She intuitively understands how people need to be treated, and she can respond to those needs. However, as some of the cast members needs are greater than others, and some behavior becomes abusive, we see Michelle draw a line at how much she is willing to tolerate. She seemed to become more assertive while still serving as a counselor-mediator.

PAGE
75

THE CAST
AND CREW on

MICHELLE: It's hard to say if I changed after *Road Rules*, because the truth is that I am an intuitive person about other people but completely clueless about myself. I do know that watching the show will have an effect on me. I remember seeing a snippet of myself on a monitor. I was thinking, "Oh, my God! I look just so happy and so excited; it looks like I need to take Ritalin."

I did actually learn about roughing it when I was on *Road Rules*. There were times when we had no running water in the Winnebago at all, so you couldn't use the toilet. And the bathing thing: I can go a day and a half, but when you're going a day, a night, a day, a night, a day, and that night you don't know if you're going to shower—that really bothered me. For a lot of people in Europe, like Belou, shaving is not a big thing. Legs are not a big deal for me. But armpits! Absolutely! This sounds so awful, but I guess I'm not as hygienic as I used to be. I don't freak out anymore if my hair's a little greasy.

All said, I think that only really good things came out of *Road Rules*, even if I didn't change in any major way. I'm still the same Michelle. The most important things to me are love and God and friendships. Those are my priorities, really, just kind of smelling the flowers as you go along.

TRAVEL ✉ LOG

Handsome reward in hand and TV-ready, our telegenic travelers find themselves ensconced in the luxury of a hotel suite as they embark on their last evening as a team.

PATRICE: The last night was not as I expected it. I wish it could have been better. I decided to go back to the National Palace of Spain, back where it all started. I wanted the others to come with me, but they wanted to stay back at the hotel. I was right up there at the top of the palace by myself. There was this beautiful fountain there, with all the lights, and the classical music was so beautiful. The thing is, I was missing the others. **I was like, "Hey, why the heck are they still in the hotel and not here with me—just to have this moment."** I was sad I couldn't share that moment with the others—or that they didn't bother that much about it. But I was sort of used to being the one who is more into things than the others.

The Last Night

BELOU: On the last night, Antoine wanted to get together with me, and I didn't really feel like it. Chris, Michelle, Antoine and I were all in bed together, just like the first night. Chris and Michelle were next to us, and I could hear that they were doing something. I was, like, there in the middle, with one guy wanting to get together with me and two guys almost making love to each other. I was like, "I have to get out of here." I said, "Antoine, I'm sorry. I can't do anything with you. I can't handle it anymore. I gotta find out who I like, who I want to be with." I just didn't feel anything anymore for Antoine. All my feelings for him were gone. They were absolutely gone.

So I got out of bed and went downstairs, where Patrice was sleeping. And I said, "Patrice, can I lay next to you tonight?" And he said, "Yeah, of course," and he just shuffled to the side, and I lay with Patrice for the rest of the night, just sleeping. I knew that Patrice wouldn't come on to me, wouldn't do anything, wouldn't make noises or whatever. That's what I liked about Patrice. He was always far away, but he was there for you when you really needed him. It was just nice, that last night. I remember that Antoine came downstairs and slept on the couch.

The crew came in the next morning, and they must have been like, "What's going on?" It must have seemed strange that Chris and Michelle are lying upstairs; Belou is lying in one bed with Patrice; and Antoine is lying on the couch.

Final Letters

ANTOINE: Belou said she was not feeling good, so she moved to another bed or something, and I can't remember where I slept.

CHRIS AND MICHELLE GET TOGETHER: **5**

CHRIS: Michelle and I stayed up together for quite some time, talking and kissing. It was really calm, relaxed and very much the way I wanted the last night to be.

MICHELLE: The last night was really intense. I was so happy to be with these people, and I felt so close to them. I stayed up all night and wrote them this letter.

To my dearest CAST members:

I'm sitting here writing this in the dark, so forgive me if I'm just way out of the lines. I know I've already said it a thousand times, but I just need to make sure y'all understand how important this experience and you guys are to me. You've put up with so much of my crap—Pepe's wreck, PMS and the many days I seemed to wake up without a brain.... The list could go on. I can't deny we had some really rough days, but I wouldn't change a single moment. I still can't quite figure out what I did to be so blessed to have an experience like this. I mean, there are so many beautiful people in this world, inside and out. Then I stop and take a moment to look at each one of you....

Superburschi—Your beautiful smile, how you can make us all laugh, when you lean over to kiss my cheek or hold open the door for no reason....

Twanner—Those two big intelligent blue eyes, your gift of sharing your knowledge, my father figure, always looking out for me....

Belou—My sister, your big gorgeous smile and beautiful golden locks, your passion for life and love and your desire to share it with the world, my Bubba....

Christopher—(My stability) Your ability to look at a situation from every angle, your crazy sense of humor, the fact you can give and give until you have nothing left to give, and yet you never ask for anything in return....

Then I understand there are no four people more lovely in this world than those I have spent the last two months of my life with. I would never change a thing about any of you ... bad habits and all. I don't exactly know when, but somewhere along the line, you became my family. I love you all so much, and I know I'm going to miss you something terrible. I wish everyone all the blessings in the world for whatever he or she decides to pursue.... With you four, the sky's the limit. I will think of you guys often, and I definitely expect some of you to come visit soon! Have a safe trip home or to Rome!

All my love,
Michelle

CHRIS: I Loved Michelle's letter. It affirmed everything I ever thought about her. I wrote my own small letter—to the crew.

To all the crew:

I never realized how hard a job all of you have. Let it be known that all your hard work and friendliness was and is appreciated by me. I'm sorry for my overfriendly nature and my attempts to "cross the line." I hope to see you all again at the premiere party, and we can party like we've been meaning to.

Thanx so much,
CHRIS

ANTOINE: I am craving for the day that they will put us back together for a reunion. I'd love to have that. I'll have so many questions to ask.

Michelle,
You should be all set for your trip. If there any probbms give me a call. Have a great trip down

BELOU: When I got home from *Road Rules*, Pablo and I spoke all the time. He was in Chile, and sometimes we'd stay on the phone for six hours at a time. I knew I had to go to Chile; I had to see if I still felt the same for him. We traveled around Chile, and we had a wonderful time, and, well, we are still very much in love. I would like to find a way to live with Pablo. I know that with him I could absolutely handle it. He gives a lot of support. He can give me many things.

One time on the phone I said, "You know what's funny? I just remembered that when I was very little I had a dream one day that I would get married in South America." And then he said, "That can happen, if you want." And I just started trembling on the phone. I was just like, "No way," you know? "No, let's not talk about it, we're too young, and no way." And he said, "Yeah, let's stop dreaming. First let's see each other and see how it works out."

Once I was in Chile, all my fears were gone. I really felt ready for marriage. One night, we were outside, and we saw these three stars called the three Marys.

He said, "With the three Marys as our witnesses, let's decide to get married." I said yes.

We wanted to do it in a place where it was beautiful, and where it was spiritual and we could be alone, so we said, "Let's go to the desert, to Moon Valley." Valle de la Luna, it's so beautiful there. There's salt coming out of the ground, which turns into rock, and after a while the rock makes crystal. At night, when the moon shines, the crystal shines all over the valley. It's beautiful.

We went to Moon Valley with these two Indian friends, who threw us this celebration with music and stuff. We all ate this special cactus, and then they left us alone. We walked around for a while, and finally I took these smooth round stones and lay them on the ground in a circle, and I asked Pablo to come inside. And he stepped in the round, and I said, "I don't know what to say. I mean, we know what we want. And I think that the stars know, and the moon knows, and the desert knows, so what can we say?" It was so exciting. "You know," he said, "I only want to say one word ... forever." And then I said, "Forever." And then we were ready. We walked out of the rocks, and we walked around the valley for a couple more hours, and then we took the car home. That was it. We were married. Not in any legal way, but spiritually. Spiritually, Pablo and I are married.

Belou and Pablo

STAYING ON

Belou's Wedding Ring Pablo and I each got ring tattoos. The tattoos are supposed to remind us of Moon Valley. There's one big moon, with two half-moons on either side of it. Pablo and I alone are each a half-moon. But together we're a whole moon.

UPDATE BELOU AND PABLO BROKE UP!

BELOU: I'd rather stay a B. Girl than be a Chilean widow. I have my own life to live. I wasn't ready to have that kind of connection with anyone, especially someone so far away.

ANTOINE: I am in Hanoi, in North Vietnam. I found a job after being here a week. I'm very lucky, I guess. I work in the financial department of an American construction company.

Vietnam offers a really, really, really different life. Every kind of comfort you have at home you don't have here. On the other hand, you can live like a king with one thousand dollars a month. Vietnamese food is quite something. I ate dog, which I must say is not very good. You dip the dog meat into a rotten shrimp-shell sauce. Apart from that, everything's great.

You can seriously go wild here and end up in the police station every night. Some of the people I hang out with, respectable as they are, they impose very few limits on themselves. I've seen people I hold in high regard indulge in very messy activities, such as drinking and going around and seeing prostitutes.

My life is a lot harder now than it was when I was on **Road Rules.**

This is probably one of the biggest challenges I have ever put myself through. Every day is really hard and tough and demanding. And there are no days off.

Michelle

Back In the U.S.A.

MICHELLE: I'm in love now. A very, very odd thing for me, because I'm not used to letting myself be dependent or vulnerable. My boyfriend's name is Brandon. He's twenty-eight. He's so kind, so spiritual, so cute. He's awesome. He's so good to me. It's like we just fit—in every sense. Like mentally, emotionally, body-wise, just everything. We just fit. When we met, we felt like we had known each other forever.

I'm out here in Los Angeles right now, living in Studio City, and I like it a lot. It's a whole lot different from Dallas. Eventually I'd like to move out of Studio City and move somewhere in the country. But this is where I have to be in order to be an actress and a dancer, which is what I want to do. **I don't want to be famous—just the best at what I do.**

I've got an agent now and I'm going out on commercial and theatrical auditions. One great thing happened recently. I got a call from MTV asking me to be a guest host on LOVELINE. I did it for a few days and I loved it! It was so great. Everyone was so nice. I loved Adam and Dr. Drew!

UPDATE MICHELLE AND BRANDON BROKE UP BUT ARE STILL CLOSE FRIENDS

PATRICE: Five days after I came back from Barcelona, the same day, actually, I went to the modeling agency that organized the Look of the Year competition in Germany. **I ended up being one of the chosen ones!** And of the ten guys, I was one of the four picked to be on the cover. I got to go on another trip—this time over the cradle, down to Mauritius. I was like, "Oh, yeah! Another free trip! I just love my life!"

If I don't go on with modeling, I will do some kind of career in media, I'm not sure which.

All I know is this: I want to keep the spirit of the trip with me. I want to keep having missions. I want to keep overcoming fears.

Patrice

THE ROAD

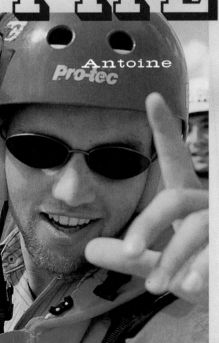
Antoine
Pro-tec

CHRIS: I'm finishing up my third year at Penn as an English major/psych major and I'm heading to NYC for the summer to do an internship. While I'm there, I'm hoping to land a bartending job, so I can pick up some cash. I'd also like to get some modeling in when I'm there. And some dating. I'm still single!

I'm not sure what I'm going to do when I graduate, probably work in entertainment—not in the acting side, but on the business side.

As far as *Road Rules* goes, I'm happy to be home, but I miss the the adventure and I miss the traveling.

I miss all the adrenaline.

Chris

Welcome to the ride of your life.

Your destination:
Your money:
Yo
And then you'll
Hands
Throw o
these a
Road

One Two Three!

Anywhere.
Gone.
ur mission: Survive.
be rewarded:
omely.
ut your rules,
re
Rules

ROAD RULES, Season 4 Islands

JAKE

In the beginning, there was really just me, Kalle and Vince. We'd say we're the Double-C-Double-R, the Cool Clique from ROAD RULES. Over the course of the trip, we kind of became more of the five of us, but still, there's always kind of been an inner circle to the group.

BRUCE TOMS
director

This cast understood from day one what we wanted. They knew that we weren't just looking to see them complete missions, but to come in and look at what's going on in their lives.

MARY-ELLIS BUNIM
executive producer

After what went on in Europe, there was a tacit understanding that we were going for a kinder, gentler, younger group. The greatest contrast to the Europe experience is that for the Islands cast, all five kids were very typical Americans. American kids are different. They are less cynical, they're more open, they're less worried about being cool, they're more attached to their parents. And maybe that's why the process of becoming independent is more dramatic with American kids than it is with European kids.

VINCE

It's just been such a blast, and I love my cast so much, but it has been strange. I was such a fan of the show. I've watched it so many times that I'd find myself watching the camera taping other people, and it would hit me how amazing it was that I was now a part of it. It's great, but it's weird — surreal. I feel like I've been in one great, big, long dream.

Say hello to Erika, Jake, Kalle, Oscar and Vince as they set out on the trip of a lifetime! It's planes, boats and Winnies as ROAD RULES Islands hops around the good old United States and the dazzling Caribbean!

It's hard enough getting along with someone you love.

OSCAR

Just imagine someone, four someones, you've never even met. It's crazy.

KALLE

Our cast was able to pull together when it mattered. I'm proud of that. Unfortunately, there was also a lot of backstabbing going on, myself included. I think it began with everybody's personalities, and then it just kind of built on itself. I wish we would have started out having everything out in the open, just blatantly honest, even if it hurt people's feelings.

ERIKA

They could all make me laugh so hard. I mean, they could just kill me. Those times when we were just all screwing around, laughing. That's the part of our group that I'd like to remember forever. I'd rather forget a lot of the fights. I would rather have that fade into the background.

ERIKA

JAKE

KALLE

OSCAR

VINCE

SY1

Episode One Kalle, nineteen, a bubbly, blond fireball from Colorado; Jake, eighteen, a wise guy from Philly; Vince, twenty, a moody martial artist from Florida; Erika, twenty-two, the sophisticated Big Sis from San Diego; and Oscar, nineteen, the Puerto Rican poet and patriot, meet on a pier in San Francisco to begin the adventure they'll never forget. In the ROAD RULES tradition, Michelle (from ROAD RULES Europe) passes the torch, confiscating their funds and handing over the keys to the Winnie. And so the adventure begins! The gang's first clue directs them to Mare Island Naval Shipyard, where they'll be battling an all-star team of former Road Rulers in a paintball war—for cash! Sadly, our new Road Rulers fail miserably against the all-stars and must manage on four hundred dollars for the next two weeks. Tattooed on Timmy (from ROAD RULES Season 2), is their next clue: It's time to be all they can be with the U.S. Coast Guard!

On the Coast Guard base, Oscar complains about the fit of his pants, forcing the no-nonsense petty officer to tame his 'tude, military-style. The cast successfully performs a series of drills, including bobbing in the icy waters sporting "Gumby" suits, but suffers desperately from seasickness. Jake threatens to leave the boat. Group reactions are mixed, but Kalle's compassionate concern proves most persuasive, and Jake decides to endure. Mayday! The radio alert calls our amateur coast guardsmen to action. It's time to suit up and save a life!

Episode Two The cast gears up to rescue a man from a burning boat and bring him aboard the cutter LONG ISLAND. The captain congratulates them on successfully completing the drill, and delivers the next clue—in Morse code! The gang puzzles over the clue but presently deciphers their destination: Balboa Island. Returning to the Winnie, Vince discovers the trademark cattle skull has been kidnapped from the grillwork. In retaliation, Jake and Oscar capture the Coast Guard flag. When an officer comes to reclaim the emblem, the cast clashes over what to do. Jake reluctantly returns the flag, betraying his partner-in-crime, a sulky Oscar. Erika bids happy birthday to her mother, who lives nearby, and Mom invites the whole gang over for a celebratory dinner. Kalle shyly bonds with Erika's mom and warmly remembers her stroll with Jake, when she confided in him about her own mother's death. En route to Balboa Island, Erika gets snippy with Oscar, and when Oscar takes the wheel, she reams him for driving like a madman. The incorrigible Oscar aggravates the tension on board, bickering with his cast mates. The cast lets off steam with a group scream.

Episode Three Morning on Balboa Island: Oscar has staged another disappearing act. His cast mates are sick of his sulky behavior and threaten to leave him behind if he doesn't materialize soon. At Wilma's Patio, they learn that they will compete in an amateur comedy competition for cash. The cast splits into pairs, leaving Oscar the odd man out. Oscar, depressed and homesick, sits alone in the Winnie, crying as he reads a letter from his family. All is forgiven, temporarily, when the cast returns to find Oscar has cleaned the Winnie in their absence. Jake reaches out to Oscar, promising to be a better friend. He and Kalle invite Oscar to be a part of their comedy team, and the cast members work on their acts. At the competition, Vince and Erika steal the show with their bickering husband and wife shtick, overshadowing Jake's bold streak across the stage with a serving tray as a loin cover. Vince and Erika take second prize and a much-needed two hundred dollars! That night, the cast receives their next clue, sending them to Key West.

Episode Four Our restless Road Rulers pass the time at the airport making predictions about their next mission. Erika ventures they may be wing walking, but Vince naively counters that you need special training for that. In the morning, the anxious adventurers report to the Key West Airport, where it so happens that just that sort of training awaits them. They will learn to wing walk, and one lucky daredevil will do the honors at three thousand feet! The group performs training maneuvers on the ground, and Kalle and Oscar are recruited as rivals for the stunt. The others take turns flying the biplane, executing loops and barrel rolls. Mission accomplished—for the moment!

Nighttime on the beach: Erika offers Kalle big sisterly advice during a heart-to-heart about her future. Then Kalle and Jake cuddle up for the night on the roof of the Winnie. Kalle confesses she's never been this close to anyone but Brian, and Jake admits to having a crush on Kalle. New dawn, new dangers . . . Back at the airfield, Kalle is chosen to wing walk, while Oscar will perform a standing stunt inside the plane. Kalle straps herself to the wing of the plane and surfs clouds to the thrill and admiration of her cast mates, especially Jake. Overdosing on adrenaline, Kalle gushes that this is the best thing she's ever done.

Episode Five In Key West, the kids bemoan their empty bellies and pockets. Pouty and preoccupied, Jake wheels into a KFC drive-through and wedges the Winnie beneath the overhang. When officers arrive on the scene, Oscar sweet-talks their way out of trouble and then charms the restaurant crew into donating a bag of fried chicken to the cause. The next day, the cast meets their contact from Kokomo Cabs in the pouring rain. They will pedal and peddle for a day to earn money driving pedicabs. After mastering the maneuvering of the vehicles, our pedicabbies really get into it. Oscar dominates, cashing in on tourism to the tune of $139. The cast races back to the Winnie to uncover their next clue: They're off to Grand Cayman!

They arrive at the youth hostel, which their host explains is haunted, making them slightly ill at ease. In the morning, it's off to Treasure Island Hotel, where they learn that they'll be shooting a swimsuit calendar. The kids do an excellent job modeling the suits and shooting all over the island, and they finish the project just under the wire. As the cast mates select the twelve best photos, Vince rescues a stray dog and delivers him to the vet for care. The cast reunites with their finished calendar, earning praise and payment from their professional contact. The cast celebrates with their hard-earned cash, partying at a dance club.

Episode Six The cast makes a beeline for Otto Watler's honey farm on Grand Cayman. While briefing the cast in the ways of harvesting honey, Otto is stung and shows them how the stinger continues to pump poison into his flesh. Oscar soon experiences this sensation himself when he is stung on the forehead. The cast dons bee suits and learns to retrieve the trays of honey, careful not to upset the queen bee. They are all successful, except for Jake. He doles out the smoke but gets stung anyway. The kids extract their next clue from the bee box: A three-hour tour . . . in St. Thomas! At the dock in St. Thomas, the Road Rulers meet Kenny and Vania and discover that they are going to be trained to survive on a deserted island. The gang learns how to set up hammocks and find food—all fun and games until Kenny and Vania leave the kids alone on the island for three days. Tired and hungry, the cast members talk about homesickness. Oscar seems to be the only happy one. He says he feels as though he's found his roots and that the island is paradise. On day three, Erika spots a rescue boat. It's Bob Denver, star of the show GILLIGAN'S ISLAND—they're saved! The kids are thrilled to be on their way back to civilization. When Denver's hat flies off into the water, Oscar doesn't hesitate to jump in and rescue it. Once safely in the harbor, Denver gives the cast the clue for their next mission. Oscar is blown away: They're going to Puerto Rico. That night on the beach Jake and Kalle acknowledge that their romance is heating up, and Kalle finally consents to Jake's suggestion that she get tested for HIV.

Episode Seven

Next stop is Puerto Rico and Oscar is bursting with excitement. But his travel mates head for Oscar's homeland with a bit of unease. They think the country will never match Oscar's build-up, and they worry that by staying at his home, they will owe him something. Oscar's dad welcomes the Road Rulers with open arms, food and friends as he throws a party for the travelers. But Oscar's new friends do not seem to mesh with his old. One of Oscar's buddies has a special interest in Kalle, but Oscar steps in to caution him. The next day, a new clue arrives and the kids depart for the small town of Isabela, where they learn of their mission: They must milk a goat, eat an eggroll and pitch a penny into a haunted well. If they can prove they've done all three, they get to stay in a little beachside cottage for free. Jake suggests he just roll an egg on the counter and eat it for the eggroll. As for the goat, the gang scours the countryside until they find one they can manage to wrestle some milk from. At every stop, it's Oscar with his Spanish and winning charm who keeps the cast closing in on their goal. Two down, one to go. Unfortunately, Oscar's aggressive driving lands the van's tire in a big hole, which leads to a new mission—getting the van free. After some amazing coincidences and more help from Oscar, the van is free, and the kids are at the well, pitching their penny in as thanks for the luck they've had. Back at the cottage, Oscar gets the best bunk bed and is suddenly very much a part of the group.

Episode Eight

With their clue of a miniature raft and a global positioning system (GPS), the kids drive around the Puerto Rican countryside in search of their next mission. Near a river they run into Rosano, who informs them that each must build a raft from scratch, then race them down the river. The winner will be served a gourmet dinner by a sexy waitperson. Using inner tubes, bamboo and rope, the Road Rulers each concoct their own unique creation, but before the race can begin, Rosano has a surprise. The race is to start with a pendulum jump off the nearby bridge. Jake gains an early lead and soon realizes the irony of his situation: Although he is winning, he is sorry to be alone while everyone else is just having fun floating down the river together. Ditto for the prize of a gourmet dinner for one, so Jake invites Oscar to share the meal with him. Their next clue tells the kids that they're going to Martinique, where Captain Christian will teach them to sail. Before the sailing lessons, Vince and Erika—both away from serious relationships—let off a little sexual steam by wrestling in bed and throwing pitchers of water at each other. In Martinique, Christian informs the cast that not only are they going to learn to sail, but they get to live on his million dollar yacht for two weeks. The Road Rulers can't believe their good luck, but then they have trouble understanding Christian's Norwegian accent, and it's only Jake who really gets the hang of sailing. It's no surprise when he is elected captain. During a break, Oscar discovers the next clue. They're headed for St. Lucia to plan and orchestrate a wedding. En route to St. Lucia, Jake is enjoying his command, until he fails to tie a sail down, and it comes loose and flaps wildly in the wind. With the sun down and the boat sailing into the darkness, Christian has to climb up and cut down the sail, nearly cutting his thumb off in the process. Just when they think they are out of danger, Vince steers the wrong way and the boat goes into a dangerous jibe, sending the boom flying across the boat and nearly taking some Road Ruler heads with it. The kids are scared, but they're pulling together.

Special Two-Part Episode–Road Rules/The Real World *Challenge*

Rafting is not the end of the fun and games in Puerto Rico. Before their journey to Martinique the Road Rulers defend their good name:
At the end of Jake's gourmet meal in Puerto Rico, there is another clue—a chocolate cake that does not want to be cut. Underneath the fake cake is a two-part mission. The Road Rulers are to deliver challenge cards to competitors and then meet and compete with them the following day. Vince deduces that they are going up against THE REAL WORLD, which brings on the trash talking. The kids write down their favorite disses on the cards, and Jake, Kalle and Oscar successfully deliver the challenge. When the REAL WORLD crew—Elka, Genesis, Jason, Kameelah, Montana, Sean and Syrus—see the challenge cards, they are ready for battle. On the day of the competition our Road Rulers have reason to be wary: THE REAL WORLD has some big boys, including a lumberjack, in their court. Rosano, of the rafting mission, is in charge and explains that the two groups are going to compete for money in a series of events that test not only strength and skill, but also intelligence. And the fate of the losing team? Rosano will allude only to "severe humiliation."
THE REAL WORLD cast gets off to a quick start, winning The Plank, The Net and The Box. Team ROAD RULES is looking severely down, remembering all too well the paintball humiliation that started off their trip. As they break for lunch, it's THE REAL WORLD 3, ROAD RULES 0. While the two teams sit down to eat, the competitors start feeling a little friendlier. There's lots of mingling going on, most significantly between Oscar and Syrus, and Erika and Sean. But too soon, Rosano blows the whistle and it's time to return to the hostilities. The Road Rulers are looking a little better after some food—they had started the day without breakfast. The second half begins with The Wall, which is neck and neck until Vince manages to finish first. The Road Rulers are freaking with their first victory, and it's a whole new competition. The Four-way Tug-of-War is next and doesn't bode well for the Road Rulers, with Syrus and Sean against them, but Oscar turns superhuman, and they pull it out. An A for effort and two wins are not enough and ROAD RULES must suffer the humiliation. They are to give THE REAL WORLD team professional pedicures. Controversy erupts when Oscar and Montana start a mud fight. With the games behind them, the team members of each side feel pleased with their own cast mates. And both casts have promised to hook up later in the evening for some fun. While Syrus goes off to the hospital to have a battle wound stitched up, Jason and Sean look forward to seeing the ROAD RULES girls all done up. At the discotheque, things start heating up. Jake and Kalle are getting down, and Sean is putting the moves on Erika—giving a whole new meaning to the ROAD RULES / THE REAL WORLD Challenge!

Episode Nine

In St. Lucia, the cast is having fun, swinging off the mast and landing in the sea, until Oscar forgets to let go and smashes into the boat, badly cutting his toes. Freshly bandaged, Oscar and friends head to a resort, where they meet Cyndi and Zaine, a young couple who give them specifics on their mission: The kids have forty-eight hours to plan and pull off a traditional Creole wedding. If they succeed, they'll get their own posh suite and money to celebrate with. The Road Rulers are not so sure; they don't want to screw up the most important day of a couple's life. The next morning, Jake takes command. He finds the name of a place, Bridal Paradise, which he thinks will have all the answers. On the way to Bridal Paradise, Oscar is dropped off at a doctor's office to check on his toes. Bridal Paradise ends up being true to its name. Beverly, the proprietress, will take care of just about every wedding detail. Back at the doctor, Oscar gets a shock. His toes are fractured and the doctor recommends a cast. Oscar is distraught, knowing a cast could keep him from participating in some of the more rugged missions. After talking it over with his trip mates, Oscar decides to go without the cast. The next day, the wedding goes off without a hitch. The reception is all dancing, eating and toasting, but the fun really begins when the kids claim their reward, the luxury suite. The girls are the first to go in the pool, but soon Vince is swimming sans his suit, followed by Jake who does a naked crawl around the edge of the pool. Things get even steamier when everyone starts piling into the shower. When a chocolate cake in the shape of a volcano arrives, the Road Rulers have their next clue. They're going to spend the night in the crater of a volcano in St. Vincent. The next morning, the kids are slow to move, but soon they're sailing for St. Vincent. A guide named Clint starts them on their way up the volcano, but they must face the hardest part alone, and for Oscar with his broken toes the trip is very touch and go.

Episode Ten The kids are poised on the rim of St. Vincent's La Soufrière volcano and down they must go, for their mission is to spend the night in the crater. But all is not well, especially for Oscar with his broken toes. They make it successfully to the bottom and are proud of Oscar, but their troubles aren't over. Sleeping bags are lost, the tents don't seem to want to be assembled and a storm's approaching. These campers are less than happy as they eat dinner out of cans and call it a night. The next day, after a tough climb out of the volcano, the kids spot Clint, who gives them their next clue: They're off to Grenada where they will be on the radio as Love Doctors. On the boat, Jake and Kalle retreat to their cabin for snuggling, but when Jake bursts out the "L" word, Kalle gets uncomfortable. The next day, Vince asks Kalle if she thinks she would have hooked up with Jake if they met under different circumstances, and she answers no. In Grenada, it's good-bye to Christian and hello to Grenada Broadcasting where the kids are briefed about their mission by Troy, a cautious man who is full of warnings for the Road Rulers. He wants them to have fun, but also to be professional and clean. He has reason to be worried. The kids quickly steer discussion to topics many conservative Grenadians find objectionable, and when they get a surprise call from LOVELINE's Dr. Drew and Adam Corolla, it gets even more out of hand. With show time running out, the kids get a final surprise caller. It's Jake's dad calling to say that the cast must stop in Philadelphia for a visit. Jake can't believe it.

Episode Eleven Though they've loved the Caribbean, the Road Rulers are psyched to return to the U.S.A. Jake's parents warmly welcome the travelers to their cool loft home. They're full of questions for the cast and more than interested to discover that both Jake and Kalle plan to go to school in New York City. The next morning, Jake's dad presents the next clue. The cast are New York City bound where they will participate in a mystery audition with the Knicks. Kalle is especially pleased. She can't wait to see the apartment she will be moving into with her best friend, Nicki. The kids take the train to Penn Station, and then cab it to a youth hostel. Kalle absolutely loves the city. The next morning, Vince is psyched to play some hoops, but he gets a monster surprise. They're trying out for the dance team, not the basketball team. Vince is stunned. After a brief warm-up with the dancers, the Road Rulers get to see these professionals perform, and it looks incredibly hard. Vince gets gloomier by the minute, while Oscar sees a bright side: The dancers are beautiful. After giving rehearsal a brief try, Vince has had it. He's throwing in the towel. Jake thinks he's a baby and Oscar thinks he's crazy. Back to rehearsal—the verdict is that only Erika has a shot. Erika will rehearse tomorrow and then give a final audition. Erika is pleased, but scared. After another day of rehearsing, Erika doesn't think she's good enough, but she keeps trying. While the audition goes well, the dancers' coach informs Erika that she's not quite ready, at which point Erika heads for the locker room for a private cry. The other Road Rulers get to run stats during the game, while Vince, as punishment for bailing, has to watch the game from the nose bleed seats. During the game, which the Knicks win easily, the cast notices something on the scoreboard. It's a clue, just for them. They're headed for Pine Valley, ALL MY CHILDREN country.

Episode Twelve Judy Wilson welcomes the kids to ALL MY CHILDREN and explains their mission: They're going to audition for three spots as extras on the show. The two who don't make it will be gofers for the show's two young stars. The Road Rulers have fun goofing around the set, have their auditions and then hear the verdict: Vince, Erika and Oscar are the extras. Jake and Kalle are bummed to be "the losers" and Oscar just can't believe he got it. Jake and Kalle then meet Mark and Kelly, the couple they'll be gofering for. It turns out that Mark and Kelly are married in real life and Kelly is pregnant with their first child. With Vince, Erika and Oscar going to make-up and costumes, Jake and Kalle start sorting Kelly's fan mail, but soon they get a perk and sit down to a lunch of French toast with the couple. During lunch, Kelly talks about fate bringing Mark and her together, and Jake and Kalle recognize fate's part in their own meeting. On the set, the others are finding extra work pretty easy, but Oscar is ecstatic that he gets a line. Meanwhile, Jake and Kalle are having a blast out in the city doing errands for Mark and Kelly. For a last errand, they are off to a hot dog cart across town. After the extras finish up, Judy sends them to the same hot dog cart, where the kids all convene around a clue. It's a charred human foot: They're going to have to walk on hot coals. That night, Kalle and Company are hanging with her friend Nicki and some others at the new apartment. They all end up checking out Kalle's audition tape for ROAD RULES. Jake gets a pretty big surprise when he sees Kalle on the tape saying she knows she wants to marry Brian, but just wants some time alone. The next morning, the kids are packing up and it's starting to sink in. The dream trip is about to come to an end.

Episode Thirteen Mark, the clean-cut firewalking instructor, sets fire to a pile of logs. He asks the kids to consider whether this experience is going to be the peak moment of their lives, or just the springboard to bigger and better heights? The kids learn that walking the coals is not just about fire, it's about doing things your mind tells you are impossible. Back in a conference room, the first thing they try is breaking boards with their bare hands. Next, Mark takes the kids through the steps of overcoming fears. Just before they head for the fire, Mark gives them a mantra to recite for power: Cool moss. Out in the park, the red hot coals are ready to go and the kids are pumped. They're screaming the mantra and hopping up and down on bare feet. One by one they make the walk, then join together in a ring of fire for more hugging and screaming. Once they are all in the circle, it's handsome reward time. They are given a box that contains a video tape and a key to a suite at Trump Plaza. In their suite, the kids go right for the VCR. They pop in the tape and press play. Their reward? A three-month trip around the world on the "Semester at Sea" ship. The reactions are mixed: Oscar is speechless, but Erika looks ill. She can't imagine heading off on another trip at this stage in her life. In Erika's room Vince talks to her about how she's feeling, and he admits that if they hadn't had significant others back home, something probably would have happened between them. During their gourmet feast, the kids are starting to feel nostalgic. They can't imagine what normal life will be like. By the end of the meal, it's clear that a deep bond has formed among them. The next day, it's off to the airport and Oscar is the first to board the plane. As he gets last hugs, the tears start flowing. Erika and Kalle can't stop crying. Vince is next. He and Jake exchange "I Love You's" and then he leaves. After Erika catches her plane, it's just the happy couple, except Jake's unhappy. He knows they're going to meet in New York the next week, but he still worries that something could happen. Kalle tells him he has to have faith, and with that, she's gone.

CASTING *ERIKA*

NICKNAME: **Pansy Ass**
HOMETOWN: **San Diego, California**
BIRTHDAY: **August 26, 1974**   SIGN: **Virgo**
ODD JOB: **Go-go dancer**
SPORT: **Rower on her college crew team**
SUPERHERO OF CHOICE: **Wonder Woman**
CELEBRITY SHE'D CHUCK IT ALL FOR:
Chris Isaak

Kenny Hull, CASTING DIRECTOR: Erika was great-pretty, likable. Very warm, girl next door, the girl you'd want to marry, the girl you'd want to bring home to Mom. I did think she was too mature for ROAD RULES. But due to other factors, it was decided that Erika should be on ROAD RULES, even though she'd already been told she was cast for THE REAL WORLD. I was asked to make the phone call, because I'm the one who knew Erika the best. Except they didn't want her to feel like she was being forced, so they said, "Call her up and say 'How would you feel if you had the choice between going on THE REAL WORLD and ROAD RULES?'"

Erika: Kenny called me two hours after I'd been told I was on THE REAL WORLD, and he goes, "Do you still want to be on ROAD RULES? You kind of have a choice right now." I said, "I want to be on ROAD RULES!" Meanwhile, the whole crew from THE REAL WORLD is over at my apartment.

Kenny Hull, CASTING DIRECTOR: There were about twelve people in the room, and they're all watching me. And I'm just acting in the midst of being upset that we're making this switch. I said, "Okay, I'm going to see if I can pull some strings. I'll call you back." So I hang up, wait for a few minutes, then call her back, and I'm like, "I did it! I did it! You can do it. You can go on ROAD RULES!" Looking back now, it's kind of funny. And it worked out well for both casts. But at the time, it was very painful.

Erika: I was so happy, because I always wanted to be on ROAD RULES. THE REAL WORLD never really did it for me.

Casting Scoop: Erika was initially cast for THE REAL WORLD. A camera crew showed up at her apartment, presented her with a rowing oar that had "Boston" painted on it, and taped her getting the call that she had been selected to be on THE REAL WORLD.

Casting Application

How would you describe your best traits? **A good sense of humor. I like that more than anything, well maybe not anything, but I like it a lot. And I know that I am a strong person. I have solid opinions, and I am very comfortable with myself as a person. Plus, I love to have fun and be adventurous.**

How would you describe your worst traits? **Sometimes I can be moody and short-tempered. I have to admit at times I can get very impatient, and I don't even realize how rude I am being.**

Describe your most embarrassing moment? **In high school, I modeled for a local store that made wedding dresses. One** time, I had to do a runway show wearing our dresses. There were probably five hundred people watching, and I came out to walk down the runway with my groom, and I fell flat on my face. I kinda ate my bouquet. The groom tried to help me up, but I was laughing too hard.

What is one of the most surprising things you've done? **When I was getting a tattoo, a pansy (my nickname), on my backside, there were about eight guys watching. They said they were all watching as students. I'm like, "Yeah right, buddy, you just want to see me with my pants down." And I was there with my friend, who had just gotten her nipples pierced. I was holding her hand because she was nervous, and she was in a little pain. And the guy looks at me, and he says, "Okay, now no rough play for a couple weeks." I was like, "What? Are you talking to me?" They thought that we were lesbians.**

CASTING CONFESSION
ERIKA: I THINK A LOT OF THE WAY I FEEL ABOUT THINGS COMES FROM MY MOTHER. MY MOM IS A GREAT MOTHER, AND SHE LOVES US, BUT SHE HAS ALWAYS BEEN TOUGH ON US. SHE DIDN'T WANT US TO GO THROUGH LIFE DOING ANYTHING MEDIOCRE, AND WE WERE NEVER ALLOWED TO QUIT. IT WAS HARD ON US, BUT THAT IS THE WAY SHE KNOWS HOW TO BE A GOOD MOM. SHE NEVER QUITS, AND SHE DOESN'T LET HER KIDS QUIT, EITHER. AND WHILE THERE HAVE BEEN TIMES THAT IT HAS BEEN EXTREMELY HARD TO LIVE UP TO THAT STANDARD, I THINK IT HAS CARRIED WITH ME INTO MY LIFE AS AN ADULT. I MAY NOT ALWAYS BE A HUGE SUCCESS AT EVERYTHING, BUT I DON'T GIVE UP. I HAVE A SENSE OF OWING IT TO MYSELF TO GET WHAT I WANT OUT OF LIFE. I REALLY APPRECIATE THAT NOW. YOU SHOULD'NT SETTLE FOR ANYTHING BUT DO THE BEST THAT YOU CAN DO. IT'S HARD, BUT SO IS LIFE, AND YOU CAN'T GIVE UP ON LIFE. THAT'S THE GREATEST THING MY MOM EVER TAUGHT ME.

Do you have a boyfriend? **I just started seeing someone [Stefan], but it's not serious yet.**

Describe your first love. **I will always love him. He broke my heart, and I did the same to him. We are too different to be together. I think that for the rest of my life, I will think of him at least once a day.**

How do you feel about sex? Do you have it only when you're in a relationship, or do you seek it out at other times? I can't have sex with somebody that I don't care about. **I talk about sex, I think about sex, but it's only something that happens in relationships for me.**

What's the most exciting/interesting place you've ever had sex? **I had sex in a closet at my aunt's house during a party.**

Describe a major event or issue that has affected your life. **When my parents got divorced. It was like my entire life was a lie. My parents not being married anymore was incomprehensible to me. A part of me still believes in love that lasts forever, but the divorce left me a skeptic.**

What habits do you have that we should know about? I am mildly prissy.

Who are your heroes and why? **My mother. She picked herself up at the lowest time in her life, and she never quit, even when it was painful. She always does what she thinks is right. And she never stopped believing in people.**

CASTING JAKE

Michelle Millard, CASTING: I went on the follow with Jake, which he kept referring to as a date. He was flirting his butt off. He said, "I could invite you to come back to my room because it's raining, and you really don't need to drive all the way across town . . ." I said, "Thanks, but no thanks. I really appreciate your heart-felt concern for my safety." He volunteered to give me his sweater, which I thought was all chivalrous. And it was. But he was really concerned about his "scrawn factor," as he called it, which is strange considering how often he was naked on the trip. But he seemed sincerely worried about showing his body. Jake also had a hard time getting beyond the camera and the microphone. He was all about being listened to and watched. He kept whispering into his microphone at first, and I had to really work to get him interested in our conversation more than he was in the camera. That should have been a big red flag that he was going to be preoccupied with how the show is taped and edited.

Kenny Hull, CASTING DIRECTOR: Jake played us like a fiddle. He's quick, and he's got a very dry sense of humor, and there was something about him that reminded all of us in casting of what we were like at eighteen.

BIRTH NAME: **Allen Jacob**
NICKNAME: **Fat-Cat-Slim**
HOMETOWN: **Philadelphia, Pennsylvania**
BIRTHDAY: **June 13, 1978**
SIGN: **Gemini**

Casting Quotable: I'd rather have a relationship than a lot of sex. I learned that in high school.

CASTING TALE
JAKE: I WAS DRIVING HOME FROM MY HIGH SCHOOL, WHICH IS IN A REALLY BAD NEIGHBORHOOD. AND I'M AT A RED LIGHT. SOMEBODY BEHIND ME HONKS, LIKE I SHOULD BE GOING. SO I STICK MY HEAD OUT THE WINDOW AND YELL SOMETHING BACK. THE GIRL I'M WITH IS ALARMED, SHE'S LIKE, "ARE YOU INSANE?" BUT WHAT'S HE GONNA DO? WE PULL UP TO THE NEXT LIGHT, AND THE GUY IS NEXT TO ME NOW. AND HE'S GOT A GUN, AND HE'S LIKE, "PULL OVER! PULL OVER! I'M GONNA KICK THE S**T OUT OF YOU!" I'M NOT GONNA PULL OVER. THAT'S NOT AN OPTION. SO WE'RE FLYING DOWN THE STREET. IT'S LIKE A LITTLE TWO-WAY, TWO-LANER. I'M GETTING IN THE WRONG LANE, DOIN' WHATEVER IT TAKES, BECAUSE HE'S GOT A GUN, AND I DON'T PLAY LIKE THAT. AND THEN AS WE'RE REACHING THE ON-RAMP TO THE EXPRESSWAY, I HEAR WHAM! LIKE SOMETHING HITS THE BACK OF THE CAR, AND WE BOTH DUCK, DRIVING ALONG ALL CROUCHED DOWN. I DEFINITELY THOUGHT THE CAR HAD BEEN SHOT. BUT IT TURNS OUT IT WASN'T A BULLET. IT WAS CELERY. I DON'T KNOW WHAT HE WAS DOING THAT HE HAD CELERY AND THAT HE DECIDED TO THROW IT, BUT I WAS REALLY HAPPY IT WAS ONLY CELERY.

Casting Application

What are some ways you have treated someone who has been important to you that you are proud of? I'm just always there for my friends when they need me. When things come to push and shove, for them I push and I shove.

How would you describe your worst traits? My worst traits are that my bad traits can be unpredictable. I might be cool with something now, and then all of a sudden flip out 'cause it annoys me. People say it's because I'm a Gemini.

What do you want to be when you grow up? I don't want to grow up. My dad said to me the other day, "I don't think you have the common sense to make it past thirty."

Who would be in your dream ROAD RULES cast? If I were going to put together my dream cast, let's see, it would be Tyra Banks, Chili and Tatiana Ali are good places to start. Then we can go . . . Alicia Silverstone. That's only four, so four and me is five. That's a road trip right there.

Describe your most embarrassing moment? My very first day of high school. They had just handed out our new textbooks—I'm in my English class. And all I hear is my teacher scream, "Don't drool on that book!" And my head flies up, and there is so much drool. There is drool on my face, and some flies off as my head comes up. All the pages are slimy, like I had soaked it through. I've always been the cool one.

Describe a major event or issue that has affected your life. I was coming home from school at 2:30 P.M. when I was stuck-up on my corner. What bothered me was this guy had a huge gun to my head in plain sight while people walked by, and no one did anything.

What habits do your have that we should know about? None really. Sometimes I act crazy. I mean out there. But that's just a character flaw.

Who are your heroes and why? My dad—just for being such a good parent and raising me the way he did. And my mom. And the Beastie Boys for being the first white guests on SOUL TRAIN.

When you do something ridiculous, how much does it bother you to have other people notice it and laugh at you? Not at all. I'm ridiculous on purpose.

DEFINITION

The Follow: Part of the casting process in which the applicant is sent out with a friend, or someone from the ROAD RULES office, and a camera to see what they're like in a less formal situation.

CASTING *KALLE*

PRONUNCIATION: **Kay-lee**
NICKNAME: **Kazel-bezel-little-blonde-diesel**
HOMETOWN: **Ft. Collins, Colorado**
BIRTHDAY: **March 8, 1977**
SIGN: **Pisces**
SPORT: **Volleyball**
ODD JOBS: **Blood lab courier, volleyball referee, gift wrapper
and a salesgirl at a T-shirt shop, a tanning spa
and a lingerie shop.**
PIERCING: **Eyebrow!**
CASTING QUOTABLE: **I'm ready to spread my wings. I
want to live someplace big, someplace wild for a while.**

Michelle Millard, CASTING: She came in wearing a glittery green shirt and shiny green nail polish. She told me she wanted to be a funky diva. And she had her eyebrow pierced, so she's doing this L.A. thing from small town Colorado. She had a mixture of sophistication and innocence. And then, when we were interviewing her, Kenny was in the room. Someone asked her, "So, do you think he's cute?" referring to Kenny. And she goes, "Do you?" Like with this *big* attitude. My esteem for her shot up about one hundred points. She definitely had a mind of her own. Then the guys went out of the room, and Mary-Ellis and I sat in. Immediately, her attitude changed. She started to reveal her soft side when it was just women. Kalle had lost her mom pretty recently before the show started. We had all admired her spunk when she was with the guys, but it helped to know that she could have a soft side, too. Then when we went on her follow, she developed a bit of a crush on the cameraman, who happens to have a great sense of humor, so I wasn't surprised when she fell for Jake, who was all about humor in his interviews.

Casting Scoop: Kalle's audition tape was only the second tape that the casting department looked at.

What are your personal goals in life? **I want to marry Brian (my boy) — much later, and have children with him. I want to be beautiful, inside and out, and be a person** people like to be around and confide in. (I wouldn't mind being in PLAYBOY just once!)

Worst traits: **I am very selfish, never on time, sometimes anal.**

Describe your mother. **My mother passed away last November. My answer to this question can't be anything but too sentimental, but I'll try. On the one hand, she was the most encouraging, driving force in my life, and on the other hand, she was my child. I took care of her when she was sick, and it was hard.**

What is the most important issue or problem facing you? **I still don't know what I want to be when I grow up. I'm at a crossroads.**

Describe your most embarrassing moment. **Last Valentine's Day, I wanted to earn some extra money, so I went to the Plasma Donation Center. After giving blood plasma for more than an hour, I stood up real fast to leave and fainted on the way out. Coming to on the floor, I discovered that I had peed in my pants!**

Other than a boyfriend, who is the most important person in your life? **Becky, my boyfriend's mom, has been important in my life since I met her. She is sincere, down-to-earth and forever caring. I know that she would do anything for me at any time. My mom died last November, and I lived with Brian's family for a while. Along with Brian, Becky was the most helpful in guiding me to heal.**

What bothers you most about other people? **The fact that so many people are so angry and rude for no apparent reason really bothers me.** Life is a super thing to have, why waste it being awful?

If you could change any one thing about your personality, what would that be? **I want to be a person who is less judgmental. I jump to conclusions all too quickly and form opinions instantly — which I don't like about myself.**

What is your greatest fear and why? **My greatest fear is of having regrets when I'm older.**

If you had Aladdin's lamp and three wishes what would they be? **My first and foremost wish would be to have my mom back — alive and happy again.**

Kalle with her dad, brother Tyson, and her mom

CASTING CONFESSION

KALLE: MY MOM DIED A YEAR AGO. I KIND OF WISH THAT WHEN PEOPLE ASK ME HOW SHE DIED THAT I HAD SOME EASY EXPLANATION, BUT IT ISN'T EASY. SHE WAS REALLY UNHAPPY AND VERY ILL, AND IT WAS JUST KIND OF A THING WHERE SHE WAS ON TOO MANY MEDICATIONS FOR HER BODY WEIGHT AND HER SYSTEM GAVE OUT . . . IT WAS REALLY HARD, BUT IT GOT ME THINKING ABOUT THINGS.

LIKE MY BOYFRIEND, BRIAN. I STARTED THINKING ABOUT OUR FUTURE AND I DIDN'T WANT TO LOOK BACK AND THINK, WE WENT OUT TOGETHER, WE GOT MARRIED, WE STAYED IN THE SAME TOWN. I DON'T WANT TO BE THAT PERSON. I WANT TO TRAVEL. I WANT TO GO OUT. I WANT MAKE OTHER FRIENDS. I WANT TO LIVE WITH OTHER PEOPLE. I WANT TO HAVE SPACE APART. IN THE PAST, I'VE BEEN REALLY COMPLACENT ABOUT IT, BUT WHEN THIS ALL HIT ME, I WAS LIKE, "THIS IS MY LIFE. OH MY GOD, THIS CAN'T BE ALL THERE IS." I KNOW HOW MUCH I LOVE HIM, BUT I WANT TO DO OTHER THINGS, I WANT TO GO OTHER PLACES, AND I NEED SOME SPACE ON MY OWN. I JUST

CASTING **OSCAR**

Kenny Hull,
CASTING DIRECTOR:

We were down in San Juan, looking for a real Puerto Rican stud. Oscar came in … not quite what we had in mind. But he sits down and immediately starts talking about going to past-life regressions, and how he once did this so that he was in his mother's womb, and he could actually hear his mother and father arguing outside of her stomach. Right then and there, I'm like, "Whoa, we gotta get to know this kid." And we would ask him one question, and he'd talk for half an hour. He was very passionate. He also was so expressive about issues that are very hard for most people to talk about. It was no effort for him to discuss any topic whatsoever. To be eighteen years old, and to also come out of your country for the rst time, and to just be so wide-eyed, yet so grounded and completely on key. He just won us all over by the end of it. I was a huge fan of Oscar's. I loved Oscar. I still do.

Casting Quotable: I came into this world alone and I'll leave alone. I've had sex, but I've never made love.

NICKNAME:
All Star or Oski
HOMETOWN:**Trujillo**
Alto, Puerto Rico
BIRTHDAY: **January 30, 1978**
SIGN: **Aquarius**
COLLEGE MAJOR:
Graphic Arts
FAVORITE GROUP:
Bob Marley!

Oscar's drawing of the tattoo he wants to get

CASTING CONFESSION
OSCAR: MY RELATIONSHIP WITH MY PARENTS IS KIND OF FUNNY. THEY GOT DIVORCED WHEN I WAS ONE YEAR OLD, AND THERE HAVE BEEN A LOT OF EVIL FIGHTS THAT HAVE GONE ON BETWEEN THEM, WITH ME IN THE MIDDLE. I WAS LIKE THE HAM OF THE SANDWICH. THIS HAS BEEN A VERY DIFFICULT SITUATION, AND I THINK IT HAS TAKEN A LONG TIME FOR THEM TO UNDERSTAND HOW MUCH I DON'T LIKE BEING IN THE MIDDLE. THE GOOD THING IS THAT I HAVE LEARNED HOW TO DISTINGUISH MY LOVE AND MY RELATIONSHIP FROM ALL THE BAD THINGS. AND WHAT YOU HAVE TO DO IN THAT KIND OF SITUATION, WHEN THERE IS SO MUCH NEGATIVITY AROUND, YOU HAVE TO LOOK FOR THE GOOD AND MAKE THAT YOUR OWN. I TRY TO TAKE THE BEST QUALITIES THEY HAVE AND TRY TO COMBINE THEM BOTH, SEE WHAT COMES OUT. AND HOPEFULLY, IT'S JUST A BETTER HUMAN BEING.

How important is sex to you? **Sex is a biological necessity! I don't go hunting for sex, but hey . . .**

What is the most exciting place you've ever had sex? **Women's room at a department store.**

How would you describe your best traits? **Very patient, understanding, sense of humor (great). I'm Latin with a great island style. Very aware of my roots and global spiritual consciousness. Very clean, very intelligent, love to read. My great sense of adventure.** I'm never satisfied with what I know, I'm always seeking for more and more.

How would you describe your worst traits? **I don't really have worst traits, but I am very moody, but I don't let it affect people.** I hate not to get along with people, **so apart from mood changes, I'm okay.**

How have you treated someone who has been important to you that you wish you hadn't done? **I testified against my mother in a custody case in court and feel embarrassed by it because I really care for my mom. I love her. I did it, and I don't regret it, but I'm never going to choose between my dad and my mom ever again.**

If you could only pack one backpack for the trip, what would be in it? **Sunglasses, Homer Simpson stuffed toy, a book (CELESTINE PROPHECY or MANY LIVES, MANY MASTERS), board shorts, my sandals and two reggae tapes (Bob Marley and Israel Vibrations).**

What is the most important issue or problem facing you today? **My biggest problem right now is trying to start that new process of independence, emotionally, economically and spiritually.**

What habits do you have that we should know about? I don't have bad habits, only customs.

Tell us about some places in the United States you have always wished you could visit and why. **I wish I could visit somewhere where I could see snow. I have never seen snow in my life.**

What is the worst thing about being on your own? **Loneliness, being alone, having no one to talk to or sleep with sometimes. But like I said, those are character-builders.**

Who are your heroes and why? **Jose Maria de Hostos = He fought for the abolition of slavery in Puerto Rico; Jesus Christ = He has been the best prophet the world has had; My parents = They fought for me, my rights and well-being.**

Clay Newbill, SUPERVISING PRODUCER:
We left open calls thinking that we had found the Aristotle of Puerto Rico.

CASTING *VINCE*

Kenny Hull, CASTING DIRECTOR: In the beginning it didn't look like Vince had a chance to make it on the show. He had the ROAD RULES book out, and he had STAR WARS figures, and he was just like, "I want to be on ROAD RULES so bad. Pick me." There was nothing to indicate that he was something more than the other three thousand kids just like that. He's a good-looking guy, and he's a jock. I kept him in the running, just in case. But I downplayed the whole thing so he wouldn't get too excited. Then we got to the semifinals. We traveled to Atlanta, and he drove up with his mom from Florida. He came in and was really on the ball and had good stories and was very funny. He's a good example of how somebody can give you a totally different impression in person than they do on tape. Then when we brought him out to L.A., and he went on his follow, we got to know even another side of Vince, a much deeper side.

NICKNAME: **Nino**
HOMETOWN: **Boca Raton, Fla.**
BIRTHDAY: **October 11, 1976**
SIGN: **Libra**
SPORT: **Martial arts**
COLLECTION: STAR WARS **action figures**
FAVORITE GROUP: **Marilyn Manson**
CASTING QUOTABLE: **"I love my mom, but she still thinks I'm four years old."**

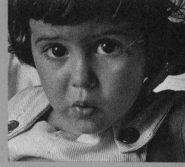

Michelle Millard, CASTING: I was taking Vince home. The follow hadn't gone very well. He hadn't been too impressive. So we're heading back to the hotel. I was lost and couldn't find my way, and he didn't seem to care where we were headed. I was making small talk, and I said something about his mother. And I swear, within five minutes, he was in tears. I was surprised because it wasn't like I had been probing him. The camera was gone, so I wasn't even thinking like that. But he was sobbing. He was telling me some intense things, revolving around a father who abandoned the family. So it's 7:30 at night, and he's just pouring out his soul in my passenger's seat. And I'm thinking, "It's Friday night, he doesn't know a soul in L.A., I cannot take this kid home and say, 'Well, thanks. I'm dropping you off at your hotel. Have a nice life.'" So I said, "Why don't we go get something to eat? You obviously need to talk about this." So we went and talked, and he told me how hard it had been on him, growing up without his father in his life. For me it was a good but normal conversation, but I think for Vince . . . he wasn't used to confiding in people. And I could tell that he was starting to look at me with different eyes. He told me I changed his life, etcetera, etcetera. I took him home, and I was like, "I don't know what's going to happen. If you don't want me to tell anybody all that you just told me . . . this went beyond work, that's fine." But he felt okay with me telling people, so when I came into work on Monday, I was like, "You won't believe what happened with Vince."

What are your best traits? **My sense of humor, my level of integrity and my lust for excitement and life.**

What are your worst traits? **Sometimes I get upset or stressed over stupid things, and I am very stubborn.** Sometimes I have the tendency to think I am always right. **AND I AM!!**

What is some way you have treated someone important to you that you wish you hadn't done? **Sometimes I yell at my mom in front of my friends. That shows lack of respect, then I feel bad.**

If you could only pack one backpack for the trip, what would be in it? **A Stephen King novel, tweezers (for my mono-brow), clothes, about four tubes of lip balm, possibly a PLAYBOY and my devil hat.**

What drives you crazy about your girlfriend? **She is soooo jealous, she won't even let me watch SINGLED OUT.**

How important is sex to you? **Sex isn't the be-all and end-all of my life, but I sure as hell enjoy it. I only have sex when I'm in a relationship.**

Describe a major event or issue that has affected your life. **When I was eleven or twelve we moved from New York to Florida. I hated it. I was in middle school, and with two weeks to go in eighth grade, I was expelled. That broke my mom's heart, so I changed my ways.**

What habits do you have that we should know about? I smoke. **I masturbate about once every half hour. Just kidding. Ha-ha.**

Where do you see yourself in ten years? I see myself as the leader of a race of Atomic Supermen. **I will rule most of the earth. Women will pass out in my presence, and I will be the first man to live underwater.**

Vince: I had my tape done, had an application out of the ROAD TRIPS book, and I sent it in, and then four days later, I got the phone call, and I was like, "What!?!" The thing is, I didn't know there were five rounds of auditioning. I thought when you get your call, you're on the show. Then they explained how long the process is. I was crushed. I didn't think I had a chance.

Head for the island with the same name as that pirate book by Robert Louis Stevenson.

First Impressions

Oscar: I was the only Latino, and they were all Americans. I was expecting a more culturally diverse group. And right after seeing Erika, I knew I'm never going to get along with this girl. Then I looked at Jake, and I was like, oh my God, this goofy-ass, annoying, always playing up to the camera type of guy. And then I saw Kalle, and I thought, she looks pretty good. But then again, she pretended to be an airhead. Then I saw Vince, and I was like, great! I got some Florida, pretty, Mama's boy. But my big mistake was trying to be friends from the start. Jake: My first impression of Oscar was that he was really fake. Really, really fake. He pulls me aside, and he's just like — his whole thing is just that he wants to have fun at all costs. So if anything that he ever does bothers me, I should tell him right away, 'cuz he's gonna stop doing it. And he's never gonna fight with

TRAVEL

Travelers to San Francisco won't find much to do on Treasure Island other than get a great view of the city. For those determined to hit an island while in the Bay Area, Angel Island is the hot tip. The island's hilly terrain makes it ideal for mountain biking. So sweat the day away on Angel, then pedal over to the deck at Sam's in Sausalito for a refreshing reward and the last of the day's rays.

Michelle: I'm nervous for them. They have no concept of what they're getting into.

Jake: When Vince and I were picking Kalle up in Colorado, we drove, and I waved to Kalle through a window, and she waved back. And I'm like, "Yeah, she's pretty cute. I can't wait to see her older sister!" Kalle looked way too young.

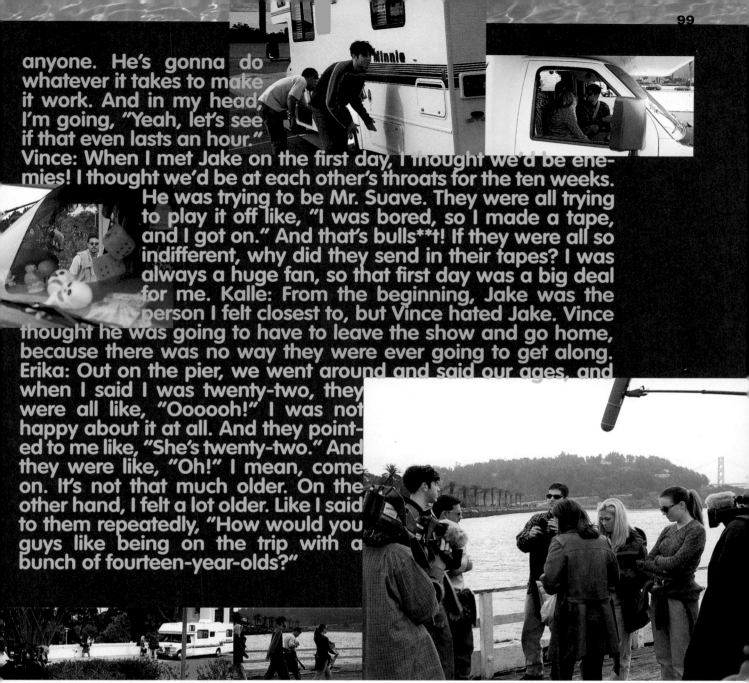

anyone. He's gonna do whatever it takes to make it work. And in my head, I'm going, "Yeah, let's see if that even lasts an hour." Vince: When I met Jake on the first day, I thought we'd be enemies! I thought we'd be at each other's throats for the ten weeks. He was trying to be Mr. Suave. They were all trying to play it off like, "I was bored, so I made a tape, and I got on." And that's bulls**t! If they were all so indifferent, why did they send in their tapes? I was always a huge fan, so that first day was a big deal for me. Kalle: From the beginning, Jake was the person I felt closest to, but Vince hated Jake. Vince thought he was going to have to leave the show and go home, because there was no way they were ever going to get along. Erika: Out on the pier, we went around and said our ages, and when I said I was twenty-two, they were all like, "Oooooh!" I was not happy about it at all. And they pointed to me like, "She's twenty-two." And they were like, "Oh!" I mean, come on. It's not that much older. On the other hand, I felt a lot older. Like I said to them repeatedly, "How would you guys like being on the trip with a bunch of fourteen-year-olds?"

CAMERA IN THE FACE

VINCE: THAT FIRST DAY, I WASN'T EVEN WALKING IN THE CAMERA SHOT. I WAS WALKING AHEAD OF THE CAMERA. I TOLD BRUCE, THE DIRECTOR, "I DON'T WANT YOU TO THINK THIS IS GONNA BE ME FOR TEN WEEKS. I'M VERY MUCH LIKE IN A SHELL WHEN I FIRST MEET PEOPLE. IT JUST TAKES ME AWHILE." AND BRUCE WAS LIKE, "OH, I'M THE SAME WAY. THERE'S NO RUSH." BUT IT WAS HARD. MEETING ALL THOSE NEW PEOPLE AND THERE ARE ALL THESE CAMERAS IN YOUR FACE, HOW COULD YOU NOT ACT LIKE A DORK?

TAKE A SHOT AT TEAMWORK WHILE BEING SHOT . . . OLD NAVAL BASE, MARE ISLAND

CLUE

Now that you've emptied your pockets, it's time to do battle for badly needed funds!
And you best be on your toes,
because your competition has been there before!

On Paintball

Erika: Paintball's just not my thing. I think competing together brought us closer, but the actual game, I didn't like it. I just don't have the urge to run out and shoot somebody. **Vince:** That mission was so incredible for me because it was the first one, I love paintball and I got to meet all those people. And the second season was my favorite season, and I got to meet Timmy, Christian, Devin, and I was just like, "Holy s**t!" I just couldn't believe it. **Jake:** I was worried that Vince might defect. Because he really, really liked them. He always loved the second season. I thought he was gonna try and go home with them or something. **Vince:** Talking with the past Road Rulers, they all had the same advice: "Just do it for you!" It's something I didn't fully understand until near the end of the trip.

The All-Stars Off-Camera

Timmy: One of the new cast runs up and is like, "My mom laughs every time you sing the national anthem." Another says, "You've got a great voice." I feel like I'm in a mall. **Devin:** Kalle's whining about everything. I looked at her and said, "Why don't you smile!" But Vince is cool as s**t. Erika looks a little bit like Emily, doesn't she? **Timmy:** Oscar's great. Jake and Oscar are going to go at it. I think they will square off. That's my prediction.

Heard Battle-Side

Kalle: Losing four hundred dollars in thirty seconds was one of the most frustrating things I've experienced. Not as frustrating as when we lost eight hundred dollars in thirty seconds, but close. **Oscar:** Kalle was like freaking out that we won so little money. She's going, "I've never been without money in my life! What are we going to do?" I tried to calm her down. People make too big a deal of money. We can get by. But she didn't want to listen.

The Money Thing

Jonathan Murray, executive producer: In the past, the cast would arrive, find the Winnebago, and in it there would be an envelope with fifteen hundred to two thousand dollars worth of cash. This year, they arrive, and suddenly they've got to compete for money. So from the very beginning, this season was very different. They were immediately challenged to make decisions that would affect their group. **Rick de Oliveira, producer:** This was probably the most difficult trip of the four seasons. It was like a "tough love" ROAD RULES. This season was about consequences. It took them a long time to understand that there had been a change. A long time.

Jake's Off-Camera Altercation

Jake: The crew needed us to shoot so they could get close-ups of the guns firing, and Effie was shooting at my foot. I told her to stop, and she might have. I don't know. I was kind of — I wanted to get her straight from the get-go. I watched her on TV, and it was just my goal to get her. So, she shot my foot another time, after I told her not to, and I was like, "Now's my chance!" And so I think I might have shot her like fifteen or sixteen times. It was pretty cool. She was all crying. I think somebody might have held her back. **Effie:** I was feeling like, we're having too much fun, something is bound to go wrong, and suddenly Jake attacks me. And he has the advantage because he has watched the show, and he knows that I'm snappy, so don't bring that side out of me. That whole thing with Jake was just posing, acting up for the camera. He's going to regret it if he keeps doing it. Not being yourself in front of the cameras, that's the worst mistake you can make.

JAKE VS. THE CREW

JAKE: BEING IN FRONT OF THE CAMERAS, IT WAS A WHOLE NEW LIFESTYLE. THE FIRST THING I REALIZED WAS THAT, 'CAUSE OF THE MICROPHONE, I COULD WHISPER AND THE DIRECTOR WOULD HEAR IT. I LOVE THAT STUFF. THEN, AFTER PAINTBALL, WHEN I LEFT OUR MONEY BEHIND, I BUSTED OUT OF THE WINNEBAGO AND JUST START SPRINTING FOR IT. I'M LIKE, "OH MY GOD, THE MONEY, THE MONEY, THE MONEY." ALL OF A SUDDEN, THERE ARE LIKE FIVE PEOPLE RUNNING BEHIND ME, TRYING TO CATCH UP. IT WAS KIND OF NEAT THAT THEY ALL HAD TO RUN WHEN WE DID. I FELT LIKE MICHAEL JACKSON IN THE BEGINNING OF HIS VIDEOS. **KARY D'ALLESANDRO, AUDIO MIXER:** JAKE KEPT SAYING HOW HE LIKED TO MAKE US RUN. WE WERE NOT AMUSED. **MARY-ELLIS BUNIM, EXECUTIVE PRODUCER:** JAKE! OH, MY GOSH. JAKE. JAKE TAUGHT US A LESSON THAT WE HAVE TO ADD A MAJOR SERIES OF QUESTIONS TO SEMIFINALS AND FINALS TO WEED OUT PEOPLE WHO ARE JUST TOO INTERESTED IN PRODUCTION. I'M SURE JAKE LEARNED A LOT ABOUT PRODUCTION ON THE ROAD, BUT THAT'S OBVIOUSLY NOT WHAT THIS IS ABOUT. I MEAN, HE WOULD WALK ALONG IN FRONT OF THE CAMERA, AND THEN SUDDENLY BREAK FROM THE GROUP, AND THEN LOOK AROUND AND WANT TO CHAT WITH THE DIRECTOR OR THE CAMERAMAN.

SAVE A LIFE.
RISK YOUR OWN.
—COAST GUARD
CAPTAIN,
YERBA BUENA
ISLAND.

Effie: Jake had better stay away from me. This is not funny. This is not friendly. This is supposed to be a game. He looked me right in the eye and fired. What is that? They got four hundred dollars. That's it. I have had it. I don't have to take this s**t! This is supposed to be a game! What's his f**king problem?!

DEFINITION

"Don't talk about production": Phrase used to remind cast that the point of the show is not for them to talk about what it's like being on camera. Most often uttered by directors, usually directed at Jake.

CLUE

MISSION 2

Saving lives, obeying orders, fighting seasickness— they're all part of the life of enlisted Road Rulers.

Jake's AWOL Attempt

I think that the guys kind of have crushes on Kalle. I could be wrong, but I get that feeling. I miss Stefan. I miss sleeping with him, talking with him. I really hope that we can make it through these ten weeks. I love him.

Erika: I was shocked when Jake wanted to get off the Coast Guard boat. And I called him on it. I mean, Kalle and I had hated playing paintball, but we stuck it out. We didn't make some big production out of the fact we were unhappy, but I guess there were some things going on I didn't know about, stuff that wasn't on-camera.
Bruce Toms, director: Jake came up to me and asked if he could get off the boat. Honestly, I didn't take him seriously at first, because he was always asking what-if questions, trying to get involved in production. Once I realized he wasn't kidding, I just told him it was something he needed to work out with his cast mates.

OFF-CAMERA
JAKE TAKES BRUCE ASIDE

JAKE: I'M NOT GOING THROUGH CRAP FOR CRAP'S SAKE. ONE WAY OR ANOTHER, I'M LEAVING THIS BOAT, BRUCE . . . I WISH YOU WOULD JUST ANSWER ME, BECAUSE IT IS REALLY BOTHERING ME, THE FACT THAT YOU'RE NOT SAYING WHAT YOU'RE GOING TO DO.
BRUCE: YOU NEED TO KNOW THAT THERE ARE GOING TO BE CONSEQUENCES.
JAKE: I DON'T WANT TO LEAVE THE SHOW, IF THAT'S WHAT YOU'RE SAYING. WHY CAN'T YOU JUST LET ME GO OFF? YOU CAN ALL FILM BEING MAD AT ME, FILM ME EXPLAINING IN MY ROOM. AND WE'LL ALL BE HAPPY.
BRUCE: WHY DON'T YOU TALK TO YOUR CAST?
JAKE: I'VE REALLY DONE MY BEST . . . AND I DON'T WANT EVERYONE ON THE BOAT TO KNOW ABOUT THIS.
BRUCE: BUT THE SHOW IS A LOT OF THIS.
JAKE: I CAN TAKE IT. I JUST WANT OFF THIS BOAT.

JONATHAN MURRAY, EXECUTIVE PRODUCER: BRUCE MADE THE VERY WISE, VERY SMART DECISION. HE REMINDED JAKE, WE'RE JUST DOCUMENTING IT AT THIS POINT. NOW, I THINK WHEN JAKE HEARD "CONSEQUENCES," HE THOUGHT THAT MEANT HE WOULD BE KICKED OFF THE SHOW, WHICH IS NOT THE CASE. MAYBE IT WAS A GOOD MISUNDERSTANDING. BUT THAT WAS NOT THE CASE. BRUCE MEANT THAT IN LIFE, THERE ARE CONSEQUENCES FOR ANY DECISION YOU MAKE. BUT THE CONSEQUENCES WOULD COME FROM THE COAST GUARD, OR FROM HIS CAST MATES.

Vince Caught in the Middle

Jake: I really never like to back down once I've said something, but suddenly it was about leaving the show. So when I talked to the group, I was hoping that like they were gonna beg me not to, which they did, except for Vince. **Vince:** I understood the others telling Jake he should stay, but I also didn't want to make him feel like he had to do something he didn't want to do. So, I felt like in a weird way, I was kind of like supporting him, by not going with the group and insisting that he stay on the boat. **Jonathan Murray, executive producer:** Vince didn't want to get involved and wanted to stay on the sidelines. Which I think hurt Jake more than the people who told him he was crazy—I think Jake felt better about the people who had the passion and who obviously cared enough about him at that point to want him to stay. Whereas I think he read Vince not taking a stand on it as basically saying, "I don't care about you. You're not important to me at this point." **Erika:** Vince is Switzerland: He won't take sides.

Jake: We trashed that boat. We threw up everywhere.

Talking to Ralph on the big white phone, in Coast Guard terminology.

Kalle: I thought there would be a steering wheel up here.

TRAVEL 415 MILES SAN FRANCISCO TO BALBOA

I have *never* done so many things in two days, and before noon! The experiences: riding in the small boat, the Gumby suits in the water, the fire-fighting, being seasick and so tired I couldn't see straight, rescuing a drowning man (for pretend!) . . . Never again in my life will I have such an action-packed couple of days on such a grand scale. Although parts of it were trying—Jake wanting to leave, throwing up through my nose, trying *hard* when I was dead tired—the feeling of sticking it out and finishing the mission was indescribable. I was very proud of our group.

Jake and Kalle's First Step

Bruce Toms, director: The irony about Jake's attempt to leave the Coast Guard ship is that Kalle was adamant that he stay. That was a huge step forward in their relationship. Things might have worked out very differently if that hadn't come up so early. **Jake:** She had already almost cried when I almost left the Coast Guard boat. Then we went on that long walk, and I told her, "Tell me something I don't know about you." I thought she was gonna tell me like a favorite color, or her favorite kind of ice cream. But she just tells me all about her mom. And I was happy she did, because it kind of let me in a little bit more. Then we had this moment, where we were both like, "I have something to tell you." And we just told each other we thought we'd be lifelong friends, no matter what happened.

The Inside Scoop

Jake: I never wanted to leave the boat. No, no, no. Even at the time, I just wanted to sleep on shore. There was this big sailor, Del, who I'd nearly gotten in a fight with. I called him "farm boy." I don't know what I was thinking. He was big! All those guys were like big, meaty. So, it was this awkward situation. I just didn't want to be sleeping on the same boat with that guy. **Del:** We were just doing that thing that guys do, just challenging each other, sizing each other up. I didn't take it seriously. People make that stereotype about people from Arizona all the time. I've worked on a ranch, but I'm not a farm boy. I wasn't going to hurt him.

Oscar says he feels "out of place." I think friendships take a little longer. The group is starting to come together, and we are starting to have a good time together. I'm sure Oscar will start to feel better when we get rolling again.

CLUE
DROWNING AT SEA IS NO LAUGHING MATTER, BUT YOUR NEXT MISSION IS! YOUR NEW PORT IS THE ISLAND NAMED FOR THE MAN WHO DISCOVERED THE PACIFIC OCEAN. TO BE VIPS, SEE SHERI AT WILMA'S PATIO.

TRIVIA
A source of some confusion to the cast: the name of the Coast Guard's man-overboard dummy is also Oscar.

MISSION

Comedy is the key to badly needed cash, but with the audience as judge, you've got a serious challenge ahead.

TRAVEL LOG Jake and Vince are off to a less than friendly start, while for Jake and Kalle there's already a hint of something more. But where do Oscar and Erika fit into this mix? Questions abound as the Road Rulers head for the competitive comedy lounge.

VINCE'S JOURNAL

Today we are entered in an amateur comedy contest, and first place is $250. The group could really use the money. I have always thought about trying stand-up, but never thought I would have the chance, until now. Things are going great. I'm so happy that I have a chance to be on my own, no parents, no teachers. Just Vince. I feel myself changing already, and it is a positive change.

Jake: For the first part of the trip, Vince had been this quiet, brooding karate guy who wouldn't take his sunglasses off. But in Balboa, he just came alive. You could almost hear his shell crack. **Erika:** Vince is a natural. He was hilarious out there, and totally comfortable. He was getting his jokes right, even checking how the audience was feeling. Vince was in his element. It was such a blast doing a comedy routine with him.

HEARD STAGE-SIDE
JENICA (HOST AND FUTURE STAR OF MEN BEHAVING BADLY): AREN'T VINCE AND ERIKA CUTE TOGETHER? ARE YOU GUYS A COUPLE? NO? OH, DID I START SOMETHING?

Vince and Erika Bonding

Mary-Ellis Bunim, executive producer: As the trip was beginning, Vince was pulling away from his girlfriend, Kim, while things had progressed between Erika and her boyfriend from when we first cast her. But Vince and Erika's attraction for each other was so clear. Physical attraction, but also, I think they liked each other a lot. **Rick de Oliveira, producer:** There was chemistry —I think there was chemistry between them from the very start. But they both also had a lot to lose at home.

INTERVIEW TRANSCRIPT FROM THE ROAD
ERIKA: OH, I LIKE VINCE A LOT. I REALLY DO. HE'S A REALLY NICE GUY, HE MAKES ME LAUGH, AND WE HAVE GOOD CONVERSATIONS. HE GENERALLY SEEMS INTERESTED IN A LOT OF THINGS THAT I HAVE TO SAY, AND I'M REALLY INTERESTED TO FIND OUT MORE ABOUT VINCE. HE'S JUST A FUNNY, NICE PERSON WHO'S EASY TO TALK TO. AND HE'S SO EASYGOING.
BRUCE: THAT'S IT?
ERIKA: YEAH. YOU WANT MORE? THERE IS NO MORE.

DEFINITION
OTF: "On The Fly" — mini-interviews done in the heat of the moment (as opposed to the weekly interviews) that give cast members a chance to say what they are feeling right then.

Sheri: What's weird is that eventually they'll be real well known, but right now, no one knew who they were, so it didn't help them win.

Mirror, Mirror . . . Who's the Funniest of Them All?

Vince: One weird thing between Jake and me, at times I felt like he was in competition with me for who was gonna be the funny man. And it kind of bothered me, because it was just like, "Jake, you're very funny! And it's not a competition." He'd say things like, "Oh, man, you shut me down. I thought I would be the funny one." I'm like, "Jake, there's no comedy trophy on the last day!" **Jake:** Somehow, Vince's being funny did shut me down. At my interview to get on the show, I had been really over-the-top, and I could hear the casting people laughing in another room as they watched me on a monitor. So I was thinking, "Why would they put two funny people together?" I got really insecure about it. It made me never want to speak again. **Oscar:** Nobody likes to attract attention to himself more than Jake. So I think losing in the comedy mission was hard. Come on, he was out there naked and we didn't get the big laugh we were expecting. What's worse than that?

Oscar the Outsider

Sheri, Wilma's Patio: When they first signed up for the comedy, Oscar was all alone, so I had to go back and tell them that everyone had to be part of a team. **Gary Pennington, director:** At the RV park, Jake, Kalle and Erika went on this power-walk. They were uniting against Oscar. Tired of him sulking, tired of him borrowing things and not returning them. **Vince:** The thing with Oscar is he's really up and down. One minute he's extremely polite, the next he's really inconsiderate, so he's someone who's harder to live with than people realize. **Erika:** Oscar just did things that would drive me crazy. We'd be grocery shopping, and he would be eating off the aisles. He treated the place like a buffet line. I would say something to Oscar about it, and he would tell me to mind my own business. **Gary Pennington, director:** Back at the Winnie, Oscar was alone again. He was cleaning up when a letter arrived for him from his family. It was just this letter saying, "We think you're great, and we love you," and all this, and he started crying. In an OTF he said, "It's great to know that people back home love you. And it's nice to know you're wanted." After we got all that on tape, I broke down, too. I started crying, we hugged each other. He didn't know how he was going to go on. **Vince:** He would talk to me about what was going on, and I would talk to him, because I used to be an outcast, up until high school. But then I started to feel that I was sacrificing my good time just because things weren't going well for him, so I kind of gave up on him. But looking back, I should have said something. **Bruce Toms, director:** All four of the others revealed that though they may be out of high school, their clique skills are still well-honed. There was a bit of a mob mentality, and unfortunately for Oscar, he was different, so he became the scapegoat. **Oscar:** At the beginning, I was so excited to meet four great people who I was gonna go on the trip with. And then all of a sudden, they're telling me, "Oh, friendship takes time." Then again, they're all already hugging and kissing. What am I supposed to think. "Oh, okay. It takes time." I mean, it didn't bother me if they don't want to be my friends. But don't tell me friendship takes time and then turn around on me and kiss the person next to you. I've never had this problem before. I love making friends. I mean, what's

Jake's Off-Camera Move on Kalle — Strike One

Kalle: I look back and I wish more than anything that Jake's first seduction attempts had been on-camera. The way it is, nobody but the two of us really understands how things went. Jake really wanted to get together with me, and he totally came on to me like three times, and I'm like, "No, this isn't it. No, no." I just wasn't ready. I'd come on this trip wanting to be free, and here is this guy wanting me to get involved. **Jake:** We were in the RV park's swimming pool, late at night and things were not going smoothly. We had to climb this kind of spiked, gated thing to get over. And my shoes were wet, and I end up just like straddling it in the most painful way! So it's pretty obvious by that point that like nothing really suave is gonna happen. We're swimming around in the pool, just me and her. I just swam up to her and tried to kiss her. And it was just like this big, awkward grab at her. It was a completely awkward move. She went, "Whooooa, there!" She rejected me with this big, two-handed push away. We're talking two hands, kinda up around the facial area, like full-body flinch— I mean it was bad. I was thoroughly embarrassed. And then the police showed up and booted us out.

Erika's Visitor

Erika: One part of my life that really doesn't make it to the show is my boyfriend Stefan. We'd only just started dating when I applied, but by the time the trip started, things had gotten serious. I was definitely crying when I said good-bye. So Stefan came up to visit me in Balboa, which was great because I was having a rough time. He came into the Winnebago for a little while, and there was Jake, rapping to himself. And Oscar's just sitting there, silent, with his cap pulled down over his eyes. Stefan looked at them, then looked at me as if to say, "Oh, Erika. You poor thing." He just could tell that they're not the kind of people I click with. I looked at him like, "Don't go! I love you so much!" I don't think I ever had anything in common with Oscar or Jake. I mean, we've never had anything in common. Even if I was younger, there would be a big difference. **Jake:** I think Stefan might have been making fun of us. He called me "Greg Brady" and Kalle "Marsha" and stuff. But I didn't really get it—I never watched THE BRADY BUNCH. And we were kind of making fun of him, too. He'd say something, and Kalle would be like, "Wow, that wasn't funny." I love it when she shuts people down.

I think I really like this trip . . . All except Oscar. It's not that I don't like him, it's just that I cannot handle him. Last night he pouted for over four hours because we just missed Troy Aikman on Balboa. Who cares? It creeps me out because he reminds me too much of my brother when he acts like that. If he keeps this up for another week, I wouldn't think twice about voting him off the trip. No kidding. I'd be glad he was gone. We'll see—I'll give him another week.

Jake: I asked Rick and Clay about kicking Oscar out. They said, "Yeah, you can vote anyone out that you want to." I guess they were kind of kidding. But I was really eager about the whole thing. I wanted to do it before dinner. And Erika was into it, too. So I was like, **"Great, you know, we can use Erika's vote to vote Oscar out. Then we can all vote Erika out. Teach her a little lesson for voting people out. Where does she get off?"** But then later, Rick was like, "You can't vote people out. You were all chosen to be here. What gives you the right?"

"PUCKing" Oscar

Erika: The weirdest thing about that is that Oscar saw Jake as the closest to him, and Jake was the one talking about kicking him out. At this time, I was not getting along with Oscar at all. He was being a real little s**t, and I was having a lot of problems with him. I didn't like hanging out with him, but I don't think I ever wanted to kick him out. **Vince:** I thought that was so friggin' harsh. Just because one kid's different, or he does stuff we don't like, we're gonna take away this amazing trip that he earned! But the night I heard that, I guess I was playing the neutral side, once again. I was just like, "Oh, really? Okay." Then the more I thought about it—I'm just like, how can you even investigate something like that? I think sometimes Jake was kind of worried how good our show was gonna be. It's like, "Damn, there's not enough fights yet. Beat someone up!" **Kalle:** I feel bad now, because looking back on it, if any one of us had just sat down with him and been like, "We're frustrated because of this. We feel like if you don't want to be here, then you shouldn't. And if you really want to be here and have fun, then let's try and work on it." But instead, we just all got together, and we ganged up, and we're like, "Let's kick him off! Yeah!" **Jonathan Murray, executive producer:** Basically, you can't just kick someone out of your group just because you don't like them. They would have to do something wrong—steal your money, threaten you physically. There has to be a real, rational reason to ask us to support you getting rid of someone. I was never concerned that they would actually take it that far.

YOU'VE CONQUERED COMEDY, NOW SOLVE THIS RIDDLE: HOW MANY ROAD RULERS DOES IT TAKE TO WALK INTO THE WIND AT FIVE THOUSAND FEET? CHECK YOUR ANSWER WITH WALT PIERCE, KEY WEST AIRPORT, IN TWO DAYS.

TRAVEL
1853
MILES
BALBOA TO
KEY WEST

CLUE

TRAVEL LOG

Jake's making the moves, and Vince is busting out, while Erika and Oscar have both found reasons to cry. And what of the fair Kalle?

Time to compete for the chance to do something truly death-defying! While everyone gets to up and pull some G's, only one of you actually gets to get up on top of the plane and walk around.

Wing Walking

Paul Buscemi, production coordinator: Forget bungee jumping, skydiving, combine them all—that's a cakewalk compared to wing walking! **Jessie, wing-walking instructor:** The best part of wing walking is when you are going straight down. Basically it's like what it would be like to be in a plane crash. **Jonathan Murray, executive producer:** We were still working out the insurance issues on it about twenty-four hours before the mission was to take place. **Jake:** At first they were saying there would be a moment when she had no safety cables on, which I was not at all comfortable with, but once they decided on more safety stuff, I calmed down. I knew she could do it. After what she's been through, Kalle is hard-core determined to live the life she wants to live. **Erika:** Deep down, I think we all just knew that not only would Kalle be the one picked, but she was the only one who had what it takes to actually get up on that wing. That's just Kalle. **Mary-Ellis Bunim, executive producer:** I couldn't get over it. No matter how many cables you have on you, the mere thought of standing on the wing as it's flying is terrifying. Kalle was so excited, she could barely speak. Something extraordinary had just happened to her, and she wasn't sure what it was. It was wonderful to see her feeling so proud of herself. **Gary Pennington, director:** I was up in the helicopter filming that. It was the most insane thing I've ever seen any human do. Looking at her, I was thinking a human being should not be doing this. **Walt:** I've had about twenty wing walkers over the years and Kalle's right up there at the top. Jessie's one of the best I've ever had and she trained Kalle to be just like Jessie.

'Road Rules' cast walks on plane's wings

KEY WEST — An MTV crew is in town this week filming a segment of its popular show "Road Rules." The cast and crew spent Monday at Island Aeroplane Tours at the Key West airport rehearsing for today's filming of some positively hair-raising stunts.

See MTV, Page 6A

Right now, I feel like I will *never* have another experience in my life that will be anything close to the "Wing Walking" one I had yesterday. It seemed so real, but like a dream at the same time. I actually ate a piece of a cloud—strapped to the top of a biplane at three thousand feet! I felt surprisingly calm through the whole experience, but it *was* the thrill of a lifetime. I'll never get over how good it feels to be presented with an opportunity like that and to take advantage of it! It was one of those experiences where you know it's possible to achieve, but in doing it, you have to give up your everyday security to feel the risk. I seriously thought about dying—because I easily could have. I'm so glad I didn't.

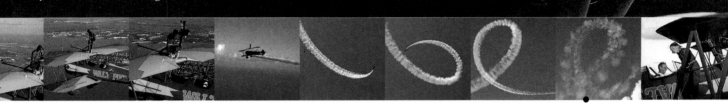

Basic Human Needs—Jake Crashes Winnie

Jake: The night I crashed the Winnie into that drive-through window, I was upset because one of the crew had made a joke about me being skinny, and I kind of flipped out. "Oh my God, I'm going to die! We don't have enough money for food! I'm starving!" That's when I started yelling about my basic human needs. I even started yelling at Bruce. I was like, "You've got to keep your crew in check."
Bruce Toms, director: What really motivates someone and what they say motivates them frequently are two different things. Around the time of the "basic human needs" outburst, Jake had just admitted, off-camera, that he was upset because Kalle had shot him down. There were things going on between them at that point that we weren't being made a part of. He was really hurting for her, and she was aloof and noncommittal. He was very frustrated. **Jake:** When I throw those big, big tantrums, I don't know how it's going to end. It's something I worry about because I'm thinking, "What's the breaking point?" Normally, I pick a fight with somebody, even if I can't win, because it just ends it. I either then get my ass spanked, or I trade blows with them. But somehow, it just ends it. So I was so happy when I smashed into the restaurant. Everybody started laughing; everything was okay. And then on top of it all, Oscar got them to cook more chicken, even though they were closed. We got like sixty dollars worth of chicken free. We were eating for the next three weeks.

It's been two weeks and as a group we've had a total of eight hundred dollars to live on. We splurged on one meal at some family chain restaurant. That's it. It's depressing all of us. We have never stayed at a motel, we have never received money as a group that we haven't won. The money situation is a big surprise. I didn't think it would be this hard, especially considering we've been in some of the most expensive places in the United States, not to mention the world. I mean San Francisco, Balboa, and now Key West. For a trailer park here it was seventy-five dollars a night. A trailer park!

JAKE VINCE ERIKA RULE

Taking

Bruce "Comes Out" to Cast

Kalle: In Key West, Bruce turned off the cameras and had a talk with us. We'd been making a lot of offensive comments about homosexuals, especially in Key West. Jake and Vince had this one expression in particular that I think he was most uncomfortable with. And they just kept saying it, and saying it, and saying it. So Bruce tells us that he thinks we should know that he's gay. **Bruce Toms, director:** I definitely crossed "the line" by having that talk. I knew they didn't mean it in a malicious way—it was just kind of immature, socialized behavior, but they were taking it very far, and at a certain point I have to be concerned that something affects how I do my job. This is a very unique show, and I think it's hard to stick to a lot of hard-and-fast rules. I'm glad I did it. I probably shouldn't have. But thankfully, it worked out really well for my relationship with the cast and their relationship with me. **Vince:** I was really glad that he opened up to us about that, because when he's interviewing us every week, we're telling him really, really hard stuff, so to suddenly have him letting us in on a bit of his personal life, it made everything much more comfortable. **Jonathan Murray, executive producer:** I'm not sure that Mary-Ellis and I would have told him that he should have done that. Some documentarians would say

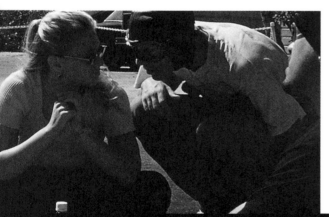

that by sharing part of your own life you will make the people feel more comfortable, and they will open up more. Others would say that by doing that you are affecting their behavior, and that should be avoided at all costs. We would have probably advised Bruce not to do it. We prefer to be the fly on the wall. But he did it without asking our advice, and we have to support him in the decision. **Kalle:** We couldn't stop apologizing, we felt so bad, but the weirdest part of that whole thing is that I totally had a crush on him! Erika had said she had heard he had a girlfriend. I had first met him during my interviews. I liked him so much.

Katy-baby—I got your message! How I love and miss you . . . I talked to Bri today, and it's not working. First, he wanted to talk about if I've made out with anyone . . . (which I haven't kissed Jake . . . yet?) Who knows. The only thing I know is that I don't want another relationship . . . I'm totally diggin' on Jake, though. We'll see . . . Wish me luck.—**Kalle**

Kalle Aside

Bruce Toms, director: We knew we weren't getting the whole story from Jake and Kalle. There's a trade-off at the heart of this show; the cast gets to go and do the most amazing things that they'd probably never do in their whole lifetime. But in exchange for that, they have to give up their privacy for ten weeks. **Jake:** It bothered me a little bit that Kalle wasn't being honest. Like, I wanted way more of our relationship to be on-camera. I didn't want to look like a moron on TV, so I kind of gave the directors some dirt in an interview. But I don't think they believed me. They were looking at me like, "Wow, he's in his own world. He's on his own road trip. What island are you on now, Jake?" **Kalle:** Jake would come on to me and try to kiss me and stuff, and then I'd sit down in interviews and be like, "No, nothing's happened between us. I don't really have any feelings for him." And then he'd interview Jake after me, and the story would be totally different. "Oh, yeah. I try to kiss her so much. I'm totally coming on to her. I think she really likes me." **Jake:** I finally got mad at Kalle. I'd figured out that she had lied to me about calling Brian, so I charged in on her, and I'm like, "Listen." And I just kind of laid it on her. And right then the camera crew showed up, so she doesn't say a word back to me. But she's like, "Let's go to the supermarket." We're walking there, and I can tell that she's so angry. And I'm trying to bring it out, but I'm just getting these looks, like "shut up" kind of looks. Just then, we pass a restaurant that we already knew production couldn't film in, so we say that we're going in for food. That was my most blatant let-production-not-get-this bull aside. I think that was the last straw for production because soon after that, Bruce had a talk with us. **Mary-Ellis Bunim, executive producer:** Kalle had such a long past with Brian, I'm sure she felt it was like trying to divorce your brother. And then for Kalle to be attracted to somebody else and worry about her former boyfriend and all that he had meant to her, of course she was going to resist sharing that with the whole country. It was so clear that she wanted to break free of everything and learn who she is. **Kalle:** There was so much going on. Bruce talked to us for a long time, and then he let me do an OTF, and that's one thing I'm so glad he let me do. 'Cuz then I like totally spilled my guts

YOU HAVE A DATE WITH SCOTT TEITLER ON SUNDAY AT TREASURE ISLAND HOTEL TO MAKE IT A PICTURE-PERFECT YEAR.

CLUE

THE CAST AND CREW ON KALLE

BRUCE TOMS DIRECTOR: I first saw Kalle when she was auditioning to get on the show. What first stuck out was just how people in the office reacted to her. I mean, there was all this flurry of activity. She was really beautiful when she came in, and she just gave off a special energy. Especially to the guys in the office. They were all finding excuses to come in. She had this kind of magnetism going on.

JAKE: One of the coolest things about Kalle is she is generally down for whatever, whenever. There is nothing she won't do, which is supercool. I think a lot of times, she realizes that she'll probably never be back in this place again, and she'll never have the opportunity to do a lot of these things that aren't related to our missions, and so she's just like ready for the action. I love that.

OSCAR: Kalle's got heart. She's got guts and heart. That's good for her. And she's funny in this Kalle way, and very sweet, but she does know how to be mean and cruel when the mood hits her. That's part of her too. It all makes her Kalle.

ERIKA: She certainly has what it takes to branch out on her own and find out what she wants to do in life. I'm happy for her in that. I kind of wish I had gotten to know Kalle better, but she and Jake were pretty inseparable, so it was very difficult. The few times that the two of us spent alone, they were great.

JONATHAN MURRAY, EXECUTIVE PRODUCER: When you first meet her, her voice gives you one distinct impression of who she is. It's almost Betty Boop. And what's wonderful is that she's much deeper, she's much smarter than that initial impression from her voice. And it's always nice to cast someone like that. Someone who is going to surprise you on second look. She's a very complex person who really seemed to be ready to break out.

MARY-ELLIS BUNIM, EXECUTIVE PRODUCER: I think from the first interview I saw of Kalle, I just loved her. I immediately rooted for her. And the more I got to know her, the more interested I was in her story, in what she was going to do next. She could have taken any number of roads, but she was clearly going to make a major life change. If it hadn't been ROAD RULES, she would have made her own opportunity. Life had dealt her some pretty tough stuff to deal with at a very young age, and she had done it. She had conquered that. And she had a lot of self-confidence because she could look at herself and say, "Wow, I'm in pretty good shape, and I can do more. I don't have to settle."

VINCE: My last interview they asked me "How has your opinion of Kalle changed?" And I said in my interview, "You know what? I really don't know Kalle." But really that wasn't true. The truth is, I think Kalle and I, we were almost like brother and sister. Because if I had a problem, I could talk to her about it, and she would really care. But we were always making faces at each other and always cracking each other up. And Kalle—she has this inner strength about her that unless people get to know her, they wouldn't know. They might think that she's just this really energetic blond who loves to have fun. But I could see it in her. Kalle has this . . . just this force inside her, that when it needs to come out, it's there. And it surprises people.

Kalle: I feel like when people from home see this, they're going to say that's not really her, because I kind of had the "bitch thing" going on in high school. My friends and I just assumed I would be that way on the show. So it was such a crazy thing to come on this trip and not be anything of who I acted like before I came. To just be myself felt so good. And to have people describe me as bubbly—I've never before in my life had anyone say I was a bubbly person! Somehow, getting away from home, having this fresh start, I realized I didn't want the role of the bitch in ROAD RULES, or in my life in general. It was wonderful. And then the whole time I was on the trip, I couldn't believe I was really there —all these amazing beautiful places I'd always wanted to go, all these adventures! And I didn't want to be the kind of person who had the opportunity to take that trip and when it was over, look back and be like, "I didn't take advantage of this. I didn't fully appreciate this. I didn't accept this, or try this." I wanted to take everything in, and do everything, and feel everything, and appreciate the scope of what I was in the middle of. And I tried my hardest, and I think I really succeeded.

FROM THE DESK OF KALLE'S DAD

I am so proud of Kalle! She is a good kid (kid defined as anyone under forty). Being chosen as a Road Ruler is her reward for being creative, persistent, outgoing and personable. I am especially happy that this success in her life came so soon after the trauma of her mother's death on November 8, 1995.

K has had tremendous family support from all of her grandparents, aunts, uncles, and cousins. I know that she has sprung back into life because of that

I've been preparing for the craziness that we may see by watching some of THE REAL WORLD Miami and ROAD RULES Europe. K said she thinks it's a good thing she will get a copy of the show a few days early so she can warn Grandma and Grandpa when NOT to watch!

The ROAD RULES experience has already changed Kalle's life forever, and of course, as a father, I hope for the better. I love you Kalle. Beth

KALLE'S LIST OF FIRSTS ON TRIP

FIRST TIME I KISSED A BOY OTHER THAN BRIAN IN 5.5 YEARS. FIRST TIME FALLING IN AND OUT OF LOVE AT THE SAME TIME. FIRST TIME GAINING MORE THAN 10 POUNDS. FIRST TIME WEARING SAME 15 ARTICLES OF CLOTHING FOR 10 WEEKS. FIRST TIME NOT WORRYING ABOUT—OR NOT FEELING LIKE I HAVE TO WORRY ABOUT—THINGS IN MY LIFE FOR AN EXTENDED PERIOD OF TIME. FIRST TIME NOT BEING A TEENAGER. FIRST TIME NOT SEEING MY DAD OR BROTHER FOR 10 WEEKS. FIRST TIME I'VE ALMOST ENTIRELY SKIPPED A COLORADO WINTER BY BEING IN THE SUN FOR MOST OF IT.

K
A
L
L E

MISSION 5

It's off to the aquamarine waters of Grand Cayman, where you must endure the nightmarish travails of...

TRAVEL LOG
Kalle conquered some major fears in the air over Key West, but on the ground, she's far from fearless. Should she give in to the pining Jake? Will she let the cameras in on her decision? What about Brian? Can these questions be answered in a bikini? The beach blanket Road Rulers are about to find out.

Life as a

The swimsuit mission was awesome. We all enjoyed it in our own way and really worked as a group. I loved being creative with the locations and poses. Kalle and I made out like bandits with a bunch of new suits. Scott seemed genuinely impressed with our work.

Scott Teitler, professional photographer: I meant it when I told them they did a great job. I remember the first pictures I took, and they were awful. If someone said to me now, "You have twenty-four hours to put together a calendar," I'm not sure I could do any better. Normally, a photographer would be given at least a week, maybe two . . . Of course, it doesn't look like Cindy Crawford's calendar, but all things considered, they did a great job. **Vince:** It was a lot more fun than I thought it was going to be, but I still hate being photographed. **Jake:** Kalle looked damn good in those suits. I was like, phew! Erika looked good too. Now me, Oscar, and Vince on the other hand, I guess we looked about as good as we're going to look. **Kalle:** Being a girl and growing up in the United States, this is kind of the dream, modeling for a calendar, and it was fun, but I'm way too overly, completely and insanely self-conscious about my body. That aspect was not so great. **Oscar:** We finally had some money after that mission, which was really good. I mean, at a certain point you do need some money, but I was even happier that we had all worked so well together. We were totally proud of ourselves and feeling good. No money in the world can match that.

supermodel

Scott: My least favorite was that one with Vince at Erika's feet. Marlon holding Erika was good. It had that cheesy, girl being rescued feeling. Kind of a BAYWATCH look.

Jake: Kalle couldn't believe that I let Erika sit on top of me, which didn't seem like a big deal at all to me. She thought it was. It didn't seem like anything to me. I was like, "Sure. Climb up on this bad boy!" It was like — it just didn't do anything for me. But Kalle couldn't believe it.

Marlon: I just hope my girlfriend's not going to see the show and want to be my ex-girlfriend.

Kalle: That picture of Erika, against the blue building, taken through the chain-link fence, that was one of my favorites. And Oscar, who I didn't have a lot of faith in, took it, but he did a great job.

To bee or not to bee, that is the question.
Whether 'tis nobler in the mind to suffer the stings and arrows, or just chicken out. Your next mission: Harvest honey at Otto Watler's.

Erika Has a Good Cry

Erika: There was a point in Cayman where I felt like I had had it, especially with Jake. He just seemed to think he had me pegged from the beginning of the trip. But there are so many more facets to my personality that don't have anything to do with arguing about money, or doing things my way. Jake was convinced though that I was this bossy woman who wanted to be den mother. And there were times where I was tired of dealing with him.

So it was just one of those days and I really wanted to get in touch with Stefan. He's a great listener. But he wasn't around when I called, so I ended up on the beach by myself, just having a nice cry, for about an hour and a half. It was hard because it seemed like no one was gonna care too much. No one really did; I was right. It's no one's fault. That's just a difficulty of being put together with people who don't know you well. They have a hard time knowing how to react when you're upset. I'm sure we all had those moments.

Vince and Kim

Vince: I got pretty upset the night I found out my girlfriend had started taking karate lessons from some other instructor. The truth is, I don't think I was so mad at her, it was just a point in the trip when things were getting to me, and I needed something to get mad at. I just felt like I was gonna go crazy and no one seemed to care. **Jake:** That was a mystery, Vince and Kim. I don't think the rest of us really understood what was going on there, so it was hard to know what to say. **Vince:** The strange thing is that Kim and I had broken up before the trip. Then two weeks before I was to leave, we got really close again. We never said officially we're together, but we hung out every night and then before I left, we said we'd wait for each other. When I met the others I told them, "I don't really have a girlfriend, but there's a girl in my life." But after a couple of weeks, I really missed her so much, I started referring to her as my girlfriend.

Kalle: Standing in the middle of a bee swarm is one of the most paralyzing things I have ever done.

Oscar: I can hear them talking to me. "I'm gonna bite you!"

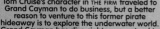

Taking Kalle Aside, Again **Rick de Oliveira, producer:** Kalle mentioned dreading talking about her and Jake in her upcoming interview, so I took her on a little walk. I told her, "Listen. Whatever you decide with Jake is really up to you. All we're asking is for you to be real." But she responded that she wasn't sure what real was. She kept asking herself if she would be attracted to Jake if they met in her real life. **Strike Two** **Jake:** We're in the shower, kneeling down, she's shampooing my hair, which I really like, so everything seems good. I kinda put my arms around her and lean in to kiss her, and it was like that full-on body flinch again. She's got a longer neck than you think. She was like, "No! What are you doing?" **Kalle:** We were talking about "us" all the time. I would tell him, "Jake, this is how I feel. I don't want a relationship. I don't wanna deal with all that. I just wanna be friends with you." And he was like, "Okay. That's all right. I respect that." But then we would talk about it, and he was like, "Well, don't you realize we already do have a relationship?" I mean, it wasn't intimate, but it was everything else. We were together all the time. We were best friends. So he was right about that. **Strike Three** **Jake:** The third attempt was by the bunk beds. We're getting ready to go have a group campfire outside the youth hostel. And this time, I got a little tactic going on. I'm not gonna just go straight for the mouth. I'm gonna start kissing around the ear area. Start over there, like behind the ear, kinda. She's really into that. She's liking it. She's telling me that she's liking it. So I'm like, here we go. We're in like Flynn. And then I finally go for the mouth, and it's like, "No!" Right then the crew come in! She shoots me one of her looks, like "Don't say a word." So I didn't, but it was way awkward. **Cold Shoulder** **Kalle:** Jake finally hit the point where he pulls that "guy thing" where they say, "Okay, I'm not trying anymore. I just wanna be your friend, and if you want anything more to happen, then you're gonna have to tell me. It's in your hands." My response was, "Fine." **Jake:** So we were on the beach at the fire, and Kalle pulls me aside and says that she wants to go for a walk. We're walking along without a camera crew, and I can tell she's finally trying to start it. I'm like yeah, man, the girl's macking me now! She was trying to figure out how to work it. And she just didn't know how to. She got me laying down in the sand, on my back, and she was kinda sitting up. We were seconds away, and then . . . she freezes and looks up. She says, "Do you see those lights?" And I'm like, "No, what lights?" But I saw them, they were the little red lights from Russ, the sound guy's rig, just floating out in the dark. He had been there the whole time. **Kalle:** We were so impressed! Because we totally thought we had snuck away. **Gary Pennington, director:** Russ and Mark actually caught Jake saying, "Yeah, those guys, man. They really miss a lot. All the good stuff . . . they're never around." They were instantly busted. Jake, Mr. Techie Guy, had to be thinking, "Whoa, these guys might be getting more than I thought." **Mark Jungjohann, camera operator:** Jake is obsessed with keeping things to himself. I caught him all the time whispering to the others. When we caught him that night, part of him may have been impressed, but most of him was really mad. **Hot Lips** **Jake:** Finally, we're back in bed, and I'm so bummed at how things have gone. The lights are out. But Kalle's being really touchy, though she wasn't kissing me. So I go to kiss her, and I'm like, "Here it comes. I'm gonna get rejected again. I must be reading this wrong." But this time the flinch didn't happen. And it was great kissing, the best. **Kalle:** Well, I hadn't kissed anybody other than Brian for almost six years, and so, there had been so much buildup and fear and frustration, and then all of a sudden, we just kiss, and it was like,

Fireworks

we should have been doing this all along. We kissed for like four hours! **Jake:** She was like, "You know, I saw fireworks. I've never actually seen fireworks." And it's on. She got really paranoid, though, about where the cameras are and where the cameras aren't. After lights out, I had to go all through the place, shut every curtain, lock every door, check every nook and cranny. **Mary-Ellis Bunim, executive producer:** I swear, it must be in the water of the Winnie. Why do the romances always happen on this show? It's wild. I've predicted a lot of them in the past, but I'm not sure I would have predicted this one in a million years. I thought for sure Kalle wanted to be on her own after having such a long relationship. **Oscar:** I'm glad they got together. I would guess that they have had more fun than anyone on the trip. It's that much nicer when you can share an experience like this with someone that you feel attracted to, and it's a mutual feeling.

CLUE

"HEY LIL' BUDDIES!
REST UP FOR YOUR
THREE-HOUR TOUR.
GO TO MAGEN'S BAY."

THE CAST AND CREW ON ERIKA

BRUCE TOMS, DIRECTOR: I fell in love with Erika at the first audition. She was poised and confident and stunning to look at. Wonder Woman is her icon, which is perfect, because I think she can do anything she sets her mind to. But she does have fire beneath that poise. She does have this past of dancing in the cage at a club, traveling in that scene in San Francisco, getting her tattoo. Erika's got it going on.

KALLE: On the trip, there are things that start to drive you crazy about the others. Erika had this thing about always being correct. But as you get to know the person, you learn their past, and you begin to see what made them the way they are. Erika lived that ugly-duckling-that-became-the-swan thing. She was really chubby, and her sister was always the popular one. She would even introduce Erika to people as her brother, Erik. Erika was always living in her sister's shadow. So now Erika always wants to be perfect. She wants to be right, and that gets old. But when the trip ends, you miss even those things. I miss Erika wanting to always be right.

RICK DE OLIVEIRA, PRODUCER: Erika's twenty-two going on forty-two, and the others were eighteen going on sixteen. She's wise beyond her years, to the point that you want to tell her it's okay to loosen up a little bit.

OSCAR: I've never met anyone like her. We're such different people. In fact, we're opposites. If you want to know what Erika is like, just imagine the opposite of me. So it was very hard for the two of us and we were arguing all the time, but opposites attract and over time we have become friends.

CLAY NEWBILL, SUPERVISING PRODUCER: She's the most polite person we've ever had on the show.

MARY-ELLIS BUNIM, EXECUTIVE PRODUCER: Erika has had more life experience. So when the others looked to her as Mom: "Mom, make the decision to hold the money, take responsibility," she got a little bored with that. Unfortunately because of that, she may not have experienced the same amount of growth that the others experienced. But she was great, especially on the missions. She always passionately embraced them and made them shine. And she had fun in the process. But I think when it was all over, she more than anyone seemed ready for it to be over. She wanted to go back to her man and her life, as opposed to the others, for whom the trip was a springboard to an unknown future.

JAKE: When she's in her fun mood, she's very fun. She's very fun to be around, and she's very lively. And she loses the whole age thing really quickly. She doesn't care. I don't understand why sometimes it's an issue, and others it's not. And she's pretty. She's a pretty woman.

VINCE: I kind of think some people on the trip had her pegged wrong. They didn't appreciate that she has a lot of different qualities, some of which don't always go together. Like she could be an extreme perfectionist with herself, but also very open-minded. And while she took money and things like that very seriously, she also has a great sense of humor and can be so much fun.

Erika: I don't know what I want to do with my life, and I never really thought of ROAD RULES as an answer. It seemed more like an escape than real life. But there was something kind of iffy and scary about it that attracted me. When I was younger, I would never step out of the normal life. I would never try new things. I would never play new games because I thought I was gonna be bad at it. And I would never play with different people because I thought that they wouldn't like me. And as I've gotten older, I purposely try things that I think maybe I'm not gonna be so good at. And even if I do look stupid, maybe I can make myself get better at it. And so this kind of opportunity was scary for me because...Like the paintball. I was horrible ... I can't aim, I have no idea of the strategy. I was so bad at it! But I still did it. And I still tried. And sure, I sucked, but I still did it. If I were younger, I would have been so petrified, I probably wouldn't have done it. But this experience ... I wouldn't allow myself to be disappointed in myself. I had to do everything to its fullest. I had to try and try and try. That was very appealing to me. Because with any experience like that, you kind of get stronger and have a bit more self-confidence.

FROM THE DESK OF ERIKA'S PARENTS

ERIKA'S DAD: I think Erika was a natural to be on the show. If I were selecting the cast members, Erika's wonderful sense of humor, her genuine interest in people, her forthrightness and honesty, and her propensity to like and be liked by a wide variety of people in a wide variety of settings would make her a strong contender. Her determination to finish what she starts, coupled with her love of life and enthusiasm for new experiences also make her a good choice. Her athletic ability and the fact that she "powers through" hard work and tough situations (she may be a princess, but never a wimp) are qualities that make her an invaluable asset to any team, especially the type of team needed for ROAD RULES. Finally, it is my totally unbiased, completely objective observation, as her father, that she is absolutely beautiful within and without.

As for being her dad preparing to watch the show, while Hillary Clinton may be anxious about Whitewater, Saddam Hussein should be anxious about cruise missiles, and the Apollo 13 crew was most certainly anxious when their spaceship was falling apart, I'm in a state of semicontrolled panic about watching my daughter on the show.

ERIKA'S MOM: From what I now know about some of the missions, I am definitely glad that the show is not being aired while they are still traveling. My concern for my daughter's welfare is always uppermost in my mind, and at least now I no longer need to fear for her personal safety when I see her flying upside down, jumping off bridges, or being left alone on a deserted island. Erika has shared events and conversations that I would edit out given a chance, but I think for the most part, I will be able to watch my daughter experiencing the trip of a lifetime.

MISSION 7

TRAVEL LOG

With Oscar hanging on his own, Erika and Vince worrying about the loves they left behind, and Jake and Kalle becoming Jake-n-Kalle, the Road Rulers arrive in St. Thomas in a fractured state. But nothing unites a group like a common enemy, and after the gang gets a load of their next accommodations, that enemy becomes the crew.

There's pampering in store for you if you can survive on the desert-island diet—conch, fish, lobster, native plants and lots and lots of coconut.
Of course, you've got to find the food (and fend off the wild donkeys in the process).

Before the Mission

Erika: We'd been traveling for twelve hours to get to St. Thomas and hadn't eaten since breakfast. We were already feeling grouchy when we see a big old tent in baggage claim with our name on it. It was weeks into the trip, and we still hadn't stayed in a hotel. We were all really tired and just wanted a little food, and then we get to Magens Bay beach where we were supposed to camp until the next mission. Ugh! **Jake:** We showed up at the beach and the guy who owns the place was like, "Well, people don't ever really sleep here, but I'll leave the public bathroom open for you." **Vince:** There wasn't even running water. Only saltwater. And there was NO food in sight. At that point, I really felt like they were messing with us to get some anger out, and I'm like, "Well, that's not right." We all woke up the next morning covered head to toe in bug bites. **Oscar:** I'm checking out the toilets and everything, and it's grossing me out. And all of a sudden this rat—like cow-sized rat, I think it even went "moo," I mean, it was huge—just like walked beside me like . . . I think it even said "Hi, Oscar." You could feed a whole village with that rat. **Jonathan Murray, executive producer:** I think they had thought that it was going to be a little easier. They didn't realize that they were on ROAD RULES TOUGH LOVE. They still thought they were on ROAD RULES UNLIMITED EXPENSE ACCOUNT. **Mary-Ellis Bunim, executive producer:** There's always a point in the trip when the cast starts to get sick of the whole thing. This show really wears you down. You're always on the go, always traveling. You can't just stay in bed when you're having a bad day. So, they were all pretty run-down and tired and hungry. And then you can't underestimate the emotional toll that it takes to have the camera on you all the time. It's harder than it looks. **Rick de Oliveira, producer:** The morning of Magens Bay was supposed to be my day off, but I get a call saying that there's a bit of a mutiny going on. The cast was apparently very upset. **Kalle:** Well, we were about ready to kill Rick personally. **Rick de Oliveira, producer:** I pull up and they start going off: rats, no food, saltwater, sand fleas. Jake's talking about being malnourished, so we had to talk. I told them, "You're gonna have a tough mission coming up. This kind of trip is about highs and lows." I was trying to keep the speech on the trip in general, but I think they perceived it as mission-specific, that the next mission was going to be a death march. As a result, the Hans Lollik mission became a waiting game, which doesn't make for great television.

Jake: I hadn't even looked at Vania, and Kalle had started in on her. Girls can be rough.

TRIVIA

Bruce Toms, director: On Hans Lollik, Jake approached the soundman and said, "Listen, this is gonna be the first time that Kalle and I are gonna be able to be together. Can you please spot us some condoms?" And Jeff came to me and asked what he should do. I told him, "Thanks. I'm glad you told me, but tell him no." The show is about how the cast handle the situations they're in, not how we help them hook up.

TRAVEL LOG
The cast arrives on deserted Hans Lollik Island and learns survival, tropical island–style, from Kenny Turbe and his lovely assistant, Vania. Kenny's eager pupils catch on fast, but the middle of the night disappearance of Kenny, Vania and the boat, transforms the cast into castaways. One day follows another until . . . is it a mirage? Off in the distance, isn't that a rescue boat?

Hans Lollik
(A.K.A. Donkey Island)

Oscar: That mission brought out instincts I didn't know I had. I loved it. And I kind of secluded myself from the others because I didn't want to hear what a bad time they were having, how disgusted they were with the island, like "Wow, I feel like s**t here." I don't need those negative vibes around me. You don't get to go fishing every day, or gather your own food from native plants, or even spend time on a deserted island. **Vania, Kenny's assistant:** Oscar was made for this type of thing. He was going crazy, he was enjoying it so much. He was touched spiritually. Some of the things he said, it touched me. It touched Kenny, too. I almost cried. **Kenny:** Oscar was like my mascot. The thing about Oscar is that he connects with nature, the natural resources. He believes, "Look around at these natural surroundings, this is richness, this is what matters in life." **Bob Denver:** I've had this hat for thirty years now. After I rescued the kids and we were heading back on the boat, the hat blew off and started sinking into the sea. I said to myself, "Denver, it's just a hat." But I felt like I'd lost something very important. It was funny. But Vince and Oscar, they went right in. I didn't think there was any chance they'd find it. Oscar got it. I said, "Oscar, anything you want, it's yours." **Bruce Toms, director:** For much of the trip, when Oscar wasn't getting along with his cast mates, he was able to make friends with the people running the missions and the locals on the islands he visited.

CLUE

BOB DENVER: I GAVE OSCAR THE NEXT CLUE. IT WAS A LETTER FROM HIS LITTLE SISTER TELLING HIM TO COME HOME TO PUERTO RICO. PEOPLE USE THE WORD "SPEECHLESS" LOOSELY, BUT OSCAR REALLY WAS. HE COULDN'T SPEAK, COULDN'T MAKE A SOUND. HE WAS OVERCOME WITH EMOTION.

Oscar: I saw Vania, and I was like "Ooooh, I want to marry her."

TRIVIA
Oscar amazed all by taking Kenny up on his challenge to eat the conch's private parts.

ERIKA'S JOURNAL

They weren't kidding when they said our reward for the survival mission would be pampering. I'm sitting in a posh hotel overlooking Sapphire Bay. We've had an endless supply of food, as well as a massage, manicure, facial, haircut and paraffin treatment. Only a few hours ago I was dirty, wet, cold, hungry, totally disgusting. It is so beautiful here. I only wish that Stefan was here with me on Valentine's Day, but you can't have it all, I guess.

Pampering

Jake: For Valentine's Day I got Kalle a calendar just like the one of hers I had accidentally thrown away and a copy of a book that she had lost two days earlier, but the timing of when I gave them to her was so bad. Erika was on the couch between us. It was the most awkward thing. Everybody was like, "Aww…" And then nothing. She had no reaction. It was pretty amazing that I had been able to get a hard-cover of that book when we didn't have any money, and that calendar, which was from Colorado, was even harder. We went upstairs later, and then I heard her REAL thank you, but I was pretty irritated. **Kalle:** It did mean a lot to me, I don't know. I'm just not into displays, especially with the camera there. Maybe it was about me still not feeling totally comfortable about us. I don't know. It's hard to say. But I did appreciate it.

Later That Day

ERIKA'S JOURNAL

My f**king boyfriend is going to dinner with some girl, alone. What is going on here? My day was going so well. How could Stefan think that I wouldn't mind? My mind is going to explode. I am thinking too much, imagining what could happen tonight. I totally trust him, but why did he do this today?!? My blood is boiling!

Erika: The food! I wish I had four stomachs. The desserts, the prime rib, the cookies! It's absolute heaven.

Vince: I needed this pampering very badly. I was really dirty, hungry—I was starving. Lost some weight on the island. So this is exactly what we all needed. Food and shelter and showers.

Oscar: It's funny 'cause the only thing I could fantasize about while we were staying on the island was like, all I want right now is just a full-body massage. And I actually got one. That was amazing.

Jake: At first I'm a little shy about it. She wants me to get naked. She wants to scrub down my butt, even. I'm like, "I don't know, lady." But I'm giving in to it, and it's feeling good, and I'm likin' being pampered a lot.

TRIVIA
Vince abstained from the massage and paraffin treatment, citing an aversion to being touched by strangers.

TRIVIA
To get the calendar for Kalle, Jake called the Ft. Collins airport, and paged an airport employee (whom he'd met at the beginning of the trip when the employee asked Jake, Kalle, and Vince for their autographs). Jake asked the employee to buy the calendar and send it to him for Kalle.

Erika: It bothered me on the trip that Vince and I were always being asked if something was going on between us. But there were times when the camera was following Jake and Kalle and missed seeing what we were about, like in St. Thomas. We just went out for dinner and had the greatest conversation, for hours. It was nice. Vince was a great friend. **Bruce Toms, director:** The night they went out in St. Thomas, that was Valentine's Day, and they had just come off the deserted island. They had spent the day being pampered, and then Erika found out that Stefan was out with some other woman who had the hots for him. I wasn't working that night, but I ran into them heading to the restaurant, and they both looked great. I was hoping that they would let loose and jump each other's bones, because I think there was a part of each of them that wanted to. But I believe them when they say nothing was happening. **Jake:** I think stuff went on. There was some kissing and some touching. But I'll bet there was a lot more going on than they even told me. And that's where I knew that Erika lied to herself. I knew they had kissed a couple of times, and they had kind of fooled around. She'd tell me, "I'm sick of being asked about my relationship with Vince like there's something going on that I'm not telling them." "Erika, stuff's going on. Who are you lying to? I know it, and you know it!" That's what I thought. **Gary Pennington, director:** One problem on our end was production's over-interest in what was going on between them. I think that was a big part of Vince's decision not to get involved. **Jonathan Murray, executive producer:** With interviews, we try to ask them each week about what's going on in their lives, but there's a danger of coming off too heavy in terms of asking things like, "So, Vince, what's happening with you and Erika?" You want to encourage people to be open, but there's the inherent danger of actually scaring some development away. **Oscar:** They were always playing pinchy, pinchy games, touch here, tickle there. And they sleep together every night. I have to say, there are nights when I wake up, and they're not sleeping. That's all I'm saying.

Erika and Vince:
Are They or Aren't They?–You Make the Call!

V I N C E ' S   J O U R N A L

This experience is half-way completed. Every day that goes by, I feel myself getting happier. I am not home-sick, but I miss my family and friends. I wonder what this will all look like on TV? There was a period where I was getting so depressed, which I realized was all about me worrying about my family watching this when it airs and criticizing me, but I think I have gotten over that. This trip is about me, not them. I also wonder if the editors play with the story at all? I just hope they do not make it look like Erika and I have a thing for each other, because we don't.

TRAVEL

St. Thomas is the kind of island where you can look out of your hotel window and see a model on the beach in the middle of a fashion shoot, which in fact was the case the day the Road Rulers were being pampered at Sapphire beach. Some of the island's best night-life is just down the road in Red Hook at Duffy's Love Shack, home to a spectacular variety of tropical drinks. On Thursdays, Duffy's usually sedate cocktail-hour crowd swells to mob size, spills out onto the parking lot, and starts boogying down. Don't miss it.

TRAVEL
72 MILES
ST. THOMAS TO
PUERTO RICO

T R A V E L   L O G   In light of Oscar's ROAD RULES experience thus far, the word "ostracized" might well be changed to "Oscarcized," but with the trip moving on to his home turf, what will Oski do with the roles reversed?

Erika: That first day in Puerto Rico, Oscar's family throws a big party for us. Oscar's feeling good, partying with his friends, and then he starts making this speech. He warms us up by saying how glad he is that we're here, then he slips in this bit about we've been big hypocrites in how we've treated him. It wasn't malicious, but he knew he had the upper hand, surrounded by friends and family. He was like, this is my chance to tell you what I think of you guys. **Oscar:** I would walk into a

Oscar's House

room, and I would know they'd been talking about me. I could hear them from the hallway. Then when I'd walk in, they'd change the subject. I don't like that. I don't. If you want to say something, say it to my face. **Vince:** We were talking behind his back, a lot. It just seemed like more trouble to talk to him and have it become a big issue with him being all mad. But then again, I guess that's not giving him a chance to have a reaction. **Gary Pennington, director:** What would the average person do after how the group treated Oscar? They would say, "Screw you guys. You're on your own in my country." No, Oscar invites them into his house. "You're part of my family now." They had a nice meal. They had showers. Food. Warm house. Clean beds. At one point, Erika said, "Oscar's family, they're so different from mine." I thought, finally, they're starting to realize Oscar is from a different culture, and it's not necessarily a bad thing. You just wanted to tell them, you're not in San Diego anymore. **Jake:** One way or another, he knew how I felt, so I didn't feel like a hypocrite. I just didn't take him seriously. That's not to say that Oscar was all bad. In a lot of ways, he got a bum rap from us. At times I really felt bad for the kid. I mean, he must have felt so alone—so isolated. He liked to say it was a cultural difference. I thought it was just a poor excuse, until we went to Puerto Rico. After that, I agreed with him. **Kalle:** Seeing Oscar in his element in Puerto Rico and us as a group being in the position of needing him, it changed my opinion of him. It's not that he's a bad kid. He's just as lost as the rest of us.

JAKE'S OFF-CAMERA ALTERCATION—ROUND THREE

OSCAR: MY FRIEND DANNY SAW KALLE, AND HE WENT CRAZY, "HAVE YOU SEEN THE LEGS ON THAT GIRL?" I'M LIKE, "YEAH, I'VE SEEN HER FOR A COUPLE OF WEEKS." HE KEPT SAYING *PENTHOUSE*, SAYING STUFF IN SPANISH, MAKING LIKE PERVERT FACES. KALLE WAS TRYING TO IGNORE HIM, AND JAKE WAS GROANING. **KALLE:** I WAS EMBARRASSED FOR THAT KID. HE WAS TOO PATHETIC TO TAKE SERIOUSLY. **JAKE:** THEY WERE MAKING FUN OF US, PRETTY MUCH, IN SPANISH. AND COMING ON TO KALLE. THERE WAS A LOT OF KALLE-COMING-ON-TO. **OSCAR:** JAKE WAS PISSED! AT FIRST I THOUGHT IT WAS FUNNY, BUT AS SOON AS I NOTICED THAT KALLE WAS UNCOMFORTABLE, THAT'S WHEN I SAID, ALL RIGHT, DRAW THE LINE. JAKE TOOK DANNY INTO THE OTHER ROOM, AWAY FROM THE CAMERAS AND HAD A TALK WITH HIM. IT'S GOOD THEY DIDN'T START SOMETHING, BECAUSE DANNY'S FRIENDS WERE ALL THERE. THAT WOULD HAVE GOTTEN UGLY. THEN MY STEPMOM MADE ME KICK DANNY OUT.

SAY *"ADIOS"* TO *LA FAMILIA* UNTIL SATURDAY, PACK YOUR STUFF, THEN HEAD NORTHWEST, TAKE THE ROUTE CLOSEST TO THE SEA TO A TOWN WITH THE SAME NAME AS THE BEAUTIFUL BRUNETTE LANCÔME MODEL (THE ONE WITH THE FAMOUS PARENTS).

CLUE

TRIVIA
During the party, Jake started a game where any time production said, "Don't talk about production," the cast would start kissing each other: Jake and Kalle, Vince and Erika, Jake and Vince?

TRAVEL 65 MILES
SAN JUAN, P.R. TO ISABELA, P.R.

How does a gourmet meal, served by a sexy waitperson sound? Unfortunately, there's only one meal, and it awaits the first Road Ruler to build a raft, leap off a bridge and cross the finish line.

ERIKA'S JOURNAL The raft race was a joke, but what a fun mission! We spent all this time building rafts that didn't work. We started the race with a pendulum jump off the bridge, which was like a dream, a flying dream. Jake won because he could carry his raft. The rest of us had a blast just ditching our rafts and swimming down the river. The scenery in that canyon was so beautiful. Kalle and I couldn't care less that we were not going to win, we were having such a cool time just floating along the river.

Kalle: That was weird. We were laughing so hard, having such a blast. Somehow that race just turned into Kalle and Erika bonding day.

Missing Oscar's Mom

Oscar: When I had planned to see my mom, we suddenly had to go to Isabela. And then when we came back, we didn't have enough time. And it really, really sucked. I was upset. Now, if people see this show, they're gonna see my dad. And they're gonna be like, "Where's his mom? That's his mom? No, that's his dad's wife. Where's his real mom?" And that's gonna be upsetting for me, but . . . I tried. **Vince:** No one was quite sure what happened about Oscar's mom. Maybe it would have just been too emotional for him. Maybe he just thought there was going to be more time. I don't know. That's something Oscar never seemed to want to talk about. **Oscar:** After the trip, I talked to her, and she tried to understand. But she's a mom. "You can't even spare some time for your mom!" I told her I tried. "You tried, all right! I also tried to raise you up like a fine man!" I was like, "All right, that's it. I'm outta here." I need to work on that with my mom. I feel like s**t about it. I'm so self-conscious about my relationship with my mom, it's not even funny. I need to spend more time with her, talk to her, look her straight in the eye, and tell her I love her. After all the weird stuff between my mom and my dad, I can't help feeling bad that she has to see the TV and see my dad playing this big-hero-father role.

CLUE

LET'S SEE IF YOU REALLY DO TAKE THE CAKE. FIRST, FIND THESE TOURISTS AND DELIVER THE ENCLOSED CHALLENGE WITHOUT BEING SEEN. THEN BEAT THEM AT IT. AT STAKE: SEVERE HUMILIATION.

TRAVEL

A trip to Puerto Rico will quickly explain Oscar's unbridled patriotism. The island has an astounding variety of activities beyond the usual Caribbean beach fare: world-class surfing, a rain forest, cave diving, casino gambling, a European-style old capital, and crazy night-life.

CHALLENGE

Climb the wall, walk the plank, scramble through the net, and stand on the little box!?! They're all games with a twist, and the biggest one is that your competition is the gang from THE REAL WORLD!

TRAVEL LOG
Team competition and a new supply of cash seem to have brought some unity to Team ROAD RULES, but Erika and Oscar are still looking for some friendly companionship outside the group!

Road Rules /
The Real

Kalle: The first person I saw from THE REAL WORLD was Syrus, and I was scared—he's a giant, and we had written all these harsh things about them when we dropped off the challenge. I was thinking, what if he took it personally and he's just coming down to kick our asses. **Elka, Real Worlder:** They were a bunch of ruffians that were supposed to be out on the road, killing live tigers and eating their flesh, and trying to start their own fires, things like that, while we were coming from a luxurious hotel and a nice continental breakfast. So it felt great to kick the butts of those ROAD RULES fools at their own game. **Erika:** We felt good, we felt confident, then they kicked our confident asses the first three games. It was a flashback to paintball. But then we took a break and ate lunch, which was key, because we hadn't had any breakfast. **Bruce Toms, director:** It was so hard to watch our team getting stomped by THE REAL WORLD. I really wanted them to win, it was killing me. It's funny how you could tell that the two crews were both rooting for their own teams. Our team came back from lunch ready to go and right away they won that wall game. Finally. That was big. **Erika:** We were over that wall like a well-oiled machine. We broke the losing streak. We couldn't believe it! We were screaming, we were going crazy. **Oscar:** The last tug-of-war was insane. Syrus and Sean were in front of us, and they were like the two biggest guys, and I was with Jake. I was like, "Ohh, man. All right, Jake." We started pulling. All of a sudden I see Jake fall. He's like break dancing on the floor. And I was like, "Get up, man." And then I had to hold the thing for him to get up, and at the same time, I had to pull. I went crazy. It was one of those adrenaline things. After we won, I looked at who we beat. I couldn't believe I had pulled those huge guys. **Jake:** Oscar holding those guys off—I was truly amazed. When I fell, I felt for sure we would be dragged. That was amazing. They won more events, but we won more money, which is what we really cared about. **Jonathan Murray, executive producer:** The competition was fun, because I think both groups came away from it convinced that they had the best group, that they were the best people. So it was actually a bonding experience, which I think helped both casts move forward with their own respective seasons.

Oscar: I was so proud when we won an event—that wall thing. Wow, that's a moment I wish I could live again.

We are going to compete against all the cast members from *The Real World*. They will all die and turn to ash at the sight of us. We will bury them within two-tenths of a second. They will be our slaves for all eternity, and we shall make them suffer.

World Games

SYRUS: TELL ME, HOW IS IT?

OSCAR: I MEAN, IT'S BEEN HARD FOR ME.

SYRUS: WE'RE IN THE SAME BOAT, BRO. IT'S KINDA WEIRD. I'M LIKE AN OUTCAST FOR NO REASON.

OSCAR: THAT'S IT. THAT'S JUST HOW I FEEL. LIKE SOMETIMES, LIKE THEY'RE LIKE OFF IN THEIR LITTLE GROUP, AND I'M HERE, AND JUST LIKE KICKING IT ALONE. WHAT THE F**K?

SYRUS: WE WERE DESTINED TO MEET, BRO. WE'RE BOTH INTO REGGAE. WE'RE BOTH OUTCASTS. YOU KNOW WHAT I'M SAYING?

OSCAR: THAT'S RIGHT.

SYRUS: BUT MAYBE THE LAST WEEK AND A HALF, WE'VE BEEN GETTING CLOSER.

OSCAR: S**T! IT'S BEEN HAPPENING THE SAME THING TO ME, LIKE . . .

SYRUS: GROUP DYNAMICS, BABY!

Vince: I liked the guys a lot. But those girls. Genesis and Kameelah! They were the bitchiest girls I've ever encountered. It just seemed like they enjoyed being hostile. Thank God they weren't on our trip. **Erika:** I tried being friendly with the women from THE REAL WORLD, but boy were they rude. The guys were a different story. They were so cool, all of them. Syrus was so friendly, Jason was so soft-spoken and sincere, and Sean just really sweet. It was so nice to talk to someone who was twenty-five and going through a lot of the same things I was. Just to have an actual conversation, I was really starved for that. At one point, I told Jason that I'd never had such moments of loneliness as I'd had on the trip, never in my entire life. **Bruce Toms, director:** There were a lot of interesting things happening between the two casts, the different ways that everyone interacted was very revealing. Oscar and Syrus as the two outsiders, Erika finding a friend her own age in Sean. **Oscar:** Syrus, he's my man, my boy. He's this huge big guy. He walks over to me—boom, boom—sits down, starts talking, and we go from there. It was cool to just talk, not have to deal with all those judgments, because those things can wear you down.

Kalle: I was pleasantly surprised by Sean's toes. Not bad at all.

Kalle: Syrus was a huge sweetheart.

Oscar: Montana looked much better after I smeared that mud on her face. It really made an improvement.

Erika and Sear

Mary-Ellis Bunim, executive producer: Erika's fidelity to Stefan was tested by a second man on the trip when they met up with THE REAL WORLD. Sean made such an overt play. Oh, he was working it! He wasn't giving up. He was just not going home alone. **Erika:** Oh, that was nice! I hadn't been that lonely in a long time. And I think part of the thing that just bothered me the most is that I kinda got the feeling that people on the trip just kind of assumed they knew me, and that . . . I felt like they never asked me questions about myself. And I met Sean, and he was really interested, and it was just so nice to talk to somebody. He is one of the nicest people I have met in the past few years. **Oscar:** Man, he was buying her drinks all night long. Just talking to her for hours and hours. You would really have to have a whole bunch of s**t to say to want to talk to a girl all that time. **Vince:** Erika may get mad at me for telling this, but . . . She didn't do anything with him, but she was coming out of the girls' bathroom, and Sean just grabbed her and planted one on her, right on the lips. He just laid one on her, right on the lips. She said she just pulled away and was so embarrassed and taken by surprise, she just started laughing. And Sean was like, "What? What are you laughing at? Come on, baby." **Kalle:** It was funny, Sean kept trying to give Jake money. We'd been making them feel guilty for taking the money we have to live off. Like for the cab, he tried to give him fifty bucks. He said, "Just keep the leftover. Just get something to eat, you guys." And so we get to the guesthouse, and he keeps trying to slip Jake a fifty. **Jake:** I made a point of sneaking that money back into his pocket. He was like, "And just leave Erika." So suddenly I felt like I was Erika's chaperone, but I said "No, no, no," because I don't just rent Erika out to anybody. **Erika:** I don't even remember anything. I don't remember how we got home. I fell asleep in full clothes, even shoes. You know you've overdone it when that happens. I'd been out for maybe two hours when Oscar's little sister started banging on my head. I was a wreck. I kept my sunglasses on all day. I came down and the others had big smiles on. They go, "Erika!" I said, "No, don't even talk to me." That was a funny night.

Vince: One weird coincidence in Puerto Rico . . . when we got off the plane, there was this young woman waiting for us. Production would hire a local on every island, someone who knew their way around. But when Oscar saw this woman, he almost passed out. **Kalle:** That was wild. He told us he had had this huge crush on her when he was in sixth grade, and she was in eleventh, or something, and he would write her all these love poems all the time. He had been totally in love with her. She was his dream woman. **Oscar:** I went up to her in the van, I'm like, "I know you—do you know that?" She's like, "I don't know you." And I said, "I've changed a lot." And she's like, "How do you know me?" And then I started explaining to her, and she was truly red. She totally remembered the poems. I mean, they had been extreme love poems and I had just been this little kid. But we couldn't talk any more because she was part of the crew. I'd be like, "Venemos hablar." [Come on, let's talk.] But she wouldn't, because she didn't want to mess up her job, "cross the line" they call it. I'm like, "Come on, just talk to me!" **Vince:** When we went to

A Blast from Oscar's Past

that club, I was kind of like bored out of my mind, and Oscar and I left. It was late, and Oscar was going to some girl's house. But I didn't know which one. I couldn't keep track of his women in Puerto Rico. **Oscar:** I called her, I was like, "I want to see you." And she's like, "Now?" I'm like, "Yeah." And she goes, "I was just sleeping . . . in my underwear." And I'm like, "You're done with your job, and I want to see you. Give me your address." And she's like, "All right." So, I finally got to hang out with her, which was great. She was like this idol for me.

My dear one. Today. I have the privilege to say that I've been not only a witness, but a participant in a miracle. A star combined with my own and answered my dream. The same dream, many years ago. I put in the hands of the Lord. Over me, a rain of blessings, which each drop carries a letter of your name, and every wind I feel hugs me with your spirit. God bless life. God bless you. Oscar

A Letter to Oscar's Mystery Woman

NEXT STOP'S MARTINIQUE, WHERE YOU'LL GET A CHANCE TO MAKE SOME CASH AND WORK ON THOSE TANS.

Petit Saint Vi... Island

Petit Martinique

TRAVEL 428 MILES
PUERTO RICO TO MARTINIQUE

CLUE

THE CAST AND CREW ON OSCAR

BRUCE TOMS, DIRECTOR: Oscar has this philosophical thing about him. And you either buy it, or you don't. And none of the others bought it. Which is too bad. Because I think that Oscar is a pretty wise person. It's just that sometimes the package that he delivers the message in is a little too warm and fuzzy, especially for teenagers.

JAKE: I suspect that Oscar is much easier to get to know if you're not living with him. Everyone we met along the trip loved him. Even my parents were like, "Oscar's such a sweetheart!" But from our perspective, there were a lot of parts to Oscar that we had to get past before we could appreciate that he really is a good person and can be a lot of fun to be with.

KALLE: It kind of makes me sick what happened with Oscar and the group, because so much of that amazing trip must have been very lonely for Oscar. Early on in the trip, we started shutting him out, and he started distancing himself, and those two things fed on each other. But when we were in Puerto Rico, he was suddenly in control, and we had to rely on him. That changed things. He was really important to our group.

RICK DE OLIVEIRA, PRODUCER: Oscar is a great traveler. He always wanted to go out and meet the locals all along the way. That's something that I think the others really could have learned from Oscar, because they tended to stick with their group.

VINCE: Oscar's an extremely loyal person. When you're friends with Oscar, I think he's there for you like one hundred percent.

JONATHAN MURRAY, EXECUTIVE PRODUCER: I think we were surprised that the other cast members from the trip didn't fall in love with him immediately the way we did. But then again, when we saw him on the road, we saw sides of him that we hadn't seen in the casting process. He definitely marches to his own drum. He didn't need their approval, and that can get to people.

MARY-ELLIS BUNIM, EXECUTIVE PRODUCER: What stands out about Oscar on the trip is that, though he was often being tested by his relationship with the cast, he was still able to meet every day with such full emotion. Oscar was genuinely, deeply moved by the experiences of that trip.

ERIKA: Oscar and I have a weird relationship, but I really do like him. We have an unspoken understanding that we are both going to irritate each other, and neither one of us is going to change. So there are gonna be times when we fight, but when it is over, we're going to make up and be friends. I'm proud of how our relationship grew. And when we were at the airport that last day, I was really sad to see him go.

Oscar: They were the ten funnest, most special weeks of my life, but they were also the hardest ones. I just wish I would have had another kind of cast. I'm not saying I regret having them at all. At the end, I made friendships and everything, and it was all good. But who cares what happens at the end? At the end, everyone always tries to be nice. It's while you're there that you have to care. It was like Vince was saying, "Oh, 'cuz we have like a week left, and I don't want to leave with bad regrets about anything, and I want all of us to be friends." I'm like, "Now? You should have thought of that when I was telling you, like the first week, 'We should all be friends, we should all have fun, because I don't want to leave here with any regrets.' Remember that?"

FROM THE DESK OF OSCAR'S DAD

Yes, of course he changed. He expanded his cosmovision. He is more mature. He grew in his human dimension. His spirit flew beyond the boundaries of his reality. Different people and cultures got into his soul and heart. He took stock of his capacity and potential, and placed them in perspective and in relation to those of others. I lost a kid and gained a man. The arrow flew away. He is still a miracle!!

TRAVEL LOG
Before the cast set sail with Christian, they had a beach job in Martinique. The guys were spraying people with suntan oil, and the girls were selling bathing suits. Of course, not all cultures share definitions of modesty, and in Martinique the cast confronted the French twist.

Sell that swimsuit!
Spray that tanner!
Fight that language barrier!
There's money in them beaches

Martinique: Work It

Annica, swimsuit salesperson: The girls were a little shy about taking their tops off. I would be as well if I were them, with a camera right there. But that's how we sell the suits here. If a customer is interested in a suit, you try it on and model for them. And on the beach, there's nowhere to change, so you just change out in the open. **Erika:** I had to warn my mom WAY in advance about this one. She was just like, "Well, you didn't HAVE to do it." I told her, "It wasn't that big of a deal." She was not pleased. And I was a bit irritated myself. I don't have any problem taking my top off, but there was something about being told to that I didn't like. But Annica said, "It's part of the sale, that you change in front of everybody." **Jake:** I didn't want Kalle to change, to do that whole thing, because she didn't want to. I knew she was already a little self-conscious about gaining weight on the trip. I was uncomfortable for her, and I was hoping she'd say no. And then, I became uncomfortable for me. I started thinking, "I don't want everyone to see her naked." **Kalle:** I was not comfortable at all with having to flash it all to the entire beach, but having done it, I'm glad I did. **Erika:** At first it's nerve-racking, but by the end of the day, you start seeing it like the French do. There's nothing to be ashamed of. Everyone is different. The thing to be ashamed of is that in America, they would have to blur it out on television, that's what makes it strange, like there's something wrong with being naked.

Vince: So far, this has been really disgusting.

TRAVEL
Not only is the island gorgeous, but the French influence has brought to Martinique a rare level of cool and sophistication. Anyone interested in the bathing-suit selling job should go to Sainte-Anne beach and talk to local vendors. It's a way to finance an extended stay while brushing up on your French, but it's not recommended for the modest.

Jake: That was horrible. We were spraying point-blank at anyone and everyone.

Erika (to Kalle): You talk, and I'll get naked.

CLUE

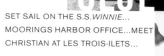

SET SAIL ON THE S.S. *WINNIE*...
MOORINGS HARBOR OFFICE...MEET
CHRISTIAN AT LES TROIS-ILETS...

MISSION 9

**Raise the main sail! Unfurl the jib!
Take your seasickness pills! And watch out for that boom!
It's life on the high seas and *Road Rules* is at the helm!**

S.S. Winnie

Mary-Ellis Bunim, executive producer: Replacing the Winnie with the S.S. WINNIE brought us some stunning visuals. And it was a very dramatic challenge for the cast, maybe more so than we were able to catch on tape, especially a couple of those weather situations where they were probably wondering if their own safety was on the line. **Captain Christian:** The cast started off strong, but after we had a couple moments of crisis, they became tentative, which is understandable. Actually, it was even more dangerous than they realized. Jake had been the most interested, but by the end, even he was expecting me to whisper to him what to do, and then he would tell the others. Learning to sail takes a lifetime. **Jake:** Our first problem on the boat was not our fault. We were just going across the bay on our first sail and suddenly there was this huge thud and the boat lurched—we'd hit some reef. Christian was shocked, he said it wasn't on the charts. **Gary Pennington, director:** I was really scared. I mean, I thought we were going down. **Kalle:** I screamed. I'm like "Oh, my God!" I was so scared. I had no idea what was going on. Everything was going haywire, and none of us knew what to do. **Jake:** I didn't really think it was that big a deal, but Vince was like, "I don't trust this guy! What does he really know? Anybody can just buy a boat. Are we going to entrust our lives to him?" He may have been overreacting, but it did get things off to a weird start.

VINCE'S JOURNAL

The *Road Rules* cast will go aboard a kick-ass boat for the next two weeks. I am so excited to get on that boat. We all must operate, maintain, and sail the boat, as well as cook our own meals. We are coming closer and closer to the end of this experience, and it saddens me. I love the cast and crew so much, and I will miss them when this is all over. I think I am the luckiest twenty-year-old male on the planet earth. I have joy attacks every five minutes. That is something I thought I would not find back home. I have so much more confidence now, and I know I can do anything I want.

CLUE

**TRAVEL
32
MILES**
MARTINIQUE TO
ST. LUCIA

NOW THAT YOU'VE BROUGHT US TOGETHER, HELP BRING US TOGETHER FOR REAL. COME TO ST. LUCIA AND HELP PLAN OUR WEDDING!

MISSION 10

Find a dress! Hire a band! Bring a cake! And don't make a mistake, because it's "'til death do us part" when ROAD RULES has to pull off a wedding!

Kalle: Jake saved us on that wedding. If we hadn't found that bridal place, I don't think we could have pulled that whole thing off in that short amount of time. **Jake:** I had been looking through the phone book under the various things we needed and kept seeing the name of Bridal Paradise. Erika was dead set against it. And it was kind of a dive, but that place totally hooked us up. They saved our asses. Erika also had another place in mind for the reception, but we wanted Pigeon Island. Then when everything went off so well, I kind of felt like she was quick to take credit for everything with the bride and groom.

HEARD RECEPTION-SIDE
JAKE: I GUESS THINGS WERE GOING TOO WELL. IT WAS EITHER UPSET THE BRIDE AND GROOM, OR MAKE ERIKA CRY. JUST ONE OF THOSE THINGS.

Jake and Erika's Last Straw

Vince: We had just pulled this mission off. We're celebrating and everything is going well. And out of nowhere, Jake just drills into Erika. I told him, "Jake, your timing was horrible! You should have done that when we were on a down." **Jake:** She was talking again about her latest ghost encounter, and I was thinking how the story had changed quite a bit. I was already angry with her, so I called her on it, but she got way more hurt than I ever wanted her to, or thought she would. I go to apologize to her later that night and she just bursts into tears and runs away. I was like, "Whoa!" And stuff was never quite the same with her. **Erika:** Even to this day, that really hurt my feelings. It seems to me that he didn't like me, and he loved to prove it. He loved to tell me in some way or another that he didn't like me. That night he saw that I was off-guard, and I was having a good time, and he was like, "Okay, this is where I'm gonna get her." The worst part is that I let him see how upset he made me. That's my fault. I hate that. But I learned something that night. I learned that Jake is not a friend of mine. Jake will never be a friend of mine, because friends do not treat people like that. And friends don't try and make you feel bad about yourself. One of these days, I think he's gonna see that. **Vince:** That night Erika and I talked by the pool, and it's one of the times I tried to go beyond being Neutral Man. I tried to explain to her that sometimes she does come across like she feels superior and does have to be right about everything. But I think Jake could be way too concerned with what other people said or did.

Oscar: I loved that band. That's the cutest band I've ever seen. They're like a hundred years old, like death itself, but they're playing. They were great.

Kalle: Cindy is the epitome of a blushing bride. She looked so beautiful.

TRAVEL
St. Lucia is the birthplace of Nobel Prize–winning author Derek Wolcott, as well as being host to a surprisingly raucous Carnival. St. Lucia is also one of the most popular departure spots for Caribbean sailing trips. The Moorings Company rents completely outfitted boats, with crew, out of Marigot Bay for anyone interested in sailing like the ROAD RULES cast.

I can't believe we pulled it off in that style with that budget, and in that amount of time! We pulled together like none other. They were so happy and lovey-dovey and totally sappy. THE BEST. The fun really began at our suite, which was a thank you to us from the bride and groom. That evening was a night of naked, crazy, unleashed, uncensored pandemonium. On the one hand, it was fun, and I was so caught up in the moment. But on the other hand, I really don't want my grandparents, etc. to see that on TV. Oh well . . . You're only young once. Hope I don't eat my words on that one.

Nude, Nude, Nude

Gary Pennington, director: They were rock stars that night. They were total Road Ruler rock stars. **Captain Christian:** They have this thing about running around naked. They say, "Christian, get your pants off." I'm not going to do that. After some time in the pool, they were all naked. **Jake:** Kalle took my underwear and threw it in a field. I was going to get them, but I wiped out, right in front of security. I start crawling away on all fours, and Vince thinks I'm doing it on purpose, like I was trying to be Neanderthal guy or something. He was dying. **Erika:** Kalle and I were in the shower washing our hair. It's a big shower—lord knows I'm not attracted to her. And the weird thing is, I had underwear on, and Kalle had a bra on, so together we made an almost full-dressed girl. Then Jake decides to come in, and I'm just like, "God!" He's naked, but I still need to condition, so I'm not leaving. Then Vince shows up saying, "I wanna come in!" I'm like, "The only way you can come in here is if you're totally naked!" But he starts getting insecure, saying he wants to keep his shorts on. And it's right about that moment it occurs to me the camera is right there. I'm like, "Hmm, maybe I should get out now." **Jake:** It was a little weird, 'cause Kalle was standing right there, and I couldn't be looking at the other girl. **Oscar:** There was a whole lot of nudity going on in that shower. I kept my undies on. And then in the living room, after the volcano clue where Vince and Christian got in a cake fight, we had a living room that ended up like chocolate. A chocolate-covered living room. You could eat off the chairs, off the walls.

VINCE AND OSCAR

VINCE: IN ST. LUCIA, I FINALLY HAD A TALK WITH OSCAR, AND I PROMISED HIM I WOULDN'T TALK BEHIND HIS BACK ANYMORE. I'D SAY IT RIGHT TO HIM IF I HAD A PROBLEM, AND HE PROMISED THE SAME THING. I JUST WISH I HAD SAID SOMETHING SOONER, BECAUSE I REALLY LIKE OSCAR A LOT. I THINK THE MORE WE DIDN'T TALK TO HIM AND LET STUFF EAT AT US, THE MORE WE KIND OF PUSHED HIM OUT OF THE GROUP. AND THE MORE HE DIDN'T REALLY CARE, THE MORE HE WOULD ACT IN WAYS THAT HE KNEW BOTHERED US.

THAT RUMBLING YOU HEAR ISN'T YOUR STOMACHS. IT'S THE SOUFRIÈRE VOLCANO. YOU'RE CAMPING INSIDE ITS CRATER TOMORROW NIGHT. COP A PLEA FOR HELP AT THE GEORGETOWN POLICE STATION.

CLUE

Kalle: We were having so much fun, being just crazy. It's times like that when you're like, "Oh, this is what being a kid's all about."

TRAVEL
72 MILES
ST. LUCIA TO
ST. VINCENT

MISSION 11

It's a brutal climb to the top, and a dangerous climb down into the crater! But how many people can say they spent the night INSIDE a live volcano!

KALLE'S JOURNAL That hike was hard. I guess just for bragging rights and the fact of saying that I did it, I'm glad I completed the hike and spent the night. It sucked losing my sleeping bag off the back of the *Lady Jane* yesterday and not having it to sleep in. The tents sucked and kept practically blowing in because it was windy on the crater floor. Jake and I tried to share his sleeping bag, but it didn't work too well. Too hot, too cold. Not enough room. Hard floor, no pillow. Oh, well. Something I'll remember for a *long* time. The view of the crater from the rim was spectacular—that'll be a redeeming aspect of the entire journey. The clouds moved so fast up there, and they came right at us. There also wasn't *any* sound. That was wild.

Jake's Love

Dear Kalle, I couldn't afford anything due to our situation and all, so I thought I'd write my very first love letter to you. I care so much for you. I can only hope some day you'll understand. Every day that goes by, I fall a little more in love with you. I never would have thought someone like you would be with a guy like me, but fate has brought us together, and if I have my way, nothing will ever draw us apart. I feel like I could stare into your eyes for days. You look into my soul, and I like to think you understand me in a way very few people do. We only have two weeks left, but I'm not scared because I think it's just the beginning, not the end. All my love, Jake
P.S. Happy Birthday. I love you. Don't ever forget it!

Vince: I'm so happy that Jake is head over heels for Kalle, but my big concern is that he holds back with her. He's never openly angry with her and always laughs at what she says. It just seems like he'll agree to whatever she says, which can be a problem when you start making major decisions about your life. Suddenly Jake was planning to move to New York, which is where Kalle already had an apartment.

Matt Sohn, camera operator: It rained so hard, and their tents weren't set up quite right. Things were drier outside the tents than in them. And that night, they were eating food straight out of the can. It was a festival of botulism.

VINCE'S JOURNAL

I am sleeping in the middle of a volcano. I never thought in a million years I would be in a volcano. The view is stunning here. Of course, I don't have my camera. We had a five-hour hike to get here, and it was brutal and dangerous. I'm not sure what we have to do here now, but I am having a great time. Oscar and I talked about our differences, and now I feel we are good friends. He is a great guy. It seemed like no one in the group wanted to give him a chance until now.

TRAVEL LOG
Next up for the cast is bestowing relationship advice to Grenada's youth. But
before all that, Jake's got some issues of
his own, and in the midst of a two-day
sail, there's a lot of time to reflect!

Letter

Mary-Ellis Bunim, executive producer: There was a period where Jake was wearing his heart on his sleeve. I'm very glad and relieved that he didn't get hurt. **Bruce Toms, director:** We were sailing and Jake was acting very moody. Something was obviously bothering him. But once again, Jake was telling me he was upset with something someone in production had done. **Jake:** I told Bruce that if I was this unhappy for a couple days at a time, I would want to go home. But I thought that if I could just spend a couple hours alone, I would just get over it. So, I'm up front crying, which — whoa! — I'm not at all comfortable doing. **Bruce Toms, director:** Jake was the most aware of how he wanted to be perceived, and he didn't want anyone to see him in that state. I tried to reassure him that we already had two months of wisecracking, man-with-all-the-answers Jake, but there is this vulnerable, confused side of him that people are going to want to know. It's what makes us human. But he wanted to create the situation the way he wanted it. Finally, I had to send a crew up there. **Jake:** I just flipped out on Bruce when the crew started taping. What I didn't realize was that like about two and a half hours had elapsed since I asked for time alone. I thought it had only been minutes. Whoops! **Bruce Toms, director:** Finally, Kalle went up to talk to him and he turned off his mike, which just isn't cool. So, I went and turned it back on again. Unfortunately, that's a situation where no one wins. Only Jake really knows what he was really feeling, but it seemed obvious he was feeling vulnerable about his future with Kalle.

Lamar Damon, story editor: It seemed like Jake and Kalle were in trouble. The closer

Jake on the Verge

they got to the end of the trip, the more the pressure was building. Here she is having to realize that she came into this trip wanting to be free and exactly the opposite happened; she was involved and he was going to follow her to New York. **Vince:** At that time, I asked Kalle if she thought she would have gotten together with Jake if it were under different circumstances, and she said no. But what she was saying — she didn't mean anything about the future, just the past. I mean, if Jake and I had just met on the street, we probably wouldn't be friends. We're totally different people. As for him leaving the show, I never would have let him do it. No way. **Kalle:** The only real difference in our feelings was that it wasn't my first time to feel this way, but it was Jake's. So he was feeling uncertain because it was new, and then he was just really, really scared that things would change between us when we were in New York without the show. But I wasn't worried. Jake has always said that if I want to date other people, or date him and other people, that that's okay, because he just wants me to be happy. So I was thinking that whatever happened in New York, it would be okay.

CLUE

THE CAST AND CREW ON JAKE

VINCE: Jake is a great friend. He's someone who will do anything for you. He'll carry your cross, whatever it takes. He's not just there when it's easy. And he says what's on his mind and is very honest. I love Jake.

OSCAR: When Jake goes for things, he goes all the way, and I think that's impressive. He also was whispering a lot on the trip, so another person couldn't hear, or the camera couldn't get something, and I didn't like that. Even if you aren't telling a secret about a person, it's not polite to whisper in front of them. If you have something to say, say it out loud. You're man enough to say what's on your mind, man enough to say it for the camera.

JONATHAN MURRAY, EXECUTIVE PRODUCER: Jake has an amazing ability to be caught up in being eighteen years old and making the mistakes that an eighteen-year-old makes, and at the same time be able to look at it, observe it, and comment on it. That's a really amazing quality for someone of that age. The danger of that, which I think did come out a little bit on the trip, is that he was very much aware of what was going on in production, but I think he was a risk worth taking.

KALLE: Jake has a side of him that enjoys being really loud and outgoing and very abrasive. He kind of revels in the fact that he's only eighteen and that excuses any behavior he wishes to have. But he really is one of the most sincere people I've ever met, and he's very, very caring. It's just that when you don't reveal a side of yourself like that, it starts to feel like a lie.

MARY-ELLIS BUNIM, EXECUTIVE PRODUCER: Jake is someone who has never wanted for the creature comforts, so he expects everything to be given to him. I had the sense that, no matter what was given to him, whether it be accommodations, or money, or the mission itself, it was never enough for Jake. So his first instinct often was to complain. As the trip went on, I think the situation improved a bit as the others encouraged him to let go of that side of himself and enjoy the ride. Jake is a very intelligent, very funny young man, and the more he learns to see the positive in life, the happier he is going to be.

BRUCE TOMS, DIRECTOR: I was a little gun-shy after Europe, and as the Islands trip began, I began to worry that Jake was going to be another Antoine and treat the crew like his enemy. His first interview was painful, he kept wanting to re-answer questions, trying to get it right. But my Antoine fears were groundless. He was simply dealing with the puppy-dog enthusiasm of an eighteen-year-old who is suddenly surrounded by cameras and not really sure how to react. Doing the show requires a lot of trust and confidence, in the crew and yourself, and Jake came a long way.

ERIKA: I've had some very good times with Jake—there have been times when I really liked him, and there was a time when I thought we were heading toward friendship. But at a certain point, I started to feel like he was insisting on letting me know that he disliked me, which is too bad, because I felt like he made a judgment on me without really getting to know me.

Jake: Somehow during this trip, I stopped telling people how excited and happy I was about things, and I became all about the negative, which was not a good thing. I don't know where that came from, but I'm glad I realized it and snapped out of it.

There were days when my insecurities came out hard-core. I have so many insecurities you couldn't fit them all in the ocean. Piles and piles and piles. I have islands of insecurities. And when one comes, they all come, and boom, there they are. And the next thing I know, I'm feeling like I'm not part of the group, and I don't fit in, and I'm not an attractive person, and I'm not intelligent, and I don't have initiative, and everyone's laughing at me. Then I get angry and feel sorry for myself and feel sad. Now I feel like there's at least a piece of me that knows that it's going to end if I can just sit it out, deal with it, be alone, let it out. Do what I have to do.

The best thing I'm taking away, though, is how I deal with intimacy. That has not been my strength in the past. I don't even think I knew what it was. But with my relationship with Kalle and my relationship with Vince, I have been able to open myself up in a way that I haven't with most other people.

FROM THE DESK OF JAKE'S PARENTS

We've noticed wonderful changes in Jake since his trip. His vision of himself and his potential is greater, and his understanding of what it takes to make his dreams a reality is more focused. If it were possible, he's become even more outgoing. He seems to have a new sense of purpose and follow-through when he wants something and has learned all sorts of new communication skills. His relationship with Kalle has taken him beyond himself; it has been good to see!

Finally, he seems ready for college—we think the ROAD RULES experience played a large part in helping him understand the value of an education.

We can't wait for the show to air and are wondering what the "instant fame" might be like for Jake and the others. Jake has told us that we may not like some of the things that we will see, but at this point, we think nothing can surprise us about him.

MISSION 12

Testing one, two, three—the microphones are on and the islands are listening! Bestow advice as best you can when LOVE RULES goes on the air!

Jonathan Murray, executive producer: We found a new line to cross in Grenada. We crossed the cultural line. I guess the nature of some of the questions and answers was a little too much for some of the listeners of that radio station. They were used to much tamer fare. **Jake:** Before the show, we were talking to Troy, the station manager, about what would be inappropriate in terms of music. There's a line in a Jodeci song that uses the word freakin'. He says that's way inappropriate. And this is before we go on the air, and I thought, "Oh, boy, is he in for a surprise!" **Oscar:** That was crazy. We're all going off about AIDS, and oral sex, and abortion. People are like freaking out and calling the cops, the fire department. Troy was racing in and out, saying, "No, no, no, no . . ." We were like, "Hey, man. You had no idea what you were getting your-self into." We tried. We did. We really tried, so if we offended anyone, we didn't really mean to. That was a funny night. **Troy:** If I did it again, I wouldn't take it for granted that just because they are twenty years old, they are going to be mature. Radio in Grenada is something seri-ous and productive, whereas in the United States it is more about en-tertainment. They needed to be well versed in other cultures, but they mostly wanted to talk about themselves. Of course, the link up with Adam, the host of MTV's LOVELINE, in L.A., was the biggest problem. There are certain subjects we don't discuss openly here. **Erika:** I've grown up listening to LOVELINE, so I couldn't believe it when they called in. They did say some pretty rude things about Grenada, and I have to admit I laughed, but it was not cool as far as Grenada goes. Knowing the show, I know that's just the way Adam is. He doesn't hold back, but it didn't mix well down there. He was giving us advice about dealing with sexual tension among the members of our group.

ADAM'S WORDS
My advice to you all is "masturba-tion." It's your only hope. Really. Un-less there's constant masturbation by the entire cast—and crew . . . unless you do that, it's going to be one big Roman orgy.

DR. DREW'S WORDS
My advice to you guys: don't get romantically involved. Because the kinds of experiences you guys share together, the kinds of rela-tionships—the quality of relation-ships both among members of the group, individuals within the group, are such that if you let intimacy sort of creep in, it's going to get very chaotic . . . I'm just saying that if you're gonna get the most out of these relation-ships, it's best that you don't let intimacy—physical inti-macy particularly—come into this. Because it just adds a level of intensity that's not what this is all about.

Vince: We left the radio station feeling like the whole island wanted to lynch us. We got to a bar to get some food. We're just trying to keep a low profile. But on the television, there's some American comedy special on and this comedian is making jokes about the U.S. invasion of Grenada—and we're the only Americans in the place. Oh, my God! I was just waiting for the knife to go into my ribs. We're all looking around, and then Gary's like, "I think we should go now." And it got worse! We run out to our cab, and our cab driver had a huge beer in his hand. I asked him, "Are you drunk?" And he said he wasn't. Then he was peeing for like an hour by the side of his van. But we were so tired, we just got in. He takes off at warp speed. I'm like, "Sir, can you slow down?" He was seriously like flying. At the hotel, we think he's charging us too much, so we try and talk him down, telling him there should be a drunk-driver reduction. I thought he and Oscar were gonna get in a fistfight. Oscar's like, "You endangered our lives!" I felt like, "Oh, here they go!" There's something about being in those islands that just brings out the craziest moments.

Jake and Gary Miscommunicate

Gary Pennington, director: I told Jake we had all this footage of him and Kalle living together. A young couple, sleeping together in the same bed, snuggling, but then during the day it's like denial. And I just wanted to make sure they knew that was how it was coming off. **Jake:** I was telling Gary that we just didn't feel comfortable, and then I got what I thought was a great idea. I was like, "Why don't you set up a tripod in our hotel room." I'm like, "Set up a tripod and some lighting, so it's like mood lights, and we could turn it on and off whenever we want." But when I told Kalle, she just flipped out! It didn't even occur to me how it was going to look. **Gary Pennington, director:** She's like, "A camera in our room! What do you wanna make, a porno?" And I started to think, "Yeah, Jake. What do you want to make?" I'm envisioning when I give him this camera they'll turn it on for some nice, intimate, great dialogue, stuff that we're not getting. And lying in bed, and "I love you." "I love you." "What are you gonna do after the show?" I'm thinking, "What have I done?" I told Kalle, "Sorry, you're right, dumb idea."

TRAVEL
Referred to as "the island of spice and nice" by the locals, Grenada, of all the islands the Road Rulers traveled to, is the least visited by tourists; but it is no less beautiful. Visitors who feel like going native should make a reservation at Mama's for authentic local cooking, served family style (though it's not a good bet for vegetarians or the gastronomically timid), while those with a case of homesickness can party with Grenada's famous American medical students. They hold a well-attended talent show every Saturday night. Call the medical school for details.

The past few days have been very hard for me. I finally got in touch with Kim after about two and a half weeks. I was going to tell her how much I missed her, and that being with her again when I get back is my favorite thought. But Kim told me she is seeing another guy. When I heard her say that, I felt like a trillion maggots were munching on my stomach and heart; it was awful to hear her say those words.

I could not wait to get back home and start over with her. I really felt that things would be like a Hollywood love story. Instead, it is a pain I am all too familiar with. I don't know what will happen, and I am scared, but like many other times in my life, I will pull through with or without Kim. She feels I have betrayed her because she found a letter I wrote to another girl across the country. Kim did not really find the letter. She searched my room until she found it. I need more time to think about what has happened and what I want to do.

Kim Dumps Vince

Kalle: Well, the deal with that was that Vince didn't want to talk about it, because he was worried that the letter could get someone back in Los Angeles in trouble, because it was written to one of the people who interviewed him for ROAD RULES. **Vince:** I told Kim, I said, "This girl and I, we talked. And I've never really talked to someone like that in my life. I just met her once, and I ended up sharing a lot about myself to her. We just talked, and I never really connected with someone like that right off the bat, ever in my life." But Kim is really jealous. She said, "I'd rather have you sleep with twenty girls than share an emotional connection with another girl." **Kalle:** It came out later that she was already dating this other guy before she found the letter. The way it seemed at first was that she was seeing this other guy out of revenge. I only know Vince's side, but he's such a hurting little boy inside that it was really hard to see that happen to him. **Michelle Millard, casting:** Okay, this is what happened. Vince sent me a letter that was very effusive. I was very moved by that meeting with Vince. I was very affected by his story. And I didn't want him to think that I was just like in job mode. But his letter was a little too much. I felt like he was looking to me for the answers to his life. I was flustered. So I sent him a letter back, telling him that I think he's an amazing person, but that's not what this experience is all about. This is about Vince discovering things about himself. And I told him to just have an amazing trip. That was the end of our correspondence.

Kalle's Letter to Brian

Dear Brian,

I'm writing you this letter for many reasons. First, I don't think that I could effectively communicate what's going on in my head and my life now over the phone. Plus, it would just end up ugly. I know it. Second, I'm hoping that in this letter, I can tell you everything about how I feel in the order of importance it is in my mind, without interruption or guilt trips. Lastly, maybe I'm just a little chicken, but I want to tell you all of how I feel and what I think—and it'll be easier for me to put it in writing than say it to your face. I know how spineless you already think I am, so maybe the fact that I'm writing you a letter won't come as a surprise. Who knows.

Before I tell you about my trip, I want you to know that I do love you as a person and will care for you always. We've practically grown up together, and I feel like I'm a part of your family as well. That is such an important piece of who I am and how I've survived the last year and a half. You know how much it means to me that you were such a support after my mom died. Nobody can ever take that away from me. But this isn't about what was.

You know that I came on this trip to have my own time, spread my wings, have my own space, to be Kalle, to find out who I am. After leaving, I realized that I wanted to reassure myself that I wasn't one of those people who always needed to be in a relationship. I wanted to find out that I could stand on my own, survive by myself. I wanted to find that I was as strong as I see myself.

I brought all of this to the trip, and I had no intention of having a relationship with anyone while I was gone. But I've grown to care very much for one of the guys on our trip. I think it's fair that I tell you, because you'd find out sooner or later.

This hasn't been an easy issue for me to deal with, though. I've been dealing with a lot of guilt surrounding the whole situation. But I really don't know why. It's not like this is a betrayal of your trust, because we talked about it before I left.

Maybe most of it comes from knowing how bad all this will hurt you. I don't want to hurt you, but I do want to be happy. I've felt happier and more free on this trip than I ever have before, and it feels good. Too good.

Kalle

TRAVEL
2133
MILES
GRENADA TO
NEW YORK

THE CAST AND CREW ON VINCE

MARY-ELLIS BUNIM, EXECUTIVE PRODUCER: Vince has the most amazing eyes. Beautiful eyes. Some people allow you to see through their eyes, and some people don't. Vince does. And so much of what he is feeling always projects, plays right there. But with Vince, I think we just began to scratch the surface, so he is someone I wish we'd had more time with; he is going to change and grow so much in the next few years. That really is what this show is about, that transition to independence.

RICK DE OLIVEIRA, PRODUCER: So much of what will happen to Vince depends on his ability to let go of that nest. When you grow up with a lot of privileges, the question becomes, are you going to be able to take advantage of them?

OSCAR: Vince is a very creative guy who has rich blood—he's Italian, which is a great culture. He is my friend, and I hope we are always friends, but it did upset me that he changed toward me. He apologized late in the trip, but I hope he understands that it's a two-way street, and it's not totally easy for me on my side to erase all that time he wasn't being straight with me.

JAKE: It's kind of amazing how completely Vince and I wrote each other off at the beginning of the trip, because we grew to be so close. No matter what happens, Vince is someone I will be friends with for the rest of my life.

ERIKA: One of my goals for this trip was really to just laugh and have fun, and good lord, Vince made me laugh. And there were some times I really needed it. He's just so funny, and we had so much fun together. I know he has some regrets about staying in the middle and not stating his feelings, but I don't think he should feel bad. Vince is just a great guy.

KALLE: When Vince and Jake first came to pick me up in Colorado, my friends thought for sure that Vince and I would hook up. But what is so great is that he is really one of my first true platonic male friends. I miss him so much. My first impression, though, was so different. He just seemed to think he was so cool and aloof, but that totally changed. The real Vince is so different from the person you first meet. He just has such a good heart and such a beautiful smile. He has had a lot of pain in his life, though, which I think makes it hard for him to get perspective on his life, concentrate on what he does have. It keeps him kind of wild and unsettled inside.

JONATHAN MURRAY, EXECUTIVE PRODUCER: I think over the years, Vince has learned to distance himself as a means of protection. And I hope he feels that as the trip progressed, he was able to give some of that up and allow himself to get caught up in people emotionally. And maybe get hurt, but still feel one hundred percent. Those blocks may keep him from feeling emotional pain, but they also keep him from experiencing life to the fullest. It's difficult, but you can't feel the highs without letting in the lows.

Vince: This was the first time I was totally by myself in my entire life, and a big part of me just wanted to have fun and not think about anything else. But as the trip went along, I had to start confronting things, and in the process, I think I was able to accept myself so much more. I don't always need to solve everything by making people laugh, and it's okay that there's a side of me that isn't always together, and I don't have to be afraid of my emotions. In the past, I've felt guilty for having a dark side, for liking dark movies and dark music. That's just part of who I am. But it was so hard to see that. For a while I would call home and say, "Mom, they're probing me in these interviews. It's getting really hard . . ." I was so afraid. And then at a certain point, my eyes just opened, and I realized that everyone has different sides to their personality, some that scare them a little. The trip helped me say, "F**k it! I'm twenty years old. I'm a man now. I can't be afraid of consequences."

FROM THE DESK OF VINCE'S MOM

From the moment Vince walked and talked, I knew that he would always march to the beat of his own drum. Those qualities that made him stand out in a crowd—tenderness, honesty, shyness coupled with extreme daring and physical courage—made him, then and now, an outstanding youth. This is not just his mother talking! These very qualities of daring and courage, along with an outrageous sense of humor, probably led him to be chosen as a Road Ruler.

Now that it's over, Vince has basically remained the same unassuming guy but he has also changed. He is more mature and more patient and more tolerant of others. And

while I would love to shout to everyone I come into contact with that he is a Road Ruler, he stops me all the time and is very embarrassed if I try to talk about it with people who may not know. Knowing Vince the way that his sister and I do, we're fully prepared for some real shenanigans and are really looking forward to seeing the show. Vince has pretty much told us what to expect, but I'm sure we're in for some surprises and, who knows, even shocks. It wouldn't be the first time for me. Vince has pulled a few stunts without my knowing (such as skydiving) only to tell me later. He is quite a guy, and we love him deeply.

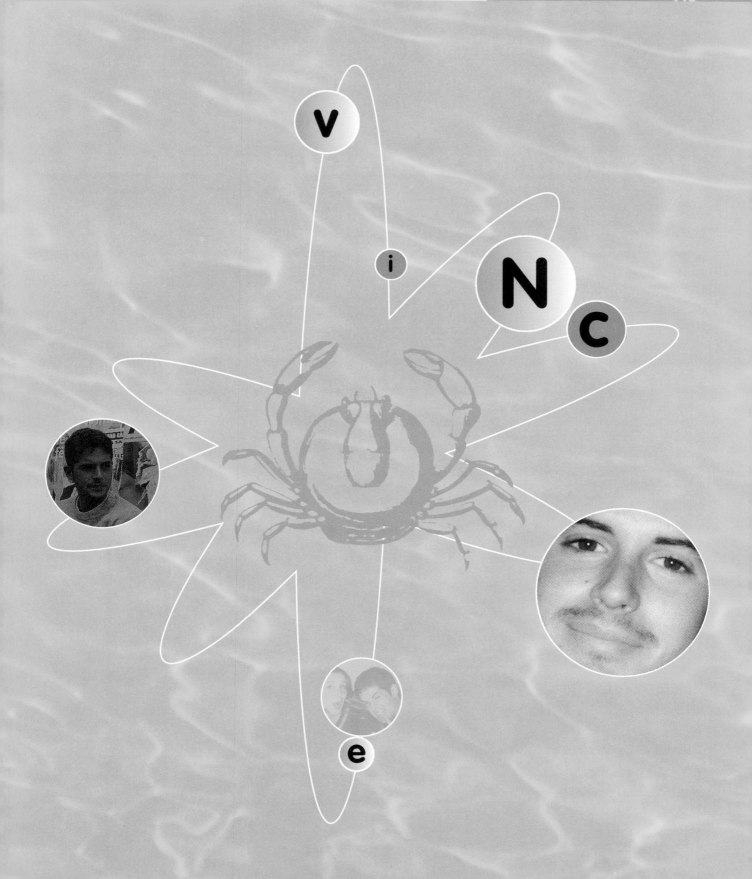

MISSION 13

We would like to try you out before the draft.
Meet me Monday at 9:30 A.M. at Madison Square Garden.
Don't drop the ball. Sincerely, Coach Pope.

Heard Madison Square Garden–side

Mary-Ellis Bunim, executive producer: I went to scout a game before the mission. I guess I had seen the dancers before, but I don't think I'd paid any attention to the difficulty of the routines. And when I saw them, saw how professional they were, how complicated the dance was, I thought, "These poor kids. How are they going to be able to do this?" I was hoping that at least one could pull off at least part of a routine. **Kalle:** I could see how people would think that this mission would look good on TV, but I felt like it was almost an insult to these women. It's their profession, and they've been dancing for ten years. And to think that we could suddenly bust out and move like them . . . it seemed wrong. **Erika:** Kalle was crying a couple of times. There was one dancer who wasn't very nice. She comes up to Kalle, and she's like, "You know, if you would really try, you would get it." And Kalle gave her one of those looks. I thought, "Girl, you better get away from her, because she's gonna kick your butt." **Jake:** It's ironic that this is the first mission where I had kind of a new attitude, I wasn't going to complain and was just going to let it happen, and somehow I enjoyed it, while everyone else hated it. **Clay Newbill, supervising producer:** Jake was actually a lot closer than he thought. Petra was considering having him try out with Erika. But I was a bit disappointed with Vince, because he just seemed to quit. **Vince:** I stayed there for a couple of hours, and I tried to have fun with it. But I had a lot on my mind, and my sense of humor was stretched pretty thin at that point. So when the dancers started trying to psyche me up to do something I think is kind of degrading, that was it. I was out of there. **Oscar:** I didn't understand that. How many days do you get to spend with the New York Knicks dancers!?! Vince was like, "I'm not gonna make a fool out of myself dancing." I don't know. I was in heaven! They were gorgeous.

TRIVIA
Though she had never been to New York before, Kalle and some friends from home had already rented an apartment in NYC.

TRAVEL
What can be said about the mother of all islands—Manhattan has it all. While in the city that never sleeps, the Road Rulers made the Banana Bungalow hostel on the Upper West Side their base. Banana Bungalow is not only affordable, but staying there is a good way to meet young European travelers. For late-night carousing, the cast went dancing at the Tunnel.

Clay Newbill, supervising producer: In four seasons, we've never so completely misjudged the difficulty of a mission. To do as well as Erika did says so much about her. **Mary-Ellis Bunim, executive producer:** To be honest, I thought after Erika had worked so hard, and gotten so close, that they would just give it to her. But they didn't, and I'd much rather things go that way and be real than have the show be predictable. The way it worked out, I think the audience will love Erika and get to see what she was about. She just worked so very, very hard. And she did such a great job. **Jonathan Murray, executive producer:** We had not anticipated how hard this mission would be, but the unexpected can be so much more interesting than the expected. The way it worked out, Erika had to confront this question of success and failure, which is a central issue in her life right now. **Erika:** I do hate to fail at anything, so I'll work and work and work at it, but that dance, no way. I mean, it was obvious I wasn't going to make it, but I still charged ahead. So when Petra told me what I expected, that I had not made it, I headed straight for the bathroom and lost it. Poor Bruce had to deal with me. **Bruce Toms, director:** Erika was devastated. She was hysterical, and she wanted to break down in private. I told her that I totally understood her feelings, but I wanted her to know that far from feeling like a failure, she should be extremely proud of herself. She took it as far as just about any nonprofessional could. **Vince:** I can be a perfectionist about things too, but I need to care about the thing I'm doing. It seems like Erika's struggle is that she's a perfectionist about everything. Once she starts something, she's going to succeed, or die trying, which seems like a hard way to live life.

Erika's Wild Side

Bruce Toms, director: During auditions, we'd gotten a sense that Erika has this wild, fiery side, and it's unfortunate that the way things worked out with the group, with her often having to feel she needed to be the mature one, we didn't get to see much of this other Erika. We did hear about one night in a strip club, but our cameras weren't allowed in. **Erika:** Vince's cousin Richard took us to the strip club. It was so funny. At one point, this woman with these really big breasts was dancing on Vince, and she just shakes them right in his face. And Vince is kind of a shy guy anyway, so he just looks at me, like, "Help!" Then I look over at Oscar, and he's got this Big Daddy smile on his face. Oh, my God! Then Richard ordered me a lap dance. So she's dancing, and we're talking and laughing, because it really was a joke—I have no interest in women that way. But then I look over at the guys, and they're not laughing. Their jaws are practically in their laps. Richard said, "You're getting the rest of the lap dances for the rest of the night." I said, "No, no, no. I don't think so." Vince said, "Seeing you with that stripper just…that was awesome!" I'm like, "Please. You guys!" **Oscar:** That was interesting. Very, very interesting! I'm just glad I was there. I had front-row tickets to see something. I think Vince and I shared the same opinion. It was interesting. That's all I'm saying.

Erika: I worked really hard, but you can't get talent in twenty-four hours.

MISSIONS 1415

Lights! Camera! Action! Act like a waiter!
Three Road Rulers get their breaks on the little screen, while the other two get to spend the day as personal assistants to some daytime stars!

Vince: Oscar, Erika and I got picked to be extras on ALL MY CHILDREN. We were just kind of waiters in the background, but Oscar got the big break. He actually had a line. **Oscar:** I was so happy to be picked, and then to even get a line. I got to say "Sir?" and then "Thank you." I couldn't believe it. My mom, she'll be so proud of me. She's an actress. **Erika:** Poor Vince, he's kind of a pretty boy, so with makeup he looked like a mannequin. The makeup person had to kind of color in his whiskers so he would look more real. **Jake:** Just when I was thinking I was going to get discovered, that casting woman told me I didn't have the look. Whoa, did that hurt my feelings. I got slammed hard-core. I mean, I can't act well enough to be the waiter?!

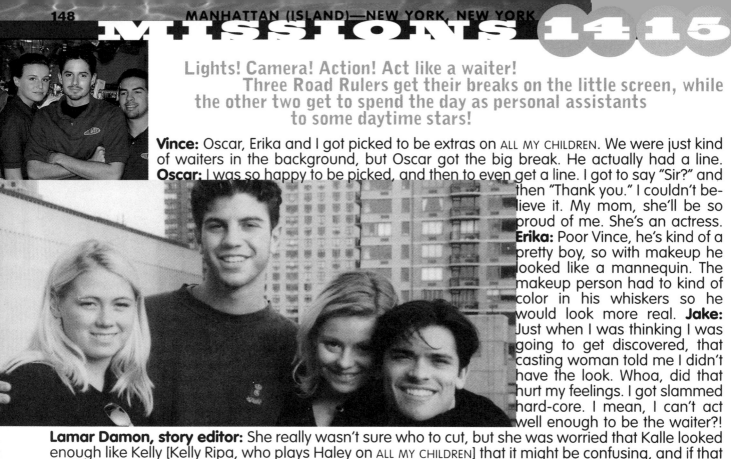

Lamar Damon, story editor: She really wasn't sure who to cut, but she was worried that Kalle looked enough like Kelly [Kelly Ripa, who plays Haley on ALL MY CHILDREN] that it might be confusing, and if that was the case, it made a lot of sense that she cut Jake as well. Here are Mark [Consuelos] and Kelly, who met on this soap, and Jake and Kalle, who met on ROAD RULES, who are going to work with them. Those couples were parallel universes, and it ended up significantly affecting Kalle. Coming into New York, she'd been having these doubts and second thoughts about her relationship, when along come Kelly and Mark. **Kalle:** Kelly and Mark met on their show, and Kelly really thought it was fate. She told us that she believes in fate, and that they are very, very happy. And it seemed like fate that we would get to meet them. I believe in fate and destiny too, so it does seem to me that there's a reason that out of fifteen thousand people, Jake and I were picked to be on ROAD RULES and spend ten weeks together at this point in our lives.

Kalle's Love Letter

Jake

From the second that you asked if you could take a picture of my bathroom for your bathroom book, I knew we'd get along. I've always liked your style. I was so relieved that there was someone who I instantly bonded with. When you said you'd leave the Coast Guard boat the second night, I thought I'd cry. Even then I already knew—whether we were always close friends or ever became lovers, I was drawn to you. Because of that, you've played a major part in such a monumental time in my life. Everything is changing for me now, and you're one of the few constants. You'll never know how good that feels. I always think about the millions of kids in the world and the thousands who we were chosen from to be here. There's a reason it was us and that we met this way. You've confirmed my belief in destiny, Jake. I'm not in a position to say what will happen in the future, but I can tell you this now—I love you with all of my heart. You are such a beautiful person, and I feel so lucky to have shared this entire experience with you. Thank you for letting me in and sharing your world. Love, Kalle

Erika: I don't mean to be mean, but all that happens is that they say "action" and everyone gets a funny look on their face, then it's "cut" and everyone goes back to drinking coffee. What's the big deal?

TRIVIA
Jake began the trip by snapping pictures of every bathroom he encountered along the journey with the intention of publishing his bathroom book at the end of the show.

WALK THROUGH FIRE TO GET YOUR HANDSOME REWARD. MEET RICH AT BATTERY PARK AT 2:00 P.M.

TRAVEL LOG

They've laughed, cried, fought and loved, but with the big-boned lady warming up to sing, there's only one last mission between the cast and the answer to that final mystery—just what is the handsome reward?

Making goals! Breaking boards! Walking on hot coals! One last test before claiming the handsome reward!

Final Test and a Handsome Reward

Vince: At first I was really skeptical of all that positive-think stuff, but after awhile I just sat back and started listening and some of it started making sense to me, the whole positive thinking and the visualization of what you're going to do, because we do that in karate, and it does work. But Kalle wasn't into it at all, so I thought, if she doesn't get into it, she's going to burn her feet on that fire walk. **Kalle:** The guy leading the training, I felt like he was pushing something on me that I didn't feel, so I was kind of irritated and was giving him a hard time. It's not that I don't believe in the power of our minds and positive thinking, it just felt like we were in the middle of this Tony Robbins seminar. **Oscar:** It was my turn to walk the coals. I was supposed to think about cool moss, so my feet wouldn't burn, and everyone was supposed to chant, "cool moss," but instead they started to scream "Puerto Rico, Puerto Rico." Oh, that really got me fired up! So, I'm like, "That's it. It's about my country now. I don't care if I burn my feet!"

Handsome Reward

Jonathan Murray, executive producer: One of the things that has bothered me personally with ROAD RULES and THE REAL WORLD is that people take off a semester of school to do the shows, and I think sometimes they have gotten a little starstruck and not gone back to school. Semester at Sea seemed like a great idea because it would encourage them to stay in school, or to finish school. And with this group, four of them are really only at the beginning of their college careers. **Mary-Ellis Bunim, executive producer:** Psychologically I think it's tough, after ten weeks of a trip, to be told that your handsome reward is going to be a trip. The last thing you want to do is live out of a suitcase. All they want at that point is to sleep in their own beds and resume some semblance of normal life. So, they may not first react with the most excitement, but after they have been back for a little while and it sinks in just what a big deal it is, what a real growth opportunity it is, they'll be thrilled. They'll realize that what we have given them is a chance to have a second life-altering experience. **Jake:** Erika was so bummed about the handsome reward, which kind of brought all our reactions down, and I have to admit, I was kind of hoping it would be something I could sell, but really, it's an amazing prize. I mean, I seriously had asked my parents if I could go on that someday, and they were like, "Are you kidding? Do you know how expensive that is?" So, I couldn't be more psyched. **Oscar:** I can't think of a better prize than the Semester at Sea reward we got. I couldn't. One of my goals was to get to travel around the world as much as I could . . . Of course, I could have gotten a candy bar for a reward, and I would still be satisfied. We had a ten-week dream come true.

No Lights, No Cameras,

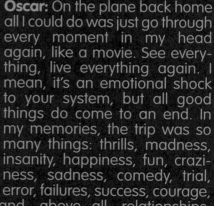

Kalle: I had major withdrawal when the trip ended. I wasn't ready to go home. And I didn't want to deal with all the stuff I had to do. Ugh, it was terrible. I'm a lot like Jake in that I never like to be alone. So this experience was my biggest fantasy. I like constant stimulation, twenty-four hours a day. And it was like a ten-week slumber party. I loved it! The last couple of years, I grew up really fast and had a lot of responsibilities, and I was always worried about everything. So it was just like a gift to have this time when I didn't have to worry about anything. Everything was so perfect. And all of a sudden, within ten minutes, I was on a plane, alone. And the last times I had been on a plane, over the last ten weeks, there had been all these people around me, there was all this commotion. The whole world stopped for me. And I just sat there by myself. And I just cried. Then I got off the plane, and I was just a normal person. It was really hard. The trip, it's such a dream world. Especially where we were, it was all so romantic.

Back in Fort Collins, I saw Brian and he really surprised me. He told me that he cares for me and he wants to be my friend, which is great, but it's also hard just because of what we were, it's hard to just go right to some intense friendship. It's another good reason for my move to New York. That was all really hard, though. I did the show for me, but I did a lot of worrying about it hurting Brian or his family. I never wanted that to happen.

In New York, things have been great. I got into the college I wanted to go to and Jake's here. We even got jobs working at the same place. We're really happy. I was so nervous to move here, just this little kid from Colorado standing beneath all these tall buildings, but I think everything's going to be great. I mean, I'm not as naive and as country as a lot of people think I am.

Erika: I was so happy to go home! I was so happy to go home! Everyone else was sad. They were like, "Ohh, I don't want to go home. I'd do another ten weeks if they'd ask me!" And I was like, "I can't wait to go home! I'm gonna go home, I'm gonna sleep in my own bed, I'm going to go out to dinner with my boyfriend, I'm going to drink wine. Just the fact that I'm gonna cook again. I love coming home. I had a great, great, great experience. But I missed my life, and I was ready for the trip to be over. About two weeks before the end of the trip, I was just kind of ready to get going with my life and go home. It was great, but I'd have to say that coming home was just awesome. Now I just want to spend time with my boyfriend and do some thinking about what I want to do with this next stage of my life.

Oscar: On the plane back home all I could do was just go through every moment in my head again, like a movie. See everything, live everything again. I mean, it's an emotional shock to your system, but all good things do come to an end. In my memories, the trip was so many things: thrills, madness, insanity, happiness, fun, craziness, sadness, comedy, trial, error, failures, success, courage, heart, and, above all, relationships. There was a period after I got home where I was feeling bitterness about those relationships. But I have to apologize for that. I'm always saying I don't

No Action

Vince: It's kinda weird. It's like going two hundred miles an hour to zero when you come home. I mean, the trip was constant excitement, and you always have stuff to do. And then, I got home, and it was just kind of like, out of warp speed. And I felt as if, "Oh, what do I do now?" And it was hard. I wanted to relax a little bit, but now it's just like, "Where's the action?" It's kind of hard coming down from all that.

When I talk to them now, it's almost really sad, because I miss them so much. I've always liked to be alone every now and then. Now, when I'm all by myself, it's like I kind of feel lonely. It's like, where's Jake making noise? Where's Kalle giggling? Stuff like that. I miss them. You kind of realize how close we all were. We really did get along well.

Jake: Leaving the show, I actually felt scared of the real world, which is ironic, because in the beginning I was so scared of the show. But the trip was just so great, something I'll remember for a lifetime. And as odd as it sounds, I think being on the show somehow grounded me some. It kinda brought me down and humanized me—which is a total surprise. I didn't expect to be changed this way going into it. It's just amazing how this experience has thrown my life into such a completely new direction. It gave it this whole new shape and form. Now I am going to a great college, which I didn't think I was ready for before. I'm going to do Semester at Sea. I moved to New York. And best of all, I'm with Kalle.

I was really happy to see my friends when I got back, but I don't always feel like I can talk to them about the trip. I'll hold back sometimes from telling a story, because I don't want to make it seem like that's all I talk about now. And at times, when I do talk about it, I can feel them getting uncomfortable, in a jealous way. That makes me miss the others that much more.

Things are better with my mom, though. Now we share a lot of things, at least me with her, that I would usually never tell her. I just didn't feel comfortable in the past. I just feel much more—I'm being much more honest with her now. Maybe that's why she finally sees that I'm ready to leave.

As for Kim, the night I got home, I went to talk to her, and she dumped me. The night I got home! I went to her house, and I was totally willing to start over, but she was like, "I think we're done." Ow. It sucked! Really bad. For like three or four days, I was trying to hold it in, like I didn't care, or whatever. But then, I broke down one day, and I just called her and now we've agreed to start over. We're taking it really, really slow.

like to hold grudges, but I was. I had a grudge about how I was treated for the first part, first half of the trip, but in the end we did become friends, we did get close. It's amazing, but true, so I want to clear that up. I want to let go of those feelings, because things did work out. I miss them. I miss the life we lived together, but it's also good to be home. I love my country. I guess everyone knows that now.

One thing that scares me is that I feel like the longer I stay here, the less motivated I'm getting. I went on this amazing trip, and now I'm all fired up, and I know what I want to do. And I have the courage to do it. And the longer I wait to do it, the more scary it seems to move out to Los Angeles and pursue what I want to be doing.

Those ten weeks were probably the happiest weeks of my life. It's just like, everything made sense to me, and I just felt so confident. I just felt so secure about myself, and I was just so happy. I just hope I don't lose that now that the show's over.

*Mission: Create a spin-off of MTV's hit show, **The Real World**!*

This is **Road Rules!**

*"Something Tells Me
We're Not in **The Real World** Anymore..."*

Mary-Ellis Bunim
executive producer

Mary-Ellis Bunim, EXECUTIVE PRODUCER:
It was actually the first episode of the second season of *The Real World* that inspired the creation of *Road Rules*. We kicked off that season with a road trip: Tami and Dominic picked up Jon in Kentucky, and the three of them traveled cross-country in a Winnebago. They were clearly affected by the smallness of the space—it was like a pressure cooker—and they found every reason to conflict with each other!

Jonathan Murray, EXECUTIVE PRODUCER: MTV was looking for a road show, so we elaborated on the REAL WORLD concept by adding a series of missions. Some are high adrenaline, some require a lot of skill, some are geared toward the phobias of participants—which is not to say we try to ambush cast members, we simply challenge them!

The Road to **Road Rules**

Mary-Ellis: We had just finished casting *The Real World* San Francisco, and we'd seen thousands of great people. We asked five of the people who didn't make it to the final cast to participate in the pilot episode, which brought them to Catalina Island for a weekend of adventures. The only one to make it into the first season's cast was Mark.

Jonathan: Believe it or not, Kit was not Mark's first on-screen romance, and during the pilot he even had a bit of a love triangle going on. We said, "Boy, this Mark's sure got potential!"

Love on the Road

Mary-Ellis: Mark was great. He and Kit proved to us that while the missions are appealing, television is about people. During the Europe season, we got glimpses into Chris that were so amazing. They'll really help teach young women in our audience how men think. He's sort of a fantasy guy. When men open up that sensitively, and really share their feelings, you can't help but respond.

Jonathan: We've been incredibly lucky as far as romance is concerned. People are always asking us if we go into the casting process looking for people who will hook up. It's not true! But, it turns out that we're really great matchmakers—if only by default

Mary-Ellis: Like my first contact with Devin and Emily from Season Two. It was the casting semifinals. First, Devin, this adorable young African-American guy with dreads, appeared. He really impressed me with how smart and open he was. And then, a few interviews later, came Emily from a little farming town in Illinois. She'd been surrounded by rednecks all of her life and had never had a conversation with a black person. I couldn't stop myself from thinking: "Oh my gosh! What if these two people meet?" I had no doubt that he was going to be attracted to her, and how could anyone not be attracted to him? That doesn't mean I knew they were going to get together. All I knew was that her life would never be the same.

About Bunim/Murray Productions

Headed by veteran soap opera producer Mary-Ellis Bunim and documentarian Jonathan Murray, Bunim/Murray Productions is currently at work on the seventh season of THE REAL WORLD and the sixth season of ROAD RULES. They are in development on a Miami-based serialized drama entitled AGE OF CONSENT, and a prime time show they imported from England called WANTED: a game show meets psychological thriller.

Jonathan: What we look for is potential chemistry. It doesn't have to be romantic. Like Christian and Timmy from Season Two. Sometimes two people just jive. It happened in THE REAL WORLD Los Angeles with Dominic and Aaron. Two people from different worlds come together, and they click.

Really, though, who can predict that chemistry? Who would have thought Belou would have gone for Antoine, the exact opposite of her boyfriend at home? And Kalle and Jake; obviously, Jake was going to be interested in any female on the trip, but who would have known that Kalle would respond!

Mary-Ellis: No! I would never have predicted Kalle and Jake! Never in a million years!

Generation *Road Rules*

Jonathan: I think both ROAD RULES and THE REAL WORLD give us insight into what it's like to be in your early twenties, or a little bit younger. For many cast members, ROAD RULES is an escape. They get a chance to go out into the world with a set of goals that have nothing to do with their real lives. Yet, as they meet the demands that are put upon them, they discover a lot about themselves.

Mary-Ellis: There's so much in each show; it takes two or three viewings to really get everything. I think the most satisfying experience is the marathon: You've seen all of the shows before, but you get to watch them again one after the other, paying close attention to the way the characters change and the relationships form.

Jonathan: After you've watched the shows all the way through once or twice, it's interesting to go back to them. It's like visiting old friends. These people have such a warm spot in your heart. It's like: "Oh, we're back to Mark and Kit. I like Mark and Kit. I feel safe. I feel good watching this."

Jonathan Murray
executive producer

Mary-Ellis: There's definitely going to be a reunion, but we're going to wait a while longer, allow the casts to move on with their lives before we come back to them.

Jonathan: But before that happens, we've got a special coming out. It's THE REAL WORLD on the Road . . . literally. It'll be a five-episode special. Five members from different REAL WORLD casts will travel in the Winnebago for three weeks.

Mary-Ellis: And, of course, there's a handsome reward!

Clay Newbill, SUPERVISING PRODUCER: When we first started production on ROAD RULES, people were always telling us that we couldn't do this, we couldn't do that. Well, why not? So what if it's never been done before? That's no reason not to do it.

Road Rules

Islands Season Crew

Rick de Oliveira, PRODUCER: Being on the road for all that time, things can get stressful, but as I like to remind the crew, this is television, not brain surgery.

Gary Pennington, Rick de Oliveira

Craig Spirko, DIRECTOR OF PHOTOGRAPHY: To do your job, you've got to find something you like about each cast member. Some are harder than others.

Rebo McFadden

Gary Pennington,
John Gumina,
Paul Buscemi

Crew

Joshua Harris,
Kary D'Allesandro,
Rebo McFadden

Europe Season Crew

Gary Pennington, DIRECTOR:
As far as the show is concerned, if something happens and we don't catch it on camera, it didn't happen at all, so the crew is pretty much on their toes at all times.

Jeff Santorro,
Bruce Toms,
Lamar Damon

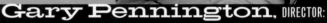

Clay Newbill and the Europe Season Cast

Bruce Toms, DIRECTOR:
Eventually the cast starts showing up in your dreams. Going on that trip is a pretty all consuming job.

Mark Jungjohann

Thank you for your interest in being a participant in the hit MTV series ROAD RULES.

ROAD RULES is about the adventures of five young people, women and men, who will travel to unknown destinations and accomplish a series of adventures. We're not interested in hiring five actors — we want real people from varying ethnic and socio-economic backgrounds — we want the conventional and the not-so-conventional. This is not an experience for a wallflower. If selected, you will be one of these five people.

So you want to be on ROAD RULES?

We're looking for interesting people who are not afraid to express their emotions and opinions, people who want to share their lives ... all in front of the cameras. You'll be living in a fishbowl, with cameras rolling almost every hour of every day, wearing a wireless microphone and having two or three camera people following you around — in the vehicle, on the street, on dates and sometimes when you're desperate just to be left alone. Consider this very carefully because we'll require you to sign a contract to commit for the full shooting period of approximately ten weeks.

This is a tough, emotionally exhausting experience. Think about whether you have the strength to endure it. If you are still interested, send in an application right away!

ROAD RULES APPLICATION INSTRUCTIONS

1. FILL OUT THE ENCLOSED APPLICATION LEGIBLY.
2. ATTACH A RECENT PHOTO OF YOURSELF, A COPY OF YOUR PASSPORT OR BIRTH CERTIFICATE, AND A COPY OF YOUR DRIVER'S LICENSE. **3.** MAKE A TEN-MINUTE VIDEOTAPE OF YOURSELF TALKING ABOUT WHATEVER YOU THINK MAKES YOU A GOOD CANDIDATE FOR **ROAD RULES**. REMEMBER, WE WANT TO SEE IF YOU ARE A PERSON WHO IS OPEN AND WILLING TO EXPRESS WHAT IS IMPORTANT TO YOU. SOMETIMES THE BEST VIDEOS ARE VERY SIMPLE. DON'T OVERTHINK IT, AND TRY TO BE HONEST AND SINCERE. (ALSO, MAKE SURE THERE'S ENOUGH LIGHT ON YOUR FACE AND THAT YOU ARE CLOSE ENOUGH TO THE MIKE TO BE HEARD.) **4.** SEND THE APPLICATION PACKAGE (MAKE SURE YOU HAVE THE CORRECT POSTAGE!) TO: ROAD RULES — CASTING DEPT., 6007 SEPULVEDA BLVD., VAN NUYS, CA 91411. PLEASE NOTE THAT ANYTHING YOU SEND US BECOMES THE PROPERTY OF BUNIM/MURRAY PRODUCTIONS, SO DON'T SEND ANYTHING THAT YOU'LL NEED TO GET BACK. **5.** WE WILL CONTACT YOU FURTHER FROM THIS POINT. PLEASE BE PATIENT.

Road Rules Application Form

Name: _____

Address: _____
_____
_____

Phone: _____

Birthdate (You must be 18 to 24 years old to be on ROAD RULES): _____

Age: _____

Parents' names, address, phone: _____
_____
_____

Brothers and sisters (names and ages): _____
_____
_____

Are you or have you ever been a member of
SAG/AFTRA? (circle one) Y or N
Have you ever acted or performed OUTSIDE of school?
(circle one) Y or N
Name of high school (with years completed): _____
_____

Name of college (with years completed and majors): _____
_____

Other education: _____
_____

Are you currently in school? (circle one) Y or N
Do you work? If so, describe your job. _____
_____
_____

What will you miss the most about leaving your friends
and family for 10 weeks? What will you miss the least?
_____
_____
_____

How would you describe your best traits? _____
_____
_____
_____
_____

How would you describe your worst traits? _____
_____
_____
_____
_____

Have you ever treated someone you cared about in
a way that makes you proud? Tell us about it.
_____
_____
_____

_____
_____
_____
_____

Have you ever treated someone you cared about in
a way that you regret? Tell us about it. _____
_____
_____
_____
_____
_____

How long does it take you to get ready in the
morning? Do you consider yourself high maintenance or low maintenance? Why? _____
_____
_____
_____

If you could only pack one backpack for the trip,
what would be in it? _____
_____
_____
_____
_____

Describe your most embarrassing moment. _____
_____
_____
_____
_____
_____
_____
_____
_____

Do you have a boyfriend or girlfriend? (circle one) Y or N

How did you meet? How long have you been together? What drives you crazy about the other person?
What is the best thing about the other person? _____
_____
_____
_____
_____
_____

How would your boyfriend/girlfriend feel about you
leaving for 10 weeks? Would you be faithful? _____
_____
_____
_____
_____

Other than your boyfriend or girlfriend, who is the
most important person in your life right now?
Describe him/her and why he/she is important. _____
_____
_____
_____

_____
_____
_____
_____
_____

How important is sex to you? Do you have it only
when you're in a relationship or do you seek it out at
other times? What's the most exciting/interesting
place you've ever had sex? _____
_____
_____
_____

Is there any issue, political or social, that you're
passionate about? Have you done anything about it?
_____
_____
_____

What is the most important issue or problem facing
you today? _____
_____
_____
_____
_____
_____

Are you physically fit? _____

Do you work out? If so, how often and what types of
activities do you like to do? If not, how do you stay
in shape? _____
_____
_____

Describe a major event or issue that has affected
your life: _____
_____
_____
_____
_____
_____

What habits do you have that we should know about?
_____
_____
_____

What habits do other people have that you simply
cannot tolerate? _____
_____
_____

Describe how conflicts were handled at home as
you were growing up (Who won? Who lost? Was
yelling and/or hitting involved?). _____
_____
_____